Death Among Strangers

ALSO BY DEIDRE S. LAIKEN

Daughters of Divorce
Listen to Me, I'm Angry

BY DEIDRE S. LAIKEN

WITH

DOROTHY GREENBAUM, M.D.

Lovestrong

Death Among Strangers

A NOVEL

Deidre S. Laiken

LANDMARK BOOKS

ABC·CLIO

Santa Barbara, California
Oxford, England

First published 1987 in the United States by Macmillan Publishing Company and 1989 in Great Britain by Headline Book Publishing.

Printed in large print 1989 by arrangement with Macmillan Publishing Company and Headline Book Publishing.

Library of Congress Cataloging-in-Publication Data

Laiken, Deidre S.
   Death among strangers.

   1. Large type books.   I. Title.
[PS3562.A335D4   1989]   813'.54   88-8072
ISBN 1-55736-110X (lg. print)

10   9   8   7   6   5   4   3   2   1

This book is Smyth sewn and printed on acid-free paper ∞ .
Manufactured in the United States of America.

For Daniel

Death Among Strangers

1

MASON KILEY did not see the legs right away.

He was lost in early morning thoughts and half-remembered dreams. Closing his eyes, he could easily picture the speckled fawn that had disappeared in the smoky mist. He could still conjure up sweet images of Peg smiling at him as he paid for his breakfast. Holding a brown paper bag that contained his second cup of coffee, he walked toward the riverbank. He sniffed the air as he gazed up at the white underbelly of a passing cloud. It was morning and he was all alone in the cemetery.

He began walking in the direction of the shed, following the familiar rut marks in the grass that led to a small wooden building, where, three days earlier, he had left his shovel and pickax. The grassy meadow with the cows grazing peacefully beside a chain link fence that ran parallel to the gray markers made the cemetery a comfortable resting place.

Mason liked the stillness and the order; he liked the scent of the raw earth as it yielded to his grave-digger's shovel. What he resented were the disruptions, the occasional practical jokes; the doll's glass eye that had once stared up at him from the damp earth, the store mannequin that had been set atop a faded tombstone. Pranks, schoolboy antics that were left for him to clean up. Maybe that's why when Mason first saw the legs he didn't bother to put down the steaming coffee, why he walked over to the riverbank as if this sort of thing happened every day. Maybe that's why instead of running, he took slow, measured steps, pausing to pick up a fallen branch as his old boots moved over the rutted earth.

He intended to poke at the legs with the branch until they tumbled over the river's bank and floated down the fast-moving water. That would be the end of it. Then he would sit down beside the shed and savor his coffee as he watched the clouds merge into shapeless white patterns. Mason liked gazing at the sky. So much of his time was spent looking down into the earth, looking at the warm soil turn over beneath his shovel, that he felt it was important to look up in the opposite direction.

The branch was thick and gnarled; it sliced through the air, just barely reaching the legs. Mason grimaced, wiping the first beads of perspiration from his brow. Moving closer he saw now for the first time that the feet were shoeless, the toenails painted a garish red. He probed harder, noting that the legs remained motionless. Yet whatever covered them seemed to yield to the pressure. The branch left small, circular impressions in the area just above the foot.

The legs should not have been real. They should have been plastic or wood, legs disconnected to anything or anyone living. Mason Kiley moved closer.

The body was not so much lying by the old plank shed as it was twisted and turned upside down, as if someone had intended to throw it over the bank and then at the last minute had changed his mind, panicked, and run away. Still gripping the branch, Mason tried to wedge himself between the shrubs and the planks of the shed. He wasn't thinking now, just moving. His right hand still grasped the branch, while the left one continued to grip the paper bag. Coffee leaked in a warm, wet stream along the seams of the brown paper. Behind the shed it was all a tangle of shrubs and weeds. Mason could hear the rushing water as he dropped the branch and, reaching out with his hand, felt the unmistakable touch of human flesh.

The body refused to reveal itself. The legs jutted out into the morning air, yet the face was hidden beneath one arm, while the other arm and much of the torso were caught up in a web of twigs and leaves. As he continued to push past the jumble of undergrowth, Mason noted a familiar paisley pattern poking up from the branches. He couldn't be sure, but it looked as though the body was wrapped in brightly colored cloth. It was then, when he saw the outline of a peacock along the border and a speck of gold glint out from a mass of dark hair, that Mason knew he didn't want to see anymore.

*   *   *

When he emerged from behind the shed, he was breathing heavily. The sound of his breathing seemed to fill all the empty spaces in the cemetery.

It seemed to reach right up to where the sky rushed between the clouds. The breathing became louder, almost deafening. For him, death had always been an orderly, peaceful process, a coffin placed tenderly beneath the pungent earth. But just now he had seen another kind of death, another kind of body. Mason Kiley clutched at his heart as he ran from the cemetery.

2

LIEUTENANT GEORGE MURPHY was not thinking about murder when the phone rang. He was sitting alone at the kitchen table. And he was feeling the loneliness. He tried to remember better times, times when he was a kid growing up in Brooklyn, times when he had an adoring wife and a baby daughter waiting for him when he walked through the door. Fragmented memories of his past moved through his mind like an old movie. Life had been sharp and clear then. There was a purpose and an order. He had been connected to a family, to a job, and to a town. Now there was only Bakersville and the department.

The town still reminded him of a picture postcard, an artist's rendering of Main Street, U.S.A. The police department, with its neat red brick headquarters, was the center of activity, still the place where people reported traffic accidents, stolen cars, and lost dogs. George knew that

Bakersville hadn't changed, that except for a new store or the temporary influx of summer visitors, it probably never would. But something was different. Looking around his apartment, at the stark walls and the bare furniture, he knew that the town and the job were the same. He was the one who had changed. He was the one who had been left behind.

George sat at the breakfast table in the early morning gloom. A grayish light filtered through the unwashed windows. He listened as the Rolling Stones sang, "Can't get no satisfaction." Satisfaction was something he had almost given up on. Since his wife had walked out nearly two and a half years ago, he had tried to avoid mornings such as these. Ordinarily, he'd be at Peg's Diner drinking his second cup of coffee, shooting the breeze with the locals, watching the door, waiting for Elizabeth to come in carrying her brown leather briefcase.

He liked the way she looked in the morning, the way her face was rested, the way her brown eyes seemed to glow when they met his. She was not the striking beauty his wife had been, but her looks were soft, appealing. She had a sensual way of moving, a quiet, confident attractiveness that he seemed unable to resist. And she had an uncanny way of sensing what he was thinking. It was difficult to hide things from Elizabeth. Maybe that's why this morning he chose to avoid her, to immerse himself in the solitude and to watch the sun burn away the pre-dawn fog.

* * *

The phone was on its fourth ring when he picked it up. It could only be an official call and he was in no rush.

It was Jean from headquarters.

"A call just came in about a body in the cemetery," she said.

"What? No 'good morning?'" George grumbled as he reached for a slice of burned toast.

The irony of her statement did not escape him. "There are always bodies in the cemetery, so what else is new?"

Jean ignored his attempt at humor. "We just received a call from a Mason Kiley. He sounded extremely agitated. Said he saw a body dumped behind the shed overlooking the river."

Kiley. George searched his mind. The name sounded familiar.

"Isn't that the same Kiley, the gravedigger, who reported the mannequin and the doll's head about a year ago?"

"Doll's eye," Jean corrected him. "That's the one. But just in case, you'd better get over there. Take your own car."

George waited until Mick Jagger had finished wailing his tale of no satisfaction before he threw on his jacket and sauntered out to his car.

He was absolutely sure that the body thing would be a hoax. He retrieved from his memory file of faces the weatherbeaten visage of Mason Kiley. The guy was a woodchuck. Murphy smiled as he said the word outloud. Woodchucks were what the transplanted city dwellers called the dyed-in-the-wool locals, the guys who hung rifles in the cabs of their pickup trucks, who got so drunk on Saturday night that they had to be pulled from roadside drainage ditches early Sunday morning. The woodchucks kept the department busy. There were arrests for drunk driving, driving without a license, domestic violence, and then, of course, there were the urgent calls reporting UFO sightings. Now a woodchuck gravedigger had sighted a body.

The cemetery was empty except for Mason Kiley, who was waving hysterically as George pulled up beside the iron gates.

"Over there," Kiley said. He pointed to the far side of the cemetery, his bony finger making vague circles in the air.

Murphy reached over and opened the door for the gravedigger. The scent of earth and coffee filled the front seat. There was no trace of alcohol. Murphy had a good nose. Not even the slightest trace of booze would have escaped him.

The car rolled slowly over to the northeastern corner of the cemetery. From where he sat, George saw only the dilapidated shed and some freshly dug earth that had been dumped there over the weekend. He glanced sideways at Kiley. The gravedigger was pale and clammy. Beads of perspiration dotted his forehead and upper lip. George was ready to acknowledge that the man had been frightened, but from where he sat it looked as if all the bodies here were safely six feet under.

"Stop," Kiley said. He wiped his brow with the ragged cuff of his work shirt. "You've got to walk there, behind the shed."

George told Kiley to wait by the car. All he needed was an hysterical woodchuck pushing him over the narrow bank into the river below.

The shed was small, its wooden sides were washed gray by years of snow and rain. A pickax and a shovel rested against the two plank doors, an ominous still life. The light closed in on him as he made his way into the thicket behind the shed. The trees seemed to grow together, forming a concealing blackness. George moved forward. He brushed against sharp thorns. He saw the legs, toenails flashing red, ankles drained of blood.

He reached out to grab the outer walls of the shed as he maneuvered along the riverbank. He looked down to check his footing. When his eyes refocused, he saw the hair. Masses of brown strands caught up in the twigs, grabbing like desperate tentacles at the weeds and branches. A bruised arm covered part of the head and all of the face. The only light came from a strip of gold that flashed dimly through the hair and weeds. As if trying to anchor himself, George dug his feet into the soft earth. But it was too late. The ground had already begun to shift. His face burned as he reached out to grab the body.

George felt himself growing smaller and smaller. He watched as another arm—one stronger and more powerful than his, one covered with curling copper hairs—tried to disengage the dead body from the underbrush. It was someone else's arm. An arm that did not hesitate for a moment. It was only when George saw the peacock print and the thin, gold cross, only when he smelled the terrible putrid smell that the scene became real.

"Police sense," George said out loud. At the sound of his voice, the other arm receded and he felt his own hands pulling at the body. The ground was still now, the body rigid and unmoving. George knew he needed help. Whoever had put the body here must have been a nanny goat. He walked out from behind the shed. Kiley was leaning against a maple tree. He looked expectantly at the cop.

"Wanna give me a hand over here?" George asked.

Kiley, still looking shaky, made an automatic gesture. Go away, he seemed to say. The only dead bodies I touch are the ones resting on tufted silk in polished boxes.

George felt the sun, brutally bright, burning away the shadow self that had appeared only briefly in that moment of fear behind the shed. It was clear he was alone. Kiley would be no help. Since, at Jean's request, he had driven here in his own car, he was without radio contact. It would take another twenty minutes to drive to the station house.

He wasn't thinking about the public phone in the mini-mall across the street from the cemetery. He wasn't thinking about the fact that dead bodies can't go anywhere. He was all electric. The charges ran like lightning from his brain to his limbs. He moved automatically back into the darkness behind the shed. He braced himself as he tugged at the body.

Red nail polish, paisley skirt, worn brown sweater, gold cross. He made mental notes as he untangled the arms and hair from the web of branches.

The body was surprisingly light. The putrid smell seeped into his skin, mixing with the scent of his own sweat and the pungent odor of grass and dirt. He carried the body a few feet, gently placing it on the mound of dirt in front of the shed. Everything clicked into a jerking slow motion. George did what he had been trained to do.

The corpse was lying on its side, a tiny fish pulled from a dark sea of brambles and undergrowth. Hoping for an instant identification, he rolled it over.

In the stark, almost iridescent morning light he saw the maggots. They crawled in and out of the hollows of the face. The features, nearly obliterated by heavy blows and dried blood, were crushed and distorted. The electricity was humming, coursing through George's body, filling him with adrenaline. The light dimmed and then grew stronger, bringing the body back and forth in crazy focus.

Police sense. George looked at the feet, the hands, the taut unwrinkled skin. Later, he would look for lividity, defensive wounds, identifying marks. But now something automatic was taking over, beckoning him to look closer.

Mason Kiley sat wide-eyed, frozen beside the maple tree. Murphy felt the electricity subside. The light grew steady, and what had once been silence was replaced by the sound of a thousand leaves rustling in the breeze.

It was precisely 8:05 A.M. A small black bird flitted across the blueness as Lieutenant George Murphy stood in the Bakersville cemetery staring at what he now firmly believed was the brutally murdered body of a young girl.

3

THE PAVEMENT HAD BECOME one long hypnotic stretch of gray. While the seamless road flashed beneath his wheels, the warm evening breeze seeped into his open collar and ran up and through the zippered cuffs of his leather jacket.

He had been traveling for hours. The old Harley was made for the road, but now his body ached and he longed to straighten his legs and rest his back. He had equipped the motorcycle with pegs on which he could prop up his legs. But those pegs were for highway driving. He never felt secure on back roads with his feet so far from the foot brake and shift pedal.

It was close to 8:00 P.M. when he saw the sign for buffalo wings. The hand-lettered placard rested in the corner of a window of a small tavern. He engaged the clutch with his left hand while he kicked down to second gear. As he drove slowly into the parking lot, the loose gravel pinged off the wheels of his bike. He parked beside an old blue pickup truck and remained seated while he ran his hands carefully over the locked luggage boxes. Before dismounting, he removed his helmet and attached it to a small sliding lock on the side of the motorcycle. It clicked neatly beside the white spare helmet he carried for riders. He decided he would take the throw-on saddlebags with him. There was expensive camera equipment inside, and although he considered getting ripped off in such a small town an unlikely possibility, it was a chance he could not afford to take.

The moment his feet touched the ground, he got the feelings. Strange vibrating sensations that ran in waves along his legs and pulsated inside his head. Now separated from the constant drone of the engine, he felt incomplete. It was difficult to walk without the familiar, lulling vibrations. He paused at the tavern door, breathing slowly, trying to find his own rhythms, trying to separate from the ones that still pounded along the sides of his face and raced into his fingertips. He knew the sensations would pass in time. But Gary did not like to feel even predictably off balance.

The place was called the Nugget, and like its name, it was reassuringly roadside. The long bar stretched into the smoky darkness. Dim lights illuminated a battered pool table, a couple of beeping computer games, and two well-used pinball machines. A woman was talking to the bartender.

Everything looked like a photograph he had taken once before.

When the bartender approached him, he gave his order slowly, letting the sound of his voice become familiar to him once again. Then he concentrated on the shadowy female silhouette. She was dressed in a business suit, but beneath the cotton skirt and blouse he could see she had a tight, athletic body. Her briefcase was resting on the bar. He knew at once she was not the usual roadside type. She was obviously waiting for someone.

She checked her watch, looked up at the clock on the wall, and then down at her wrist again. Then, with an air of impatience, she walked around to the other side of the bar, picked up the house phone, and dialed a number. She moved with a certain grace and self-confidence. He could see her legs, long and muscular, the curve of her hips, the way she cradled the phone in her hand. He strained to hear the words, but her voice was muffled in the dark space that floated between them. She was listening as someone gave her information she wrote down on a little pad. When she hung up, she checked her watch again.

The bartender's name was Fred. He knew because the woman called to him from behind the bar. She was comfortable here, using the house phone, calling to the bartender who doubled as a cook.

Gary could figure out a lot from only a few clues. He had already figured out that whomever the woman had been waiting for was not going to show up. He could sense her irritation as she drummed her fingernails along the curve of the bar. The aroma of frying chicken wings filtered out from the small kitchen. He wanted to see the woman's face. He wanted to pull the silhouette out into the light. But he was aware of the boundaries. He knew the space between them could become a chasm if he approached too quickly or spoke too hastily.

Fred was standing over him, squinting into the light of the pinball machine. He held the steaming chicken wings on a Styrofoam plate.

"I know you," he said. A foamy cloud of spittle gathered in the corner of his mouth. "Aren't you the guy who was taking pictures in front of Peg's Diner this morning?"

Gary felt an involuntary flutter in his left hand.

"That was me," he answered, "but I don't remember you."

The bartender's voice had an odd midwestern twang.

"I was the one in the blue pickup truck in the corner of the lot. I was watching you. Guess you didn't notice."

Gary had noticed. He was trained to pick up the details, the little distractions that crawled along the margins of a photograph. He remembered the blue pickup in the parking lot. The evidence clicked together neatly.

"Are you a professional photographer?" the bartender asked. The cloud of spittle lingered and then disappeared.

"Yes, I am." Gary answered.

He was hoping the inevitable conversation would not begin. Maybe Fred had a niece or a girlfriend he thought was pretty enough for Gary to photograph. Maybe he had a brother or a nephew who was a whiz with an Instamatic.

The bartender lit up a cigarette. A fly sat in the wet ring that had been left by Gary's glass.

"That's some beauty, isn't it?" he asked.

Gary glanced instinctively at the female silhouette.

"The diner. It's the genuine article."

Cigarette smoke twisted into thin spirals.

Gary waded into the conversation cautiously, testing the waters much the same way he had as a child. Without the protection of his camera, he couldn't be sure, couldn't feel entirely safe.

He smiled, looking past the bartender at a pair of deer horns that were mounted on a wooden plaque over the bar.

"It sure is," he said. "Do you have any idea when it was built?"

Fred held up a finger. "Just a sec," he said.

He called the name Elizabeth.

The silhouette turned and moved toward him. She was standing so close he could touch her. Her face, when it emerged from the shadows, was small and round. Neat brown hair fell just below her collarbone. Her eyes were almost the same color as her hair. Her lips were full and pink. There was a softness about her. No hard edges. She had the kind of face he could trust. Unlike the sharp, angular beauties most photographers preferred, her looks were real. If he tried hard enough, he could almost imagine her naked: small breasts, trim hips, long sinewy legs. And when she made love, her eyes would close, her lips part, and her face would flush with desire.

Gary looked away. If he looked too long or too intently he would break another rule. She would become uncomfortable and retreat into the darkness. Or worse, she would take his look as a stare, as a challenge that required a swift and decisive answer. And he did not want that now.

Elizabeth glanced at him as she spoke. He knew they had already begun the looking, and he held her eyes just long enough to show interest. Her voice was cautious.

"I believe it was built in 1948. I heard that the last owner refused to sell when they built the highway. That's why the road kind of curves around it."

The Bakersville Truck Stop had been renamed Peg's Diner when the trucks began traveling on the newly built interstate. Fred and Elizabeth joked about the greasy hamburgers, the farmers, and the woodchucks who started their day at 5:00 A.M., and the fan of grimy postcards that Peg tucked into the mirror over the cash register.

"Anyone who goes anywhere sends Peg a postcard," said Elizabeth. "It's become a tradition among the regulars."

Gary slipped his trembling left hand into his pocket and ordered a cup of coffee.

Elizabeth was casually close now. They could be any two people who knew each other. Any two people having a friendly drink, talking about ordinary things. He asked her if she had lived in Bakersville long. She was talking easily, explaining that although she had grown up here, she had returned to live in Bakersville only two years ago, after living in

New York City for some time. Her words floated in the darkness. But he was more interested in pictures than sounds. He checked her out, noting every detail, snapping imaginary stills in his head.

He was still waiting for the opening, for the time when he could hold her eyes a split second longer, when the phone rang. The bartender walked to the far end of the bar. His voice cut through the silence.

"It's for you, Elizabeth," he shouted.

As she walked away, he watched her black pumps click against the linoleum. She wore a skirt that hung in damp wrinkles against her thighs. And when she stood up, he could see the subtle outline of her rear end.

The conversation was mostly one-sided, and short.

"He isn't coming," she said to the bartender as she returned. "Official business," she added. "And a friend from the office dropped me off." She was irritated, angry even. She didn't seem to be the sort of woman who would quietly accept disappointment.

Gary knew this was his opening. He eased in slowly.

"Do you need a lift somewhere?" he asked.

She clutched at her briefcase, explaining that "the person" she was supposed to meet had been detained.

He knew by the way she said "person" that she had been waiting for a man. The fact that she hadn't used the word "husband" or "boyfriend" signaled a certain availability. They both pretended the signals had been neither sent nor received. But no, she demurred, she couldn't possibly go with him, stranger and all that.

Fred, who was lighting up another cigarette, pretended to look away, but he didn't move.

"I can't get off for a couple more hours," he told her. "Why don't you take the ride?"

She was tired. She wanted to go home. The stranger was hardly menacing.

"I live only fifteen minutes from here. I'd appreciate it."

Gary smiled. "No trouble," he said as he followed her to the door.

"Hey, wait a minute," the bartender called after him. "Be careful with her. No monkey business." Then he laughed, "Her boyfriend's a cop!"

4

THE MOTORCYCLE TERRIFIED HER. She had not expected it. It was simply out of the question.

Now that they were outside, he looked different. Better. His black hair curled around the collar of his leather jacket. In the glow of the parking-lot lights, she could see that he had green eyes. She had planned to look away but now found herself almost staring.

"You mean you don't have a car?" she asked. "I can't ride on that thing."

"Nothing to it," he said. "You live only fifteen minutes away, right? I'll drive nice and slow."

Elizabeth was uncomfortable, nervous. The man was obviously handsome. The motorcycle obviously exciting. She wanted nothing to do with it, and at the same time she made no attempt to leave.

"What about my briefcase?" she asked. "And this?" she pointed to her damp, rumpled skirt.

"I've got room in my saddlebag for that briefcase, and you can just tuck your skirt around your legs."

There was something embarrassingly intimate about their conversation. If he had had a car she would have slid easily into the seat and could have observed him from the corner of her eye while he watched the road. That way she would have been more in control. Now it was his ride.

"You're not afraid, are you?" he asked. His green eyes scanned her face. "Have you ever ridden on a motorcycle?"

Elizabeth was feeling that uneasy feeling again. She couldn't be sure if it was fear or excitement. Probably both, she thought as she tried to avoid his glance.

"Sure, but that was a long time ago. And it was a Honda or something. This is kind of big, isn't it?"

Gary laughed. His face was relaxed, friendly. "Believe it or not, this is a lot safer than a little motorcycle. I do some heavy traveling on this bike. It's made for the road. Look, if it will make you more comfortable, I can leave it here and ask Fred if I can drive you home in his pickup."

His alternative solution impressed her. Had he just thought of this, or, anticipating reluctance, had he planned it out in the bar? Either way, she was going to ride with him.

"Do you have a helmet for me?" she asked.

Gary pointed to the white one that was locked beside his own.

She was really going to do this. At the very least, it would be something to talk about at the office. It wasn't every day she had the opportunity to ride on a Harley-Davidson with a man who was looking increasingly like Jim Morrison.

He took her briefcase and slipped it neatly into his saddlebag beside some lenses and cameras.

"That's a lot of equipment you carry," she said. "Aren't you afraid you'll fall?"

He thought back to a moment when he had taken a turn too sharply. The delicate symbiosis with the engine had been broken. The bike had leaned. The road had become a thousand flashes of gray. In that instant he'd lost all control. Total fear gave way to complete freedom. It had been a dangerous exhilaration. But he couldn't dwell on that now. Instead, he reassured her that she was safe with him.

She watched as he straddled the motorcycle, kicking at the stand until he was balancing the machine between his legs. She was noticing everything now: his jeans, worn soft in all the right places, his leather jacket with the zippers on the pockets and cuffs. When he had pulled the bike out from the parking space, she lowered herself onto the seat behind him, tucking her skirt cautiously around her legs. She remembered she hadn't given him the exact directions. As she leaned forward and spoke, she inhaled his scent. Leather and sweat and something else. He nodded as if he knew the roads quite well. Then he waited as she tucked her hair into the white helmet. For an instant, she worried that she might never get home at all.

She was holding him around the waist, feeling his leather jacket against her palms, sitting so close she was sure he could feel the pressure of her breasts as they rubbed against his back.

The engine made a constant vibrating sound that crept along the insides of her thighs. The road, the trees, and the sky became a blur of form and light. Familiar signposts seemed strangely distorted. They rushed by and then receded into the night. Her palms were sweating. She wanted to move the position of her arms, but she was already too close to him. Moving now would only make things worse. This clearly had been a mistake. How would she get rid of him when they reached her door? What if he insisted on coming in? How would she look getting off the backseat all creased and uncomfortable, dressed in a business suit, looking and feeling more and more out of control?

At least she didn't have to talk. The helmets sealed them in private chambers. Only the warm air seeped in around the edges of the plastic face shield. She was enjoying the ride. It stirred up sexual feelings, old memories, flashes of sensations that came and went as quickly as the trees that knotted in the moonlight.

As they approached her house, the engine began to make louder and slower vibrations. He kicked at something that put the motorcycle into a lower gear. When the engine stopped, the vibrations still rippled along the surface of her skin. He leaned the motorcycle to one side, making it easier for her to get off.

It was that awkward time now. She was unsure as she watched him pull her briefcase from the leather saddlebag. Usually, by this time, she'd know just what to say. Either she'd make it clear she wanted to end the evening or she'd leave room for an opening. Maybe, she thought, she was just out of practice.

If he asked to come in, she would definitely say no. Her better judgment told her she was lucky to have arrived safely in one piece. She watched his hands as he buckled the saddlebag. Remarkable. Long tapering fingers, smooth olive skin. It did not escape her that his fingers were ringless.

"So how was it?" he asked as he handed her the briefcase and took back the white helmet.

Elizabeth was uncomfortable now, shifting a little from one side to the other.

"Not bad at all." She was afraid to say how much she had enjoyed it, afraid to give him any room to maneuver.

"Thank you," she added.

Gary was grinning. His eyes crinkled into irresistible squints.

"My pleasure." He gave a mock bow, doffing his helmet. His hair tumbled out, a mass of dark curls.

Elizabeth picked at the stitches along the brief-case handle. Well, maybe she would have him in. She hadn't done anything like this since she'd left the city. The men she had met here all knew each other. Privacy and anonymity were urban luxuries. It was rare that she met an attractive stranger. But she wouldn't invite him. That would be provocative. Let him convince me, she thought as she stared at his perfect hands. The motorcycle had left her feeling reckless, ready for a moment of abandon. She had taken the ride, hadn't she?

These were new feelings. Or were they old ones resurfacing? She couldn't be sure. The man was enticing. But the moment had an unreal, almost dreamlike quality to it. She felt as though she were standing on a threshold of some sort. A step in either direction might set her on an irreversible course.

Curiosity. New hands touching her in familiar places. It was a crazy impulse—and totally out of character.

Elizabeth was thinking about the phone call she could make if only she could get inside, when she saw that Gary was still holding his helmet in his right hand. She was looking past his eyes, hoping to avoid any meaningful contact, while she planned her strategy.

"I'm glad you enjoyed the ride, Elizabeth," he said. Nothing else. No mention of other rides to come. No references to seeing her again.

He reached up and touched her face. She thought she felt his hand tremble against her cheek. Then he was gone. The engine droned gently into the darkness.

5

IT WAS 2:00 A.M. and Lieutenant Murphy was planning his next move. He had spent all day at the murder scene. After removing the body from the underbrush, he had called headquarters, a funeral home, and an ambulance. The funeral home was for the unidentified girl. The ambulance was for Mason Kiley. When he saw the body, the gravedigger had collapsed. Murphy couldn't be sure if it was a fainting spell or something more serious. He had given the man CPR and propped him, sweating and shaking, against the nearest tombstone.

George was convinced there would be some ID on or near the body. He had processed the scene himself, making sure to check for tire tracks, torn fragments of fabric, bullet holes. The site was spotless. By the time the New York State Police Identification Bureau arrived, George had searched the bushes for the slightest scrap of evidence. The whole department had fanned out, combing the area for weapons, footprints, any possible leads. Nothing had been found. It was as if the girl's body had been dropped from a helicopter. He examined the corpse for abrasions, cuts, and defensive wounds. It had been hard to look. She was so small. He estimated her age somewhere between twelve and sixteen, maybe seventeen. Her feet had been slightly calloused, her hands smooth. Only her clothes, worn and out of date, indicated she might possibly be a runaway.

By the time the girl's body was slipped into the moss green body bag, George knew he would be up all night. He had seen dead bodies before. He had found them stabbed, bludgeoned, shot, strangled. He had seen them twisted in rigid, frozen horror, seen them decomposed and half-buried. When he had first been a cop in Miami and then later in Brooklyn, homicide was as ordinary as the morning newspaper. People would read about a murder, shake their heads, and by afternoon they would have forgotten. No one remembered the names and faces of the dead. The city was like that. It seemed to swallow its victims. But Bakersville was different. People didn't disappear here. Everything was noticed and remembered. The town had its own particular order and rhythm.

Located in the western corner of Steven's County, Bakersville was one of a string of towns arranged alphabetically. There was Aiken to the north, Beacon, Crescent Springs, and Duchess to the south. Small villages molded to the contours of the hills and valleys; they were arranged with the same precision as the corn that was planted every spring. And he had moved here for the predictability, the order, the safety. It had been his compromise with Tina. After their daughter was born she had begged him to leave Brooklyn. She couldn't bear the heat of the summers, the isolation of apartment living, and the thought of what he might confront behind a locked door or in a dark alley.

When he had suggested Bakersville, he remembered his childhood—the summers he had spent with his family in wooden bungalows on Whitehill Lake. There had been cotton candy and country fairs, blazing afternoons that were cooled by lake breezes. Autumn throbbed with color, and winters were a fantasy of snowmen and sleigh riding. He wanted to return to a place where the memories were welcoming.

He believed small-town life would help his marriage. And for a while it did. He found police work in Bakersville less demanding and certainly less dangerous. He made personal contact with everyone from the owner of the diner on the edge of town to the used car salesman on Main Street. People here knew one another. Strangers were assimilated but only after they had become part of the tapestry; only when they had learned Bakersville ways and understood that here life unfolded gradually in slow and gentle waves.

Even after Tina had left him, weary of their marriage and longing for the comfort of her own family, he had stayed on. It had been his choice. But then, subtly, things began to change. Now it was as if someone had rearranged everything, as if nature had been reshaped by human hands.

The body didn't belong here. It wasn't part of the landscape. No, this was someone's cruel and hideous trick, the work of an outsider who had stumbled upon a setting—a place about which he knew nothing and cared less.

* * *

George hadn't eaten all day. His stomach growled as he drove the squad car back over the road toward the cemetery. Tomorrow the body would be posted. After the medical examiner conducted the autopsy, he would know more. The post mortem might yield clues he and the department had been unable to find. It was impossible that no one would claim the body. She was someone's child. Someone was looking for her. It was just a matter of time.

But George was aware that time was his enemy here. Whoever killed her had dumped her body in Bakersville. She might have been murdered miles from here. Lividity had set in. So had rigor mortis. The lines of lividity, areas where the blood settled within hours after death, seemed to indicate that the girl had been seated when she was bludgeoned. There had been no red areas on her ankles or wrists, no defensive wounds on her hands. Could she have been sitting passively, unrestrained while her attacker crushed her skull?

George went over the details again and again. When he closed his eyes he saw the toenails. Red against gray skin. On the way to the cemetery he passed a dumpster. Without thinking, he pulled over. Standing on the hood of the car, he looked inside. It was bare, probably just emptied. Damn. There was always a chance the perpetrator had panicked and thrown the girl's purse or wallet into a nearby garbage can.

His mind was racing now. He thought he saw clues everywhere. A piece of something white on the side of the road caught his eye. He stopped to look. It was a Styrofoam drinking cup. He'd hoped it would be a wallet or a handkerchief with initials or bloodstains.

The chief had told him to go home and get some sleep. "Tomorrow we'll have more to go on," he said. George knew he was right. But it would be impossible to sleep. The body, so small, so frail. The face so hideously decomposed.

And there was something else. Something that kept bothering him. The hands. They were delicate and expressive. And only the fingernails of the right hand were polished. It was the same unmistakable shade of red that he had seen on the toenails. A small detail, but it bothered him. It bothered him so much that when he turned into the cemetery he imagined he saw something moving in the bushes. He slowed down long enough to see a tiny rabbit dart in front of his headlights.

He knew it was pointless, but he sat in the squad car and figured out what he would do next. If they couldn't ID her, things would get tough. He'd have every hysterical parent of a runaway from New York to California calling headquarters. He ran his fingers through his hair.

Then there was a third possibility. Suppose no one claimed her. Events would be thrown off course. The town's rhythm would be disrupted. Like a stone cast into a placid stream, the murder would make waves. It would create an environment of its own. The illusion of safety would be shattered. Bakersville wouldn't bounce back; it wasn't a sponge that could absorb such a thing while retaining its familiar shape.

If this murder wasn't solved within twenty-four hours, the ripples might become waves, and people as well as places could be engulfed.

He flashed back to the body being slipped into the moss green bag. He had only guessed at her age. But he knew he had been close. His own daughter, Sheila, was almost twelve. He had promised to visit her this weekend. Seeing her was important; he didn't want the bond between them to weaken. But he already knew he would be wrapped up in this case for at least the next few days. A quick and definite ID would make his life a lot easier. He could fill out his reports, drive to New Jersey, and spend the afternoon with his daughter. Perhaps he could even pretend that nothing out of the ordinary had happened.

As he sat in the darkness, it crossed his mind, just for an instant, that this might not be an isolated case. Maybe tomorrow there would be another dead body and then another. It was getting late. He was way ahead of himself, imagining things that probably would never happen, looking for evidence along roadsides.

His police sense told him he was fatigued. He needed a cup of coffee and a sympathetic ear. He thought about Elizabeth. She had probably called headquarters hours ago. It wasn't like her to wait.

Elizabeth set her watch with the radio every morning. It drove her crazy when clients were late. It made her furious when friends showed up five or ten minutes after they had said they would. Murphy smiled to himself. He could just picture her sitting in the Nugget, calling headquarters, insisting on getting some information from Jean, who would only answer coolly that he was on "official business." Elizabeth wouldn't push. She would probably have a glass of wine with Fred, a friend from her high school days, and drive home, miffed.

For a second he played with the idea of stopping in at the Nugget. There had been a murder and Elizabeth was alone. It worried him, but he realized he was being foolish. If he left now, by the time he arrived it would be 2:30. There was no way Elizabeth would still be there, no way she wouldn't be fast asleep by now, he thought. No sense waking her.

He smiled as he ran his hand along the dusty dashboard. He thought of her face, warm and loving, concerned. He longed for her presence. Tonight it would have made a difference. But even now, just knowing she was close by, eased the loneliness. And in the dark cemetery, where eighteen hours earlier he had dragged a dead body from the bushes, he felt strangely comforted.

6

SHE WAS NAKED. In the dark her skin felt smooth and young. At thirty-five, she still believed her body looked exactly as it had when she was in her twenties. Of course many things had changed since then. Inside. But Elizabeth was sure those things didn't show.

The shadows gathered in the curves of her hips. The light from the moon filtered through the window and warmed her breasts.

She had wanted him to touch her.

But he was a stranger, someone she had only known for an hour. He could have been anyone: a drifter, a maniac, a married man.

She cupped her breast in her hand.

If he had insisted, she would have surrendered. Like in a movie or on a TV show.

The man's name was Gary. He had green eyes and black hair. He was breathtakingly handsome. And she would probably never see him again.

She dialed Celia's number. It was 3:00 A.M., but Elizabeth knew that Celia never slept. Not like ordinary people. She catnapped between her patients; she caught a few hours in the early evening. They had been friends for ten years, having met in graduate school when they were both working toward their social work degrees. Celia was only five years older, but she always seemed to know more. She had direction. When, only months before graduation, she had announced she was pregnant and getting married, Elizabeth had not been surprised.

Celia named her daughter Leslie, but somehow the name got changed, turned inside out. Everyone wound up calling her Elsie. Within a year, Celia was divorced and Elsie was attending a very expensive day-care center. Celia went on to become a psychoanalyst. She had the patience for it. Elizabeth had dabbled at the institute, but it had been too rigid, too deadly serious. Celia had wanted her to finish. We can go into practice together, she had said. We can rent a suite of offices. Instead, Elizabeth had taken a clinic job on the Upper West Side. In her free hours she saw a few private patients. But she didn't have the discipline necessary for the endless hours of near silent listening.

Celia loved the city. It energized her. Elizabeth had grown up in Bakersville. She knew about sunsets and hills and views that went on for miles. As the years passed, Manhattan seemed to get smaller and smaller. She felt squeezed, confined, out of step. She had left Bakersville after high school because it was expected of her. She had been a good student. She was attractive. It was understood that she would grow bored with small-town life.

Go, her mother had said. You can always come back.

It had happened on a day when she was thinking about the house she had lived in as a child, the house surrounded by maple trees and tomato plants, the house with room for two children, toys, and pets. She was trying to remember if it possibly could have been that big, when the hand reached into her purse. It was an invisible hand. She never saw it. There wasn't the slightest feeling. No sudden jostle, no accidental encounter. When she got back to her apartment, she saw that her wallet was gone. Thirty dollars and all the photographs. It was as if someone had silently stolen part of her life. Elizabeth thought of it as a sign. She was too logical to be superstitious, but it seemed like a foreshadowing of some sort. She was shaken.

Two days later her brother Steven called and said her mother had been hospitalized with a stroke. As she packed her bags, it occurred to her that none of her neighbors would miss her. Within days, an eager new tenant would move into her small apartment. There would be no trace that she had ever lived there. None.

*　　*　　*

That had been over a year ago. When she returned to Bakersville, it was pretty much the same town she had left. Now the streets seemed slightly narrower, the stores smaller. But she knew that was more a distortion of memory than an accurate reflection of reality.

Elizabeth's mother lingered for a while before she died. Her brother flew in from California to help her arrange the funeral. By then, she had met George and began feeling that she might stay for a while. She was offered a job with the division of social services, and she accepted immediately, grateful for the diversion. An old friend from high school found her a cottage in the woods. It had large, airy rooms.

There were plenty of closets and a kitchen she could turn around in. It felt like home.

Celia kept asking her when she was going to come back to New York. I don't know, Elizabeth answered. It became a ritual between them. Like most city people, all Celia saw in Bakersville were the spaces. Elizabeth saw the people and the land that filled them. She had been part of this town once, and her place was waiting for her when she returned. And then there was George. There were possibilities here. Celia couldn't understand that.

The phone rang four times. Celia didn't like to take evening calls from patients, ex-lovers, or anonymous breathers.

"What's up?" she asked.

Elizabeth told her about the ride with Gary.

"Sounds exciting. What happened next?" Celia asked.

"I'm here alone in bed talking to you."

"Tell me again, how sexy was he?"

"Like Jim Morrison, only better."

Celia laughed. "I didn't know they made them better."

Elizabeth realized then, that for a moment, they weren't talking about George. She wasn't complaining about his ambivalence and his strained, but not totally detached, involvement with his ex-wife. Celia wasn't needling her about her tendency to hold back emotionally and physically. You keep a little part of yourself on reserve, as if you're waiting for someone, Celia had once said. Elizabeth didn't see it that way. She thought of it as being careful.

"Will there be more to this adventure?" Celia was asking.

"Men like him aren't real," Elizabeth said. "They sort of drift into your life and then disappear."

"You don't know that. Maybe he'll call you tomorrow."

"He never asked me for my phone number."

"But he knows where you live, right?"

"Right. But it was dark, he'll never find it again."

"Let's say he did. Would you let him in?"

"I'd probably decide not to, but with a little coaxing I might change my mind. Just thinking about it makes me crazy."

"Sex is crazy. And love is total madness," Celia said. "You always have the option of avoiding both."

"Is that your advice?"

"As a self-proclaimed expert on the subject, I'd say that a little madness every now and then is good for the soul, not to mention the body."

Elizabeth threw a thin cotton blanket over her bare legs. Tomorrow was a work day. She was beginning to feel sleepy. The man was a fantasy. It had been an accident, an impulsive moment. She would never see him again and that would be the end of it. Celia's voice had calmed her. It had been the same voice she had listened to after her mother had died.

The same voice that had always been there when she was anxious, confused, or hurt.

"I'm counting on you to help me get this all in perspective," Elizabeth said.

"Well, that's what I'm here for. Your voice of sanity. Your proverbial glass of warm milk. If he comes back, we'll talk."

Elizabeth laughed. She could almost imagine asking the man on the Harley-Davidson to wait in her living room while she called Celia.

"What would I do without you?" Elizabeth asked.

"Absolutely nothing, I hope," Celia said before she blew a goodnight kiss into the phone.

7

EVERYTHING WAS WHITE. The brightness hurt his eyes. He flashed his badge at the nurse behind the reception desk.

"I'm looking for a patient you admitted yesterday. Name's Mason Kiley," he said.

The nurse looked at her clipboard, her nylon uniform rustled against her skin. He was backtracking now. Kiley had discovered the body, maybe he had seen something or could recall a small detail that might help the investigation.

*   *   *

It was 6:00 A.M. He had been up all night. Lists. He had made dozens of them. Each one detailed a plan of action he might take, leads he might follow, evidence he might piece together. If he could ID the victim quickly, chances were he'd locate the assailant. It was just a matter of legwork—talking to friends and relatives, tracing the girl's whereabouts. Somewhere, someone was missing a daughter.

The nurse, a different one now, in white nylon pants and a white jacket, was leading him down a corridor. She was using a lot of initials: MI, ICU. He wasn't sure what she was saying, but he followed in her wake, letting the waves of white carry him down the corridor.

There was nothing else to do at 6:00 A.M. Everyone in the department had gone home to sleep. The bureaucratic machinery was grinding at its usual slow pace. The autopsy had been scheduled for later that morning.

He wasn't ready to call Elizabeth. He had been alone with this information for almost twenty-four hours. He was trying to let it all sink in. How would he tell her?

He had simply discovered a dead body behind a shed in the cemetery. But that wasn't all. It was a horribly decomposed corpse. And it might be the remains of a child as young as twelve years old. She had been murdered. Yes, he thought, that's how he'd say it. He was involved in a homicide. But of course everyone, Elizabeth included, would want to know the details. And somehow, even after twenty-two hours without sleep, the details still sent adrenaline pumping through his veins.

Moving silently down the corridor, he wondered if this wasn't one of the things that kept him going. This rush of terror. This sensation of being on the verge of something. The seduction of danger, George knew, was an experience shared by both cop and criminal. Sometimes the line between the two was thinly drawn. With a weapon in his holster or strapped to his ankle, George was capable of murder, but he also believed he possesssed an inner control. A balance that could not be tipped.

"You can only stay a minute or two," the nurse was saying. "The patient is in no condition . . ."

He let her words echo against the white tiles. Then he saw for himself. Kiley could neither talk nor listen. There was a catheter in his nose. Tubes snaked from bottles hanging from IV poles into his veins. His bed was tented in plastic. He had had a heart attack, something the nurse kept calling an "MI". Lieutenant Murphy stared at the pale face, which looked even paler against the stark white pillow. Poor bastard, he thought. He asked the nurse if the family had been notified. She shook her head and said there was no wife, but someone who knew Kiley said there was a daughter in New Jersey. Murphy made a note to check it out. It was just one more thing to do, and now he needed tasks to keep him moving.

Wobbling from fatigue, he walked back through the corridors like a drunken man. The serenity of the small-town hospital in the early morning hours gave him more time to think. Suppose he had found the girl and she had not been dead? Suppose they had brought her here and, like Kiley in the room down the hall, they had inserted tubes and catheters, fed her veins with life-restoring fluids. Suppose, then, she could talk. How could the attack be explained? Maybe a young boyfriend in a jealous rage. Maybe a rape that had gone beyond sexual assault. Perhaps she had been a hooker or a runaway, or even a victim of a serial murderer. That troubled him. He also considered the possibility of an irate father or a homicidal sibling. She hadn't fought back. There were no defensive wounds on her hands or forearms.

The lists were all in his head now. He tried to arrange them in some order. But each attempt proved futile. The body was not fully clothed. True, she wore a skirt and sweater, but there had been no undergarments, no shoes, no rings, no jewelry, except, of course, the cross. Past experience had proved that homicides committed in a jealous rage, crimes of passion they were called, had a particular pattern. There would be signs of struggle on the victim herself. If it had been a violent assault by a rapist, there would have been scratches, bruises on the inside of the thighs, the buttocks, or the vagina. He would have noticed that. Maybe the autopsy would find skin or fiber evidence beneath the nails. Any indication of sexual assault would send him in a definite direction.

Instinctively, George knew the pieces weren't fitting together. Not at all. The assailant had had a cool head. He had managed to dump the body in an inconspicuous place. He had removed or destroyed any significant clues as to the girl's identity. It chilled him to think that perhaps the murderer was familiar with Bakersville. How else would he have known when that extra dirt was scheduled to be dumped on precisely the path that had led to that sight behind the shed? Of course it might have just been lucky timing. Lucky for the perpetrator. Unlucky for the girl, and for him.

It was 6:30 and he needed coffee. He thought about calling his ex-wife and explaining that the weekend plans with Sheila might have to be canceled. No, postponed. That sounded better. But Tina wouldn't be up for at least another hour. Waking her would only make their conversation more tense, more disturbing to both of them.

He walked aimlessly around the hospital grounds. Realizing there was no place to go, he sat down on a bench and stared at the well-tended lawn. Automatically, his hand grazed the scar that ran diagonally from his left shoulder across his chest. It had been almost a year since he had been here in this hospital. Almost a year and he still had nightmares.

He closed his eyes for an instant and it was all there. The dark, moonless night, the car parked alongside the highway. He had been alone in a patrol car. The vehicle appeared to be disabled. Without thinking much about it, he sauntered over to the sedan, figuring the passengers would need some help. He motioned for the driver to roll down the window. He never had a chance to look at the man's face or to check the license plate. But he did remember the blood. It poured from his chest and ran down his arms. It formed red puddles on the highway. He hadn't seen the knife, but whoever wielded the blade had been an expert.

He could still feel the uneven pavement scraping against his knees as he knelt down and took aim. Two shots rang out. The car he had believed to be disabled sped away. He squinted his eyes against the pain. Headlights passed him. Vehicles moving down the county road saw him rolled in a bloody ball beside his patrol car. No one stopped. The lights came and went, periodically shooting through the darkness, then disappearing. He dragged himself against the damp pavement until he reached his car and radioed for help. Then the blackness moved in. It was a blackness that stayed with him for almost twenty-four hours. He recalled swimming in pools of light, hearing voices, feeling warmth.

He resurfaced in the early morning. Still fuzzy from the pain, it took him several hours to remember. It must have been during those hours, he thought now, that the man with the blade admitted himself to an emergency room not more than 150 miles from Bakersville. By the time Chief Norris had gotten the investigation underway, the man had been treated for a bullet wound in the left thigh and had escaped. No one knew where. No one had followed up. Murphy remembered the horrible vulnerability. Even now as he thought about it, the scar throbbed beneath his shirt. He had been slashed by someone who would remain nameless and faceless. The attacker's bullet had been removed. His scar would be permanent.

He scraped his feet along the metal railing that ran beneath the bench. Those days and nights in the hospital had been hellish. Chief Norris came every afternoon. When he bent down to shake Murphy's hand, Murphy had smelled the booze. It hadn't been the first time, but it gave credence to the screwups that were to come later. Tina called every day, and every day he told her he didn't want to see her. She came anyway, trailing Sheila, who seemed small and frightened as she stood in the doorway.

Why was this all coming back to him now? Maybe—and he was sure he heard Elizabeth's voice as he asked himself these questions—it had something to do with being a victim. Since that night, police work had changed for him. He was more cautious now, but he was also unsure. The cases he once would have gone through quickly and automatically now seemed to take time. They stayed with him. Since that night victims began to have faces. He knew, because he had been one himself.

He looked up at a window on the uppermost floor of the hospital. If Kiley was in that room and if Kiley were to expire, he too would be a victim. Whoever had bludgeoned the girl would have been indirectly responsible for the gravedigger's death.

The fatigue was moving behind his eyes, a thick opaque curtain that dulled his defenses. He was remembering all the scenes he wanted to forget. All he should be thinking about was the girl. In a matter of hours he would be getting some answers. He would be there when the medical examiner conducted the autopsy. He would make sure every detail was noted, every procedure followed to a tee. Then he would put the pieces together. He would begin looking for the family. His police sense would take over again. But even as he prepared himself for the events to follow, Lieutenant Murphy was aware that this case was different. He fully expected that for a while the murderer would remain unidentified but he shuddered when he realized that this time so might the victim.

8

ELIZABETH BEGAN WORRYING the minute she woke up. It hadn't occurred to her at all last night. Probably because of the motorcycle and the man, she thought as she hastily dialed his number. There was no answer. She sat down beside the bed and began to think about calling headquarters. They had been through all this before. He didn't like her to pump Jean for information. His ex-wife Tina had done it constantly. And when it finally had happened he had been alone.

That's when she'd met him. After the stabbing. She passed his hospital room every day on the way to visit her mother. It was hard not to notice him. Big, blond, and square-jawed, his chest was wrapped in bandages, but he looked as though he would still be able to leap out of bed and take on the world. He was strong, she could tell that immediately. When he told her he was a cop, she wasn't surprised. He looked the part, and there was something appealing about his tough, protective attitude.

Their relationship began during the days he lay bandaged and immobile. Still in shock about her mother, she had felt wounded too. Their mutual pain became a common denominator, a magnet that drew them closer and closer. But it was more than that. George talked to her. He told her about his life, how happy he had been as a child and how hurt and confused he had been when his marriage ended. As the days passed, Elizabeth found herself caring more than she had expected to. George couldn't always articulate his feelings, but he was aware of them. The brutality he had seen as a cop and the pain he had felt in his own life had not closed him off. He had not shut down emotionally like so many men she had known. Despite his tough veneer, Elizabeth sensed that George was not a simple man.

When he left the hospital, they slept together for the first time. It had been the culmination of weeks of talking and flirting—of wondering what the other would be like in bed.

She guessed that he would be a good lover and she had been right. His body was just as she'd imagined it. His legs, thick and muscular, were covered with coppery blond hairs. When he held her breasts in his large hands she felt like a small child, a miniature person. Sometimes he caught her looking at the scar. She would run her fingers along the raw, red ridge. He wanted to forget what had happened. He had said it was part of being a cop. She wasn't sure she agreed, but she knew not to argue. He was struggling to regain his confidence and his sense of control.

In the beginning they made love every night. Once, he undressed her in the squad car and carried her naked into the bedroom. But later, there were times when an unbearable tension existed between them. After he visited his ex-wife and his daughter, they avoided one another for days. He seemed to need the time alone to sort through his confusion. Resentful, she spent her nights wondering if he was thinking about Tina, fearful he might return to her. Eventually one of them would give in. But there was always a residue of anger. It was clear he didn't belong to Elizabeth completely.

Recently, when they made love she remained silent, refusing to give herself up to the pleasure.

*   *   *

She checked the time. It was almost 7:30. Was it possible that he hadn't come in at all last night? She padded around the small house looking everywhere for a cigarette. Finally she found one, smashed but still smokable, at the bottom of her blue handbag. Inhaling relaxed her. Only now the worry was giving way to guilt. Maybe she should have called him instead of Celia. Maybe taking that ride would have serious consequences. What if by not being there, not being home when he might have tried to reach her, she had put him in some sort of danger? She thought about that night when he had dragged himself, bleeding and alone, to the car radio. What if something like that had happened again?

It crossed her mind to call the hospital, but as she inhaled she realized she was being overly dramatic. This was Bakersville, after all. Jean had told her he was out on a case. If he ran into trouble he would call headquarters, not her. She crushed the cigarette in a nearby ashtray, making sure she couldn't resurrect it later on. If she really hurried, she could get to the diner in time to catch him. She would act totally relaxed. Her panic had a way of becoming contagious. He would definitely pick up on it and would either become angry or withdrawn.

Elizabeth dialed his number one more time. She let it ring as she considered the cigarette. She had done a good job on this one. The only part that remained intact was the filter. As she hung up, she decided she would play the entire morning by ear. Be spontaneous, she thought. And she definitely would not mention last night. That would be a mistake.

She dressed quickly, hoping she could make it to Peg's in time. Otherwise she'd have to sit under a cloud of worry all day. She only thought about Gary once—when she remembered that she had left her car keys in the blue handbag on her dresser. That swept her into a stream of associations, at the forefront of which was her eagerness to take a ride on a Harley-Davidson with a complete stranger. Now, in the light of day, it seemed like a reckless thing to have done. She made a firm decision not to dwell on it. Then she put the key in the ignition of the car and drove toward the diner.

He was there at his usual counter seat. He was wearing his blue uniform; his broad back strained the seams.

She tapped him on the shoulder. When he turned to face her, she saw thc darkness beneath his eyes. There were wrinkles on his forehead, frown lines around his mouth. He looked as though he hadn't slept in weeks.

"What's up?" she asked, trying to seem casual. She dreaded being compared to Tina.

"Been up on a case all night," he answered. There was no affection in his tone. He was all business. Something was wrong. She looked at him questioningly.

"Why don't we go out and sit in the car for a few minutes?"

Curious, and frightened, she followed.

The squad car was parked in the far corner of the lot. He walked quickly, expecting her to match his strides. She was breathless by the time she slid into the front seat beside him.

"No one knows yet," he told her. "There's been a murder. I found the body yesterday."

He avoided her eyes as he ran through the chilling details. He spoke in a continuous monotone, as if any hesitation would make going on impossible.

"You mean there was no identification at all?" she asked.

George shook his head.

It was unthinkable that such a thing could happen here. She had grown up in this town. The riverbank and the gravedigger's shed George described were places where she used to play as a teenager. Going to the cemetery at night had always been a game. On Halloween, kids would meet there and try to scare one another. Sometimes they put plastic legs behind the tombstones. But that had all been part of the fun. No one ever took any of it seriously. Finding a body, a real one, would change all that. Things would be different. Now there would be a reason to be afraid.

"You have no idea who she is?" she asked again, as if knowing who the girl was would somehow make everything less shocking.

"Zero," George said. He offered her a cigarette.

"What happens now?" she asked, inhaling until she could feel a dry burning at the back of her throat.

"I think we'll have more information after the autopsy."

"When will that be?"

"It should have been a.s.a.p.," he answered, "but thanks to Norris it wasn't scheduled until later this morning."

"Are you going?"

"You bet I'm going," he shot back. "I'm not gonna let that medical examiner screw up my investigation. I'll be there, watching every cut, making sure they don't overlook a single shred of evidence."

She knew when he used initials he was trying to sound official. Before, she had made fun of him, joking that he wasn't a real cop, that Bakersville only needed a traffic policeman. But today she was seeing a different side of his work. And he was different too. His face was a mask of control. Nothing showed. Despite their intimacy, it was hard for her to tell.

Was he frightened, angry? She couldn't be sure. He must be feeling *something*. The girl was close in age to his own daughter.

"George, is that where you were all last night—working on this case?"

"We went over that cemetery with a fine-tooth comb," he answered. "Then when they quit, I retraced every step. I was thinking of calling you, but by the time I stopped, it was after two."

She wondered what she had been doing at that moment—riding on a motorcycle in the moonlight, or lying naked in her bed, imagining being touched by a stranger?

"What can I do?" She was aware that last night while she indulged her fantasies, George had held a murdered child in his arms.

"I'll be needing you, Elizabeth. If we ID the victim, I'd like your help with the parents. If we don't get an ID, we'll want to look at some of your files."

"What sort of stuff would you need?"

"Anything. If the victim is local, we'd look for records of child abuse, runaways, anything that might place a minor in a situation like this. If she's not local, which I suspect, you can help me reach other agencies and poke around for information."

Elizabeth nodded. There was no sense getting embroiled in a discussion about a client's right to privacy. Not now when there was an unidentified child waiting in the morgue.

"Do you have any theories?"

"I don't know," he answered. The fatigue was even more evident now than it had been before. He squinted against the morning light. He was under tremendous pressure. She hoped he could remain alert during the autopsy. "I checked for signs of sexual assault and didn't see anything. Of course, that may all be reversed this afternoon. But my guess is it wasn't a rape."

Elizabeth was thoughtful. The horrible possibilies were occurring to her—one by one.

"Did you take photographs? Maybe someone saw her in the past few days. If she's as young as you think, someone would have noticed, someone must be looking for her."

"Photographs of what? I told you there was no face left at all." He shook his head. "Elizabeth, I have very little to go on."

No face. She felt sick to her stomach. How could they hope for a quick resolution under these circumstances?

"Do you have any more cigarettes?"

He flipped open the glove compartment. They sat silently as they smoked.

She crushed the cigarette out when it reached the halfway mark.

"What about Kiley?" she finally thought to ask.

"He's in rough shape," George answered. "Tubes and bottles, oxygen tent, the whole mess. By the way, do you know anything about his family? His wife passed away a few years ago, but I think I remember hearing about a daughter. Would you know anything about that?"

Elizabeth nodded. Kiley had attended a much-publicized program for alcoholics that her predecessor had initiated. It was very possible they still had a file on him.

"I'll look into it this morning. Anything else I can do?"

"Nose around. See if you can get a lead on any recent domestic violence, any reports of missing kids. Remember that cult thing? See if there were any local girls involved in that."

The cult thing he was referring to had been a group of Hare Krishnas that had made the mistake of trying to establish a residence in the heart of Bakersville's most rural district. They had been run out within weeks. She knew this was a long shot, but it was clear he needed to involve her in this case.

"What are you planning to do after the results of the post mortem?"

"I'm planning to solve the case," he said abruptly.

Even now she couldn't help noticing the blond stubble that covered his chin; he had a worn, rugged look. His blue eyes met hers for an instant before he looked away. She moved in his direction but retreated when she felt him back away.

He checked his watch. Like rubbing his scar, it was one of his automatic gestures, one intended to keep her at arm's length. He didn't want any contact now. She sat motionless, watching as another car pulled up beside them.

"I guess there's nothing to do between now and noon," she said. She didn't offer to attend the post mortem, although she could have gotten the time off if she really wanted to.

He was staring out the window at the gravel in the parking lot.

"Remind me to make sure they do a pelvic," he said. It was clear he was totally absorbed. He was thinking out loud. It was as if she wasn't there at all.

"What for?"

"It's important to know if she was pregnant or had ever carried to full term. It might help us locate her family or link her to the assailant in some way."

Elizabeth nodded. It was too morbid to think of the medical examiner doing a pelvic examination on a corpse. She tried to change the subject.

"Did you call Sheila? Are you going to cancel this weekend?"

He relaxed for a moment. "Shit," he said, "I hope not. I'm going to try my best to make it. Who knows? This whole mess might be wrapped up and delivered to the chief in twenty-four hours."

But they both knew that was unlikely. There were just too many unknowns with this case.

"It's almost nine," Elizabeth said. "I guess I'd better get moving. Is there anything else I can do?"

George shook his head. She hated herself for thinking about it at a time like this, but, still, she was grateful she didn't have to mention the ride home last night. It seemed so unimportant in the light of what had happened.

He grabbed her hand as she opened the door.

"Thanks for listening."

"Remember to have them do a pelvic," she said as she kissed him goodbye.

9

HE WAS UP TO HIS KNEES in grass, fragrant summer grass that was sprinkled everywhere with wildflowers. He had an overwhelming impulse to lie down in the green meadow and let the warm air, the bees, and the summer scents surround him. Instead, he sat cross-legged beside a cluster of mountain laurel and began to take photographs. Only he didn't reach for the camera that was slung around his neck. This was one of those days, one of those moments he wanted to capture with the other sort of photograph, the type he had been taking long before he learned to master the intricacies of shutter speeds and lens adjustments. He made a circle with his thumb and forefinger. Framed by his own hand, the meadow would be captured forever in his mind. He squeezed the circle tighter. Click. The picture was his.

Gary had camped out overnight in a field only a few miles from where he had dropped Elizabeth off the night before. His tent, a small but efficient setup, was rolled into a tight package beside the Harley-Davidson. He had ridden the motorcycle directly onto the grass, set up camp, and gazed at the stars before he fell into a dark, dreamless sleep.

Now, in the early morning he was thinking about the woman he had met in the bar. In the beginning she had been wary, but he was sure that the ride had loosened her up. He could almost sense her growing pleasure as they sped along the country roads. It might be interesting to see her again. Gary thought about stopping off at the diner. It was clear from their discussion last night that she frequented the place. But he wasn't sure he was ready. Not quite yet.

He reached for his canteen and quickly washed his face. He would have to stop somewhere to clean up if he did visit her. Sleeping in the field last night had been another impulse, but this time he had given in. The motel in Castle Corners was only a short ride away. He stayed there often. It had become a routine pit stop on his way south from Buffalo.

He plucked a pink flower from the lush mountain laurel. Camping out reminded him of the sixties. He had been a student at the university, and although he knew there had been horribly cold winters, it seemed that all he could remember from those days were the summers. He had taken a lot of photographs back then. Later he had used the black and whites to get his first free-lance job. It hadn't taken very long before he had a portfolio bulging with published works and reps on both coasts who got him choice assignments. Now the photography was less important to him, certainly less exciting. He preferred his older, more primitive method of picture-taking.

Getting up, he walked slowly through the field. Oxeye daisies, golden asters, loosestrife. He identified the wildflowers one by one. He thought of putting together a bouquet. There were fiddlehead ferns growing along the borders of the forest. He could fill in the spaces between the yellow and blue clusters with the spidery green leaves. Maybe that would be too much. She could be frightened away by such excess. She was definitely the careful type. But he was sure he had sensed another side of her during the ride. He was sure he hadn't imagined her breasts pushing against the back of his jacket, or the way she had paused, waiting for him to make a move in front of her door.

He squinted into the sun. He was between assignments now. There was plenty of time to court Elizabeth. He waded deeper into the tall grass, hoping to spot the red, swordlike leaves of a lone wood lily. The flower fascinated him. It grew alone, or sometimes with a mate, on the edges of the forest. In a single spot where the light filtered down through the trees, the wood lily spread its flaming petals for only one day. He had been lucky enough to spot the flower several times. If he saw one this morning he would make a mental note, take a picture in his head. Then he would return before the day was over. It would be better than a bouquet. More meaningful, less overwhelming.

As he tramped through the grass, he noticed every detail: the perfect symmetry of a black-eyed Susan, the white, odd-shaped flower of a nodding teaberry. He stopped to watch as the sun glinted off the iridescent wings of a dragonfly. He didn't need his camera for this, he didn't even need to make a circle with his fingers. Gary had spent years looking at the tiniest details in nature. At first, all his photographs had been of wildflowers, insects, trees, and spider webs. In order to take those pictures he had to remain undetected, to blend in with the landscape. Dressed in camouflage, he had hidden for hours behind a blind, a drape of gray or green cloth with a triangular opening for his lens.

The blind had worked well, but as time passed he came to resent it. He needed to become part of the landscape. He came to believe that in order to learn the secrets, he had to be part of them, to integrate his presence with the forests and the meadows. So he trained himself to sit beside a tree without stirring, barely breathing, for hours. He practiced walking through the woods slowly, side-stepping each twig.

Back then he had believed that the forest was good and beautiful. But now he knew that it was merely silent—a witness unaffected by the events that took place within it.

*   *   *

When he spotted the wood lily, he was on his way back to the motorcycle. He saw it protruding from a thicket, standing above the ferns like a solitary red beacon. He stopped by the grassy border that separated the meadows, green and flushed with light, from the forest. Perhaps now wasn't the time to pick it. Even if he wrapped it well, it might wither before she came home. Then he thought of driving over to the diner and giving it to her. He hesitated an instant before crossing into the darkness. He had never really succeeded in blending in with the trees and the foliage.

He remained an intruder, as he reached down and plucked the flower from the soft earth.

He knew the way to the diner, instinctively, as if he traveled there often. But in truth, he had only taken photographs of the outside. His familiarity with the place was very recent.

As he was turning the corner, he saw a patrol car pull out from the parking lot. The man inside either didn't notice him or was just a lousy driver. The car made a wide and sloppy turn, nearly pushing him off the road. Damn cop, he thought, the guy thinks he can get away with anything. Gary felt like speeding up and giving the policeman the sort of excitement he wouldn't easily forget. But, instead, he responded by leaning the Harley as far to the right as he possibly could. The patrol car accelerated, leaving him in the dust.

He wasn't wearing a watch, but it was clear by the half-empty lot, that he had missed the morning rush. His first inclination was to ride away. There were better diners just north and east of Bakersville. But he still might catch her. It was certainly worth a try.

As he entered the diner he could smell the remains of what was probably some sort of grease fire. She wasn't there. He had missed her, or she hadn't come in yet. He ordered coffee and waited. Peg, the blond waitress who filled his cup, was calling everyone by their first names. She smiled and joked with the regulars, who all seemed to be dressed alike: overalls, caps, flannel shirts, and heavy boots.

Gary had no desire to get into an early morning chat. He avoided Peg's eyes and gazed instead at the myriad postcards that were tucked into the corners of the two windows and taped on the mirror over the cash register. Many of the cards had turned yellow with age and were covered with a thick layer of grime. Two fresh ones were taped on the window overlooking the parking lot. He glanced at them briefly.

He remembered that last night Fred had mentioned something about a boyfriend. If that were true, she might come in with him, or they might have already eaten and left. He thought about the flower he had wrapped with a damp cloth and placed in his saddlebag. A boyfriend might not appreciate the offering. Maybe this won't be so easy, he thought, as he left some loose change beside the empty coffee cup.

When he returned to the motorcycle, he had already made his decision. He donned his helmet and headed west.

The day was thickening around him. A little longer and the light would begin to soften, turning the color it got as late morning melted into noon. Gary was feeling it now. He had to act quickly and carefully. The mood might not last, the impulse could fade with the changing light.

He had no trouble finding the way back to her house. He remembered every detail of last evening's ride, including the winding road, the pine trees, and the isolated location of the cottage.

No one was home. He was sure of it. The driveway was empty; there was no sign of activity. As an extra precaution, he revved the engine. If she was home, she'd come to the door or peer out through a window. If there was a dog, he'd hear a warning bark.

Gary glanced over his shoulder as he picked the lock. It clicked easily beneath his fingers. He had to believe that he could not be seen. He willed his own invisibility.

His hands were steady, but there was an internal trembling. He was an intruder, trespassing in her most private world.

*   *   *

Inside, the house was still. It was an eerie stillness—a ticking clock, the steady hum of the refrigerator turning itself on and off. Gary knew that houses continued working, obediently clicking and whirring despite their owner's absence. He believed that in this emptiness he could experience a particular kind of intimacy. Without her being there he could know her. Alone, he could leave a message suspended in the silence.

He stood in the kitchen as he stared down at the small blue ashtray that held only the brown lipstick-stained filter of a cigarette. Holding it in his hand, he inhaled. Her scent was everywhere.

He rubbed his hand across the well-worn handle of an enamel tea kettle, warming it with his own flesh. The refrigerator was filled with yogurt and cottage cheese, milk and eggs. A half-eaten danish was wrapped in plastic on the bottom shelf.

It was good that he'd started in this room. This was the last place she had been. A white cup still filled with coffee rested on a saucer. He brought it to his lips. The coffee was strong and unsweetened. This was his first taste of her. He was hungry for more.

There wasn't much time. He walked slowly, almost reverently toward the bedroom. Now the sensations were building. He felt them tighten in his groin, felt them move upward into his belly. He paused at the half-closed door, clicking his eyes like the shutter of a camera.

The bed was carelessly made. Partially covered with a hand-sewn quilt, it still bore the trace of her impression. He held a pale blue pillow in both hands. Exchanging his scent for hers, he rubbed his cheek against the smooth cotton. It would have been too easy to make a mistake now, to slip beneath the sheets or sit on the bed. But that would be clumsy. It would leave too much of himself.

His pulse quickened as he opened the top dresser drawers. They held slips and bras, panties, socks and stockings. It was clear that there had been an order once, but now the contents crowded in on one another. The socks were balled into round fists, the pantyhose scattered everywhere.

He held a soft pink bra between his fingers. Closing his eyes, he remembered how her breasts had pushed against his back as he drove the motorcycle. He tried to imagine her nipples, soft and brown beneath the pink. The sensations were more intense now. He was very close to her. He stared at the jumble of pastels. He was knowing her, invading her, stealing in a way no one could ever understand.

He lifted up the first layer of underpants and reached down into the drawer. Without disturbing the order of things, he touched them all. For a split second he closed his eyes and held his breath. Now the pictures were in his head. They belonged to him.

He entered the living room. A stack of professional journals was piled neatly on a pine table. He picked one up, and noticing an address label, saw that her full name was Elizabeth Kern. Just to try the sound, he said the name out loud. It felt good to hear his voice in her house. He was filling up the empty spaces, taking the place that had been waiting for him.

Walking into the small white bathroom, he touched the toothbrush, the cosmetics, the contents of the medicine chest. There was so much. The house was overflowing with her presence.

He left his reflection in the mirror over the sink. Knowing it would be there when he returned, he felt safe. The sensations were moving across the surface of his skin. His hands began to shake. He returned to the kitchen and picked up the red flower he had placed beside the sink. He had taken all the photographs he needed. He had left part of himself and he was leaving with part of her.

Gary slipped out of Elizabeth's house as quietly as he had entered it. He left no trace of his trespass, save the flower he attached to the front door. And he took nothing but a mysterious essence no one could possibly miss.

10

IT LOOKED LIKE AN operating room, only there were no life-support systems, no tubes, no bottles of liquid hanging from IV poles, no sterile instruments. This was the decomp room. The body he had pulled from the tangle of branches now lay peacefully on a stainless steel table surrounded by catch basins.

Two long fluorescent tubes stretched along the ceiling, illuminating the gray flesh and the battered skull. The pathologist did not wear a mask. Narrow ventilation ducts cut into the spaces where windows should have been. A small machine released a scent intended to reduce the odor. Lieutenant Murphy felt an uncomfortable constriction in his gut. The smell of decomposition—rotting human flesh—clung to the walls and filtered through the slow-moving air.

He was concerned about his own lack of composure. There were subtle signs, little things he was sure no one else could detect: the jittery feeling in his wrists, the way his scar throbbed beneath his shirt. And then there had been the close call on the way over here. He had caught the reflection of the black motorcycle in the corner of his car mirror, just as he made a wide turn. He had nearly pushed the bike off the road. Luckily, the driver had leaned to the right. Ordinarily, he would have pulled the chopper over for a routine check, but instead he had sped away, angry at his own carelessness.

The incident continued to bother him. It was almost as if a black cat had crossed his path. True, he hadn't gotten a look at the rider, but the motorcycle had seemed vaguely familiar. He knew he had been irresponsible to speed up and leave the driver to maneuver in his wake.

Now that he was here, he had to put that out of his mind. He could not afford to be preoccupied with traffic accidents or with superstitions. This was the most crucial part of the investigation, and it was all up to him. The pathologist would perform only the most basic procedures. If he wanted to avoid any slipups, any oversights, he had to remain attentive. After the post mortem, the physical evidence would be wrapped up. The only clues left now were those on, or in, the body of the dead girl. He owed it to her to be thorough.

The pathologist was talking to him. She held a clipboard and wrote down the information he gave her. His responses, like her inquiries, were automatic. He tried not to look too closely at the narrow table but concentrated instead on the sound of the medical examiner's voice. She asked him where he had found the body, the position it had been in, the precise time of discovery. Her voice became a gentle drone that seemed to make the horror of what he told her, mundane, routine.

"I'm ready to begin now," she said, as she slipped on a pair of thin surgical gloves. She unhooked the gold chain with the cross before expertly removing the clothing from the body.

"Bloodstains on the sweater," she said as she put the cross and the garments in a plastic bag that he would take with him when he left. She inspected the body for marks, scars, contusions, anything unusual or remarkable. She took samples from under the fingernails and collected maggots from the crushed skull. This all would be sent to the lab in the hope it would yield information about the assailant and the exact time of death.

Lieutenant Murphy watched as the pathologist made the incision—a neat Y that ran from the left shoulder blade to the center of the breastbone. She was open now. The girl who perhaps as recently as three days ago walked and talked, ate and breathed was now a corpse to be dissected, tagged, bagged, and classified by a pathologist and a police officer.

He felt the grinding in his gut begin to slow. He had been here before. He had watched countless autopsies. Now that the flesh was peeled back, she was no longer the girl he had carried from behind the shed. She was a Jane Doe. The pathologist fixed her age at somewhere between fourteen and seventeen. His hands remained steady as he wrote the numbers on his notepad.

"There's food in the digestive tract. I'd say it looks like your typical junk-food meal: hamburger, french fries, the whole bit. This was ingested about an hour or so before the time of death."

Lieutenant Murphy nodded. There had been no appendectomy scar, no birthmarks, tattoos, or other identifying marks. There were no signs of sexual assault, no semen in the vaginal smear. The pelvic the pathologist had reluctantly performed showed that the victim had neither been pregnant nor had she ever carried a child to term. She had been a virgin. A junk-food meal an hour before death was the only new information the autopsy had revealed.

The pathologist was curt and efficient. She weighed the organs and placed them in plastic bags and buckets for him to transport to the lab. Cause of death had been established as blows to the skull with a heavy, blunt instrument. There were no stab wounds, bullet holes, or bruises caused by strangulation.

"I guess that about does it," she said as she began peeling off the gloves.

"What about prints?" George asked.

She looked at him impatiently. "With the skin in this condition, it's iffy. We can do a roll, but there's a good chance the fingertips will peel off. There's no way we can go for a second try."

He had been prepared for this. The medical examiner's office was overworked and understaffed, but he knew what he was about to ask was within his rights.

"I want the hands removed and shot with silicone. I'll take them to the lab myself. It's the only way we can get readable prints."

The pathologist narrowed her eyes. It was clear she considered this an extraordinary request. She scribbled something on her notes and turned her back to him. He had tangled with the bureaucracy before. If the chief wasn't getting any pressure from higher-ups, he'd support George on this. George knew no one would bother making a fuss over the case. Not yet, anyway.

Approximately three hours after he had arrived, Lieutenant Murphy left the medical examiner's office with the clothes, the organs, and the hands of the body he had discovered the day before. Now he knew exactly what he was up against.

At first the case would cause a mild ripple. If he handled it right, and if the chief gave him free rein, he could get enough publicity to alert the upstate area. But that might not be good enough. If the girl was actively being sought, which he was sure she was, and if her family lived in the state, it would only be a matter of days, possibly weeks, until someone came to inquire.

But that would be leaving too much to chance. There was a good possibility that she had been murdered far from home. There were over 23,000 missing persons in the country. How could he possibly begin to track down a teenager who had no identifying marks, no belongings, and—no face? Sure, he could circulate the dentals and basic forensic information to police departments throughout the country, but that was slow, tedious, and usually ineffective. He knew that publicity would prevent the body from remaining a Jane Doe. But he also knew that getting anything other than local coverage would not be easy. This was a small story. Girl found in cemetery. Identity sought. The newspapers were filled with sensational cases. Murder, even the murder of a teenager, was hardly national news.

The best course of action, he decided, was to try and reconstruct the events on his own. He had to give the girl whose body parts now rested in buckets and bags on the backseat of his patrol car, a personality, a life, and even a name. If he could make her real, make her important, then he had a chance.

The first step was to imagine her, not as a decaying corpse in a body bag but as a lively teenager, dressed in a brown sweater and long paisley skirt.

He tried to envision her eating a hamburger at a fast-food joint, leaving, going somewhere, with someone. That's when he hit a dead end. Again and again, his imagination failed him. The clothes seemed all wrong. The sweater with the cotton skirt seemed incongruous. When he closed his eyes and tried to picture her sitting in a restaurant, or ordering from a car, he drew a blank. The only face that appeared when he attempted to conjure one up was the smiling image of his own daughter.

Maybe it was the hour, the fact that he had gone so long without sleep. He knew he needed help on this one. The other men in the department were locals, young, and relatively inexperienced. The chief had handled his share of homicides, but George was wary of him. It was no secret that Ed Norris was hitting the bottle again. Murphy knew all too well that booze would make him careless as well as vulnerable to bureaucratic pressure. Besides, he wanted to handle the police work on his own. He wanted to wrap this case up himself. All he needed was some help in imagining, in temporarily inventing an identity. If he could make the girl flesh and blood, people would care. He could buy more time, could prevent her from becoming what the department termed "actively inactive," and what he would simply call yesterday's news.

He considered phoning Elizabeth. This sort of thing was right up her alley. She worked with families every day. He could give her the forensic details and they could put together a profile, something that seemed believable. At the same time they could work on a dramatic angle—a hook to attract publicity to the case.

By the time Lieutenant Murphy reached the lab, he had most of it figured out. In a few hours, everyone would know about the girl without a face. He would recreate her so no one could forget. He didn't have every detail yet, he would need Elizabeth's help to fill in the blanks, but he did have a plan of action, and a gimmick. Somewhere between the medical examiner's office and the lab, he had come up with a way to present the evidence that would create the first small ripple of interest. He was going to handle this on his own.

Right now she was nothing, a Jane Doe. But not for long. If he did everything right, if there were no slipups, she would soon be someone. Not a hooker or a runaway or an unclaimed corpse. She would matter. The dead girl he had dragged from the bushes was going to have an identity, even if he had to invent it himself.

11

"MRS. MORGAN, I UNDERSTAND what you've told me, and I appreciate your position, but perhaps you might be able to phone the hospital. And if you're not quite ready to speak to your father, at least you can stay abreast of his condition."

There was silence on the other end. Elizabeth could hear a child crying in the background. It hadn't taken too long to locate Mason Kiley's daughter. Annabel Morgan, mother of three, lived in Warren County, New Jersey. She hadn't seen her father since she'd left home twelve years ago. For the past half hour Elizabeth had listened as Mrs. Morgan recounted the childhood she had had with an alcoholic father. It was a story Elizabeth had heard many times before.

"I'll have to think about that, Ms. Kern," Annabel replied. "You know that will be a long distance call. And, uh, I really don't know what to say to him. He's never even seen my kids. I left home when I was sixteen. Seems like I don't really have a father."

She sensed that the woman wanted to talk, but there was no time. Annabel Morgan was not a client; she was no longer a resident of Bakersville. Elizabeth drummed her fingers across the green desk blotter.

"Well, Mrs. Morgan, your father is here, and he's hospitalized. I'm sure he would want to hear from you. But the decision is yours. If I can be of any further help . . . ," she let her voice trail off, hoping Annabel Morgan would let her go gracefully.

The woman had not asked many questions about the circumstances surrounding her father's heart attack. And that was a definite relief. George hadn't told her what information was confidential and what she could share. Her co-workers already knew about the body. After the initial shock, they had come to the conclusion that the girl was a hooker or a runaway, or both, and that she was most probably en route to or from New York City. Elizabeth wasn't so sure.

After she wrapped up her conversation with Kiley's daughter, she went back to the files—yellowed client folders marked "confidential" that were jammed into a row of metal cabinets. There were thousands of possibilities here. Incest. Rape. Jealous boyfriends. Angry stepfathers. For the first time the reality of what had happened, and what might still be happening, occurred to her.

The files were filled with potential motives, potential victims, likely assailants. But it seemed doubtful that the solution would be found here. For one thing, no one had called. Neither the police department nor her office had heard anything about a runaway or a missing child. The only explanation was that she was from another county or state. But even then, wouldn't there be police reports, some description of her lying on a desk somewhere? Then she remembered about the face. That would definitely slow things down. Identifying a body in that condition would be difficult. Fingerprints. That was one possibility. But of course there would have to be matching prints on file somewhere. How the hell was George going to handle this?

She checked her watch. It was 10:25 and he was probably at the autopsy right now. She tried to picture him watching stoically as they disassembled the body he had carried from behind the wooden shed. It must be agony for him, she thought. He had moved to Bakersville so his daughter would have a safe place to grow up. Ironically, he had lost her anyway. Little by little, a distance was growing between them. She was a child of divorce. At best, he could only be a part-time father. And now he had found the body of a girl—someone else's daughter, but Elizabeth had a feeling George wouldn't see it exactly that way.

This was going to be a long day. After the autopsy there would be the local radio and newspaper reports. No doubt a mild panic would follow. The usual crop of deranged woodchucks would stop by, insisting they knew either the victim or the attacker. No doubt they'd demand to see the body or insist on speaking to someone in charge. She would send them to police headquarters, and they in turn would send them back to her for what was locally referred to as "head shrinking."

Still, this was a murder. Somewhere, not far from the cemetery she passed every day, a young girl had been beaten on the skull until she died. The murderer had removed any identification—even her underwear. Elizabeth shuddered. Perhaps while she was here, talking to a client or even chatting with

Celia on the WATS line, some maniac was peeling the underwear off a dead girl's body. Then later, while she was riding on a motorcycle in the moonlight, that same body was lying in a bag in the morgue.

She began to imagine that they all might have seen one another. She and George, the girl, even the assailant. Maybe she had passed them on the street. Perhaps they had caught a glimpse of her as she drove to work or stopped at the diner. But now the connections were broken. The girl was dead; George was left with whatever evidence the pathologist could glean from the corpse; and she was here trying to find something in the yellow folders that would link the body with a name.

She tried not to think of the murderer. They'd probably never find him. Or when they did, he'd seem so small and real, so incapable of murder. Elizabeth knew this from her work at the clinic in Manhattan. There had been a woman, a battered wife. She had come often, had shown Elizabeth the bruises, had told her of the blind rages, the horrible beatings.

Elizabeth had urged the wife to bring her husband in for joint sessions. He had refused. The brutality continued. At night, after work, Elizabeth imagined she saw the husband everywhere—on the subway, in the street, behind the wheel of the taxi she took home. He began to take on immense, terrifying proportions. Eventually, Elizabeth convinced the woman to take refuge in an out-of-state shelter. She never made it. On the night she was to leave, her husband strangled her in the garage.

At the trial, Elizabeth finally got to see him. He was a thin, dark man, not the giant she had expected. Now that she had seen a murderer in person, she understood how easily they blended in with the scenery. There would be no way to tell, no way at all.

There was a call on her private line. She put the phone to her ear.

"Eros and Thanatos. Love and death."

"Who is this?" Elizabeth asked.

"It's me," Celia said. "I've been thinking about last night. You know, that motorcycle ride. It's a perfect example of dual forces, the erotic and the dangerous."

"Celia, you have no idea what's happened since we spoke. You couldn't have picked a worse time for a discussion of symbolism."

"Is something wrong?"

Elizabeth lowered her voice. "I can't give you all the details, but there's been a homicide here, and it's pretty gruesome."

"Don't tell me," Celia said, "George is involved."

"Right. And I'm not sure how he's going to handle it."

"Is there anything I can do? Do you want me to come up for the weekend? Maybe you want to stay here for a while? Are you, is anyone, in any danger?"

"Thanks for the offer, but I think he needs my help on this one."

"*Your* help? What can you do?"

Elizabeth was whispering now. "Celia, it was a young girl."

"How young?" Celia asked.

"We don't know yet. Maybe fourteen."

Celia was silent. Elsie was twelve and a half.

"I'm not going to ask you any of the details. I'll read about it, right?"

"Probably," Elizabeth answered.

"Just thank God you're not a mother. It's my worst nightmare. I watch Elsie like a hawk. Have you notified the parents?"

"Not yet, but we will soon."

"Those poor people. They must be frantic."

"Celia, if Elsie or one of her friends were missing for let's say a day or two, what would you do? Who would you notify?"

"A day or two! You've got to be joking. If my kid is more than fifteen minutes late coming home from school I'm ready to alert the FBI. With what's going on these days, no one waits twenty-four hours."

"That's what I thought," Elizabeth said.

"Why are you asking me this?" Celia questioned. "Do you mean you haven't told the parents yet or that you haven't found the parents yet?"

"Both," Elizabeth answered.

"Shit. It's enough to make me sick."

"Later, maybe I'll give you the particulars."

"I have a feeling," Celia said, "that I won't want to hear them."

"So do I," Elizabeth responded.

"I feel like a total jerk. Here I was calling you up with this brilliant psychological insight into your character and the nature of the universe, and there you are knee-deep in reality."

"Make that neck-high. Listen, there's a call on my other line. I'll get back to you as soon as I can."

"Take it slow," Celia warned.

"Elizabeth is that you?" Someone was shouting into the receiver. It was George. He was calling from a public phone on the highway. She could barely hear him over the steady roar of traffic.

"Yes, it's me," she answered. "How'd it go?"

"Routine." He sounded strangely up, wired.

"Are you all right?"

"Listen," he said, ignoring her question, "I'm on my way back from the lab. I need to talk to you. Can we meet at your place?"

"Is this about the case?"

"Yes. Can you get away?"

She looked at her appointment book. This was murder. Everything else would have to wait. "I'll be there," she said.

"Thanks," he answered. "I think I have this all figured out."

I wonder what that means, she thought as she hung up the phone. If the autopsy had been routine, what could he have figured out?

Elizabeth made a few calls, postponed sessions with the clients she could reach, left a note for her supervisor, and slipped out the door. She didn't want to discuss the case or what George had told her with anyone. Besides, the whole place was buzzing with the news. They'd never miss her. Once out on the street, she noticed a motorcycle parked in front of the building. It was smaller. Blue. A Honda. She couldn't believe she could think of that at a time like this.

*   *   *

She saw the red thing from the road. It was on her door. Someone had been there. Whatever the red thing was, it frightened her. She parked the car and slowly approached the house. No, it wasn't her imagination. Something red *was* there.

She was almost at the door when she realized it was a flower. Not blood, not a bomb, just a flower. The note was written on a scrap of photographic paper. She crumpled it up and placed it in her pocket. Holding the flower in her hand, she entered the house. Everything was just as she had left it. Nothing had been touched. Why then did she feel as if someone had been there—inside?

She looked at the flower. The petals were spread apart like individual flames. There were flecks of black along the ridges of the red and a long, hairy stem that still felt damp to the touch. She smoothed out the note. He had signed his name. The message was written beneath the signature. An afterthought, maybe. "I'd like to see you again." That was it. No day, no time. Just the flower.

She was uneasy. It was as though something were missing or out of place. Without thinking, she checked the jewelry box in the bedroom. Everything was there. The extra fifty dollars she hid beneath the bracelets and pearls had not been touched. Yet, inexplicably, the room seemed different. It's got to be this murder thing, she thought. It's making me jumpy.

Walking into the kitchen, she paused and considered the flower. He had been here, at the door. That meant he remembered where she lived. Perhaps she would see him again. But of course that was no longer important. She went into the bathroom to splash cold water on her face and touch up her lipstick. A futile gesture, but she was too nervous to do anything else.

Looking into the bathroom mirror, she almost expected to see another face staring at her. This has got to stop, she thought. Perhaps all this talk about death and danger, and the very real possibility that a murderer was still in the vicinity, was creating her discomfort. Who wouldn't be frightened?

Elizabeth returned to the kitchen. She cleared the table of the leftover morning coffee, put on a fresh kettle of water, and assured herself that everything was as it had always been.

It was 11:15. Elizabeth made herself a cup of tea, sat on the couch, and waited.

12

HE COULD SEE EVERYTHING. The small house, the Volkswagen parked in the driveway, even her as she passed by a window. The trees across the road formed a natural blind. The motorcycle rested in the woods. This was better than watching nature.

Watching Elizabeth made him feel powerful. He had seen her pull up in the car, seen her take the flower off the door. He had even seen the puzzled expression on her face. It felt safe to be hidden. From his vantage point he could notice all the tiny details, but he was still far enough away not to be seen.

It was perfect that she lived here. Other times, when he watched people it had been difficult. Apartment buildings were the worst. Subjects were whisked through revolving doors into mirrored lobbies only to disappear into anonymous cubicles. That was one reason why Gary hated cities. But there were other reasons. The way he couldn't breathe. The way people's faces became a blur of black and white motion. The loud distracting noises that stopped him from seeing. He had to have quiet, a certain type of stillness in order to see.

Unlike many photographers, Gary never worked with background music. Silence was essential. He believed that if you looked closely enough you could hear the sound of images. Like the "click click" of Elizabeth's shoes. Like the ticking of the alarm clock beside her bed.

He'd had no choice but to go inside. It was part of the portrait. He had to see the secret places. It disturbed him that the lock had slipped open so easily. Maybe, when he knew her better, he would urge her to get more substantial protection. Someone might harm her. Someone might intrude in a way that was more violent than his.

He had been right about many things. Her living room had been orderly, her drawers messy and overflowing. There was an inconsistency about her, a duality that he found exciting. He had first sensed it on the motorcycle. Now he was sure. Of course it was a risk. But it had been important. Necessary. He had to see the secret places, all of them. And, as always, he had remained invisible.

This was the first time since the incident. That time when somehow, inexplicably, something had gone wrong and he had been discovered. Seen. Caught. Apprehended. He'd had to stop stealing then. He had lost the magic. What followed was a period of blackness.

*   *   *

Gary rubbed his hands along the rough bark. He was back on track now, doing what he did best. These photographs, the ones he was inhabiting, were far more intricate than the ones he developed under a bath of chemicals. He was creating a composition, something alive. And he was part of it, not a faceless robot hidden behind a lens. The camera had become a barrier to his growth as an artist. He believed that photography dulled his senses, pulled him out of life and into a limbo of passive watching. Gary called it looking but not seeing. Looking was done through a lens. But seeing was something far more complex.

Years ago, when he had traveled through the Atlas mountains in Morocco, the local people had known about seeing. They had covered their faces with their sleeves when he pointed the camera in their direction. They were afraid he would steal their souls. His companions had laughed at these primitive superstitions, but Gary felt guilty. Exposed. He was a thief. And they were right to shield their faces and run back to their shelters.

He crouched down beside a maple tree and hid in its shadow. Soon enough he would be out there, an actor in the play he was writing, a character in his own photograph. But Gary knew he wasn't in complete control. There were always surprises, little twists of plot that made the story more interesting. Like her coming home unexpectedly in the middle of the day. He hadn't anticipated it, which made his adventure all the more exciting.

He had been sure it would be hours before she returned from the office. He had looked forward to the leisurely wait, to the watching and the imagining. But now she was inside and she had the flower with her. She was touching the very thing he had chosen for her. It was as if the flower were a medium through which they could communicate.

He closed his eyes and imagined her there— inside. Perhaps she noticed his scent on the pillowcase, or the coffee cup he had touched with his lips. But that was unlikely. What he had left behind could be neither seen nor felt. It could only be sensed.

Elizabeth lived like a woman who was used to being alone and was comfortable with her own ways. He liked that. He liked almost everything he had seen in the house. But he knew it would be different when he returned that night. She would have the bedroom door closed, the coffee cup washed and put away. That was predictable. But knowing what had been there before gave him the edge—the feeling of control, the excitement of anticipation.

It was the perfect time for Elizabeth. The period of blackness was over. He was finding his way again. Entering her house had been part of this process, part of creating an intimacy they both could share. He fully intended to tell her. Not right away; that would frighten her. But later, when he had taught her about looking and seeing; when he had shown her the silence; when she understood that the photographs he took in his head were the real art; then it would all make sense to her. She would be shocked but not angry, not frightened. Gary knew that would take time. But if things went right, if she responded to him, he could tell her about it, and about the watching and waiting.

*　　*　　*

He had half-emerged from the shadows when he saw it. A patrol car that seemed to be heading toward him. Instinctively, he moved back into the darkness where the motorcycle rested beside a tree.

The white car weaved down the dusty road with deliberate speed. Gary recognized the driver as the same one who had cut him off earlier in the day. Probably just a routine check. But then, for a moment, he thought no. Perhaps the car had been following him. Perhaps the cop had seen everything.

He crouched down in the darkness. The engine of the car stopped. Gary reached into the saddlebag that hung behind the seat of the motorcycle. His hand rested on the cool steel.

But then the moment passed. The car pulled into the driveway behind the Volkswagen. The door opened and Gary watched as a stocky blond man walked toward the house. The cop and Elizabeth. This must be the boyfriend. Why were they meeting here in the middle of the day? A thousand ideas passed through his mind. Endless possibilities.

He took his hand from the saddlebag and moved to the edge of the road. He saw Elizabeth as she opened the door. Her chestnut hair seemed almost red in the bright light. Her face was pleasant but unsmiling. She made no effort to kiss the man who stood before her. This didn't look like a lover's meeting. There was tension in the air, in the way the blond cop held himself, the way she looked at him.

Gary snapped a hundred stills between his thumb and forefinger.

They were in there together. Maybe they were sitting at the kitchen table where the coffee cup had been. He closed his eyes and imagined it. He smiled to himself. It was as if he were there with them. Only he couldn't hear the voices. But of course that wasn't what mattered. They believed they were alone. But that was not the case. He had touched everything, seen everything. He was an invisible presence, both out here in the shadows and in there in the yellowish light.

He could almost see her standing by the tea kettle, the one with the nick in the handle. She would boil some water for coffee or tea. They would finish the danish she had wrapped in plastic and placed in the refrigerator. Maybe the cop would kiss her; maybe they would just talk. He was obviously there for a reason. They wouldn't go into the bedroom. No, Gary couldn't see them there at all. In his mind Elizabeth had closed the door to that room. She would not make love in the middle of a workday. Gary already knew that about her; and he already knew that would change.

Right now Elizabeth and the cop were talking, perhaps discussing some argument they had had last night. Gary smiled to himself. His flower was inside. It was a silent observer, his messenger. He wondered if she had put it in the living room or beside the bed. No, she'd probably left it in the kitchen. Later, when he had a chance to explain, she would know that the lily was special, and that it should be the last thing she looked at before falling asleep. He wondered if the blond man had noticed the flower and what Elizabeth would offer by way of explanation.

Gary slumped into the shadows. The pictures were forming, shaping themselves out of possibilities. He had already entered her life. Elizabeth and the cop had no idea they were being watched, being looked at. And they had no idea what Gary was able to see.

13

ELIZABETH LOOKED SURPRISED when she answered the door, almost as if she had been expecting someone else.

He smelled of perspiration and cigarettes. She motioned for him to sit down. He slumped into the chair. Despite his exhaustion, he was still irresistibly attractive.

"I'm not exactly sure what you want me to do," she said. "I went through the files like you asked, and I checked for any reports on missing kids. I followed up on that Hare Krishna group; they relocated in another state. I just couldn't find anything that looked hopeful. Sorry."

"I figured," he answered. "The autopsy was pretty much the same story. Either this kid has no past or someone did his damndest to make sure we wouldn't find it."

"Didn't you get anything from the post mortem you could use?"

"The only thing I have right now is a bag filled with clothing, a gold cross, and a body without a face. All the medical examiner found was a partially digested meal of junk food. That's it. No scars, no signs of rape, no indications of pregnancy. It's like this kid just dropped from the sky. I don't even know what she looked like. How the hell am I going to find out who she is, much less who murdered her?"

Elizabeth squirmed uncomfortably in her chair. They were talking about a person—someone who woke up in the morning, got dressed, ate meals, someone who had dreams and nightmares. She wasn't used to this. None of it had had a chance to sink in.

"George, someone's bound to contact you. After all, she's someone's child. Kids don't just disappear without people searching for them."

"Yeah, and what if her parents live in California or Nebraska? How are they supposed to know we have a body here that might be their daughter? How are they supposed to know it's their kid when I don't have a photograph to circulate?"

"Wouldn't they know by the description, by the clothes she was wearing? What about the cross?"

"There are probably hundreds of kids walking around with similar clothing and a simple gold cross with no inscription. And what if the clothes we found her in weren't the same ones she was wearing when she left home? What's worse, what if those parents or relatives in California or Nebraska never even hear about this case? Right now there are thousands of missing persons in this country. Why should this kid be special, why should anyone be interested?"

Elizabeth thought of the kind of small talk that got people buzzing in Bakersville: a car accident on an icy road, a local farmer who needed a third mortgage, a town politician who took a bribe from a merchant. None of these compared to an unsolved homicide. Maybe George was being theatrical. Everyone here would care, it would be all anyone would talk about.

"You've got to be kidding," she said. "This is Bakersville. The whole town will stand still when they hear this."

George was getting impatient. He paced the floor, stopping only to glance at the red flower in the juice glass.

"The whole town, sure. But if she was a local kid, we'd have already heard that she was missing. Don't you get the point I'm trying to make?"

Elizabeth shook her head.

"I want people to know about this. I want the story to run nationally. If I just present it in a cut-and-dried way, it'll get as far as a few local papers. People will think she was a runaway or a prostitute. They'll write it off."

Elizabeth cupped her chin in her hand. What he was saying made sense. But he was only one cop. There were others in the department. Why was he acting as if he were alone—as if the entire investigation was his responsibility?

George was standing by the window, looking out at the rows of trees that surrounded the cottage. He knew what she wanted. She wanted him to rip himself open, to lay bare every private terror. But he couldn't do that. He was a cop. Feeling too much could be dangerous; he had seen it make the difference between life and death. Sooner or later, she would have to understand.

He stared past the trees and into the dense forest. He was trying to figure all this out. He knew it was crazy, but increasingly it seemed that whoever had put the body there had had some sort of second sense. George believed the killer had known his victim had been vulnerable. She hadn't been just any kid. No. He was sure there had been something about her, something that told her murderer she was unprotected. A forgotten daughter.

And there was more. It was as if the killer had known him too, as if he could see inside to where the wounds had never healed.

The murderer had forced him to carry someone else's child out from behind that shed. He had forced him to look at the dead girl and wonder if this could happen to his own daughter. George knew the divorce had changed things between him and Sheila. He was no longer the daddy who came home every night and held his little girl in his lap. And Sheila was different because of it. Under the influence of his ex-wife and her family, his daughter had withdrawn from him. It only showed in subtle ways, small things: how she hesitated before running into his arms; the all-too-easy manner in which she accepted disappointment when their time together was shortened or postponed. There was a certain vulnerability in his child. He wanted to deny it, but he would only be fooling himself.

George felt the burning inside. He was trying to keep a lid on his feelings, but these were too close, too raw. The girl lying in the morgue had slipped through the cracks. A fatherless child, she would be buried without a face and without a name.

George could not let that happen.

*   *   *

Elizabeth was talking. He turned away from the window. She was frowning; her eyes had narrowed into slits. He had seen that angry look before. He knew he had closed her out, but this was *his* pain. There was no way he could expose it, not now.

"Murderers don't just walk away," she reasoned. "Bodies don't just lie around unclaimed. If she came from another state, eventually the police department will contact you."

"Damn it!" he shouted. "Murderers walk away all the time. Maybe you're forgetting that only a year ago some maniac tried to kill me, and not only did no one stop while I almost bled to death, but the guy who did it checked into a hospital, got treated for a bullet wound, and sashayed out—no questions asked. And the Bakersville police department sat on their fat rear ends and did nothing!"

Elizabeth stared at him. His face was twisted in anger. The veins on the side of his neck were knotted. This was the last thing she wanted. But it was impossible to reach him now. She knew he had been stunned by the homicide, but George had not always been a small-town cop. He had told her stories that made this murder seem mild by comparison. No, this was working on him personally. She could only guess, since she knew he would never tell her, that he had somehow made a connection between the murdered girl and his own daughter. You can't protect everyone, she wanted to scream. But she knew that would be trespassing on dangerous territory. Instead, she measured her words.

"Considering what you've told me, I just don't see what else you can do," she said. "The facts are the facts. You can't change what's real. Maybe she *was* a runaway or a prostitute."

"That doesn't mean anything," he said, still angry. "You don't know how it feels. I saw that body. I held it in my arms. Elizabeth, she had fillings in her teeth. Someone took her to the dentist, someone raised her and worried about her. And now she's lying in some drawer in the morgue with her skull battered and her body cut up in bottles and bags."

She didn't want to hear these details. George wanted something. She wished he'd just come right out and ask her.

"We've got to make this case dramatic," he was saying. "The more publicity we attract, the more likely it is that someone will come forward. If we let the news stay in Bakersville, believe me, that girl will be buried as a Jane Doe."

"I see what you mean. I just don't know how you're going to do that."

"I've got some of it figured out already. First, I thought I'd call Marsha's, you know the clothing store on Broadway, and get a dummy about her size, put the cross and the clothes on it, and present it dressed and headless, like she was when I found her. Now, that would have an impact. You don't just walk away from a sight like that and file a little back-page story. At the very least, we'd get some photographs."

Elizabeth nodded. It was a good idea. She remembered having seen something similar when she lived in Manhattan. Three prostitutes were found murdered and decapitated in a hotel room. The detectives assigned to the case put the clothing on headless dummies. The story had been front-page material for weeks.

"I think that'll work," she said, feeling the first tingle of excitement. "What other ideas do you have?"

George hesitated. He hated asking her, but he didn't see any other way. "I need your help with this part. I had her hands removed for fingerprinting. If she is on file somewhere, we'll get a positive ID. But that can take a long time, and my guess is we'll come up empty. So, I'd like to give her a name. We can't call her Jane Doe."

"Do you think a name will make her more real?"

"I think it'll help. She was someone. We can't take that away from her. I've tried and tried, but I can't come up with anything. I thought I'd show you the clothes. I have them in a bag in the car. Maybe if you look at them, it will remind you of a case or a kid. Maybe you'll get a feeling for her."

Elizabeth hesitated. She wasn't sure she wanted to see the clothes. Not here. It would make everything too real.

"Can't you just describe them to me?" she asked. She was backing away from him, he could feel it.

"It's not enough," he said. "Trust me."

"Are they very bloody?"

He was already standing up and moving toward the door. "Nothing you can't handle, I promise," he said.

Elizabeth watched him as he left the house and took a plastic bag marked, "Bakersville P.D." from the backseat of the squad car. For an instant she had a horrible feeling that once she saw the clothes she would never forget them, that she would be tied to the dead girl in some indelible way.

He placed the bag on the table. She didn't want him to open it. Maybe if she closed her eyes this would all disappear.

"You've got to look," he said. "Let's start with the cross. It's been cleaned off."

He reached into his pocket. "I kept it myself, didn't want the chain to get all caught up in the rest of the stuff."

The chain dangled from his outstretched palm. Small pink beads were placed evenly every few links. The cross was smooth. There were no unusual details.

"Can I hold it?" she asked.

She had almost expected it to have some vibrations, to send messages through her skin. But it was only a thin piece of metal, warm to the touch.

"I don't think it's gold," she said. "But the chain looks real. It's almost as if they don't belong together."

"Why do you say that?" he asked.

"I don't know if you remember, but when I was a kid it was the fashion to wear what we called 'baby bracelets,' wrist chains with pink or blue beads with our names on them—like the ones women used to get in the hospital when they had babies."

"I know what you mean."

"Well, this chain reminds me of that. But the cross doesn't seem to match. Especially since it's probably just gold plated."

"You know, you're right," he answered. "I'm not sure if it means anything, but it's definitely something to remember."

"Okay," she said. "I'm ready. Let's take a look at the clothes."

George unfolded the skirt and the brown V-neck pullover. She stared at the clothing. He was right. A description would never have been enough. The clothes were so small. The skirt, a wraparound style, looked vaguely familiar. The sweater was spotted with dried blood. The blood had hardened and turned pinkish brown. Little scabs, she thought as she tried to avert her eyes.

Elizabeth wanted to look at something soothing. For an instant, she thought about the flower. She had only to glance across the room. But the clothes had a greater power. She was unable to look away. She rested her hands by her sides. She didn't want to touch the clothes, even by accident. This time she really might feel something.

"Do you get an idea what sort of kid might wear these things?" George asked. "Was she stylish and sophisticated, a hick or a city girl? Anything. Anything that comes to mind."

"George, doesn't this skirt look at all familiar?"

"Are you asking me if I've seen it before? No. I don't think so."

"Well, not this skirt exactly," she said, "but this type of skirt."

He shook his head.

"In the sixties we all wore wraparounds with this kind of paisley pattern. I must have had two or three just like this myself. But the sweater, that looks like it came from a K-mart or something. This stuff doesn't seem to go together. It's like the girl just threw on any old thing."

"Or it was just thrown on her," he answered.

"Either way, all I can say is that she certainly wasn't a fashion plate."

"What sort of kid do you think she was?"

Elizabeth concentrated for a few seconds. "I'm thinking about what you told me before, about the junk food they found in her stomach. That's probably the kind of kid she was: small town, simple tastes, not much style."

"That doesn't give me much. There's only about a million kids out there who fit that description."

"I know," she said. "She really could be anyone—a kid we know."

"I doubt that," George said. "I'd have heard something from her parents by now."

Elizabeth didn't like this. A murder in her hometown. A body thrown beside a river where she had played as a child. The clothes of the victim spread out on her kitchen table. She wanted to give the girl a name. She wanted her identified, her killer apprehended. She wanted everything back the way it was, the way it had always been. She glanced down at the plastic bag with the initials "P.D." Something clicked.

"George, why don't we call her Princess Doe? That would be like Jane Doe, only different. Special."

It seemed that he looked instantly younger. The frown lines around his mouth melted, the creases in his forehead disappeared. He smiled for the first time since she'd seen him that morning.

"That's terrific," he said. "Princess Doe. I'll have that name printed on the photographs of the mannequin dressed in her clothes. Now she's real. People will pick up on that. Who knows? It might make the difference." He paused, looking blankly at a sliver of sunlight that splashed across the wall. He seemed almost hypnotized.

"Princess Doe," he said. "At least she'll have a name."

Elizabeth trembled. George had found the child and she had named her. She realized now, for the first time, that Princess Doe was indeed real. And she belonged to both of them.

14

A SLOW-MOVING FAN SUCKED the twisting smoke from the diner. Peg wiped the counter with deliberate circular motions. So it had been two weeks. She glanced at the postcards that were taped over the cash register. One, sometimes two, every seven days. Jamie had promised to keep in touch. There were lots of explanations, but the nervous feeling just wouldn't go away. What could she do? After all, she had given Jamie permission to visit her father. And she had promised herself—vowed—she wouldn't worry. Now two weeks had passed. She had even called Herb, but there was no answer.

The police. It seemed like the only place to turn. George Murphy had been in for coffee that morning. She had been foolish not to say something. But she was embarrassed. She hadn't wanted to sound any false alarms. Besides, Jamie was all the way across the country.

The diner was empty, except for Ted Lewis who sat in his regular booth, drinking coffee and reading the newspaper. She rubbed her bare arms. If she was going to call, now was the time. The best way to get over a senseless worry was to do something about it, to take action. She reached for the phone behind the cash register. The number for the Bakersville police department was written, along with the fire department and the hospital, on a label she had glued to the wall.

"Hi, Jean," she said, "It's Peg Moore, from the diner. I was wondering if I could speak with George Murphy."

"May I ask what this is in reference to?" Jean sounded strangely formal. She wanted to hang up, to tell Jean to forget she had ever called.

"It's nothing important, just that I haven't heard from Jamie, my daughter, and I guess I'm getting a little nervous."

"Are you reporting your daughter missing?"

Peg glanced across the diner at the empty booths. "Missing, no, not at all. It's just that she went out to visit her father and I usually hear from her. I thought maybe George might help me reach someone."

Jean was quiet for several seconds. "I'm going to radio Lieutenant Murphy right now. He'll stop over there in a few minutes."

She was ready to tell her not to bother, that it was just an irrational, impulsive action, but it was too late. Jean had hung up.

Peg leaned against the cash register as she poured herself a cup of coffee. Looking out of the window, she squinted her eyes against the sun. Maybe, she thought, I should have at least waited until the mail was delivered.

George had just lit up when the call came over the radio. When Jean told him there was a possible lead in the case, he smashed the cigarette into the empty ashtray. Jamie Moore. He knew the girl. She worked at the diner after school and on weekends. She was young, maybe fifteen or sixteen. But it was impossible to remember anything else. Was she small, tall, heavy? He simply couldn't recall. The diner had become a routine part of his life, and like all routines, he took this one for granted.

The important thing now, George reminded himself, was not to jump to any quick conclusions. The child might simply have forgotten to call home; she might have stayed out overnight with a girlfriend. He calmed himself as he pulled up beside the diner. If Jamie Moore was missing he possessed evidence that might instantly identify her. The clothes.

The cross. He had to mention them in a way that wouldn't cause Peg to panic. He had to remain relaxed and objective. There was no reason to believe that Jamie and the girl whose bloodstained clothes were wrapped on the backseat of his car were one and the same.

The diner was empty. Peg sat on a stool behind the register. She was nervously rubbing her chin as she stared at something on the counter.

"How're you doing?" George asked, remembering to take it nice and slow.

"Better—now," Peg answered. "Want some coffee?"

George nodded. "What's this I hear about your daughter not coming home?"

"God, I'm really sorry about all this," Peg said. "I didn't expect you to come over here so quickly. I just got this. So everything's really all right."

She pushed a postcard across the counter. It bore a photograph of a giraffe. The words "San Diego Zoo" were written in script along the top.

"What's this?" George asked.

"Go ahead, read it."

He turned the postcard over. It was obviously from Jamie. She was in San Diego with her father and having a wonderful time. She apologized for not writing sooner. Instinctively, George checked the postmark. It had been mailed from San Diego two days earlier.

"Does this mean everything's all right?" he asked.

Peg nodded. "I guess I should have waited for the mail. My daughter's a good kid, but you know how it is. Divorce and all. She wanted to see her father. I didn't expect anyone to make a fuss. All I wanted was to ask your advice, to see if you could help me contact someone out there."

"Let me ask you something. Does Jamie wear any particular jewelry?"

"Jewelry. Like earrings and stuff?"

"Yeah, that sort of thing."

"Sure. She wears bracelets and earrings, and those sweatbands the kids like, but I don't know if you'd count that as jewelry. Why? Is something missing? Is there something you're not saying?"

"What about a cross? Did she ever wear one?"

"Jamie? You've got to be kidding. That girl's been to church once in her whole life. No, she's not one to wear anything religious."

George fixed his eyes on the postcards taped to the mirror behind the cash register. Many had yellowed with age. Several were new, freshly tacked up.

"Are those all from Jamie?" he asked.

Peg was relaxed now. It was clear that whatever the lieutenant had on his mind had nothing to do with her daughter.

"Those? Sure, some are from her, others are from friends. It's sort of a custom around here. Herb, my ex-husband, used to send Jamie postcards from the road. He's a salesman. She saved them in a shoebox. So I guess I've just done the same. It beats calling, especially when you move around so much."

George nodded. He had been trained to look into things, and now he was satisfied that he had done his job. The child wasn't missing. The cross didn't belong to her. He was back where he had been earlier this morning.

Finishing his coffee, he glanced around the diner. It was odd to see it so empty, so quiet. For the first time George realized that Peg's place was run down. The backs of the plastic seats had been mended with masking tape. The walls needed a fresh coat of paint. Even Peg looked frazzled, worn around the edges. It's amazing, he thought, how many small details go unnoticed. He made a mental note to ask Peg about Jamie again in a week or two. You never know, he mused as he looked at the San Diego postcard one last time.

Peg waved goodbye. Glancing at the rearview mirror, he watched as the diner slowly receded into the background. There were no other cars on the road when he saw the black shape emerge from a swirl of dust. It seemed to be moving from side to side, hanging first on one curve of the road, then on the other. It was the same Harley-Davidson he had spotted earlier in the day. Only now the driver was directly behind him. The motorcycle was weaving dangerously. Although the bike wasn't speeding, the driver seemed to be playing with him, dancing along the road as if to call attention to himself.

Feeling fatigued, George tried to look away, but the movement of the bike had become rhythmic, almost hypnotic. The driver, whose face was covered by a tinted shield, was skillful. The game he was playing was dangerous, George thought, as his hand curved around the steering wheel. Sooner or later the guy was going to take a fall. And when that bike went down, it was going to take the joker behind the tinted shield with it.

The black Harley disappeared down a dirt road, leaving a low-hanging cloud of dust in its wake. Now it seemed that the motorcycle had only been a vision, a streak of blackness moving across the pavement. George's head was crammed with visions. He could still see the body he had dragged from the tangle of bushes. He could still picture Elizabeth as she gently touched the bloodstained garments, and Peg as she pushed the postcard over the counter. The images seemed to be closing in on him. They moved into a crazy collage of sights and sounds, smells and textures. Everything that had happened in the last forty-eight hours became a suffocating jumble.

Knowing he needed rest, George pulled over to the side of the road. He rolled down the car window and lit the last of his cigarettes. The smoke curled upward, spinning into thin streaks of gray before disappearing into the blue. George closed his eyes against the visions and the light. Within minutes, he was asleep. It was not like Lieutenant Murphy to let down his guard this way. But he was overcome by fatigue and by a rush of events that seemed increasingly beyond his control.

The motorcycle was parked only a few hundred yards away. The rider had dismounted and was aiming something directly at the patrol car. If he had been awake, George might have heard the first of many clicks. But he was asleep, and save for the clicking of his camera, the driver of the black Harley-Davidson remained silent and invisible.

15

IN THE DREAM SHE WAS wearing the dead girl's skirt. She awoke trembling. Looking at the clock beside her bed, Elizabeth saw that it was well past five. Where had the time gone? She pressed her face against the pillow. Sleeping had not refreshed her. The uneasy feelings had only intensified.

Her clothes were damp and wrinkled. Standing before the open window, she peeled off the layers. No one could see. The cottage was surrounded by trees. Her nearest neighbors were more than a mile away.

She needed a shower, but somehow the thought of water chilled her. Instead, reaching deep into her dresser drawer she pulled out a worn yellow sweatshirt. No need for a bra, she thought as she passed her hands across her breasts. She wasn't going anywhere, not tonight. She removed her underpants and slipped into her comfortable jeans.

The events of the day had been overwhelming. They had filled her to the brim and run over into her dreams. The dead girl's clothes had been here in her house. She shivered as she thought of George calmly placing them on the kitchen table.

Returning to the scene, Elizabeth noticed the red flower in the juice glass. Last night seemed as though it had never happened. The handsome stranger on the motorcycle. Had he been real? She thought about him as she gazed at the scarlet petals. No, she hadn't imagined it. Not him, not the ride, not the sensations.

Why had he come back? Last night would have been the perfect time to make his move. She had been ready then. Temporarily off balance, she could have easily been swayed. But now the real world had returned. No one, not even a green-eyed man on a speeding motorcycle, could make her forget the dead girl.

Elizabeth didn't want to be alone, but at the same time she did not have the energy for companionship. The afternoon had left her numb. She poured herself a glass of wine and sat quietly in the kitchen.

Listening to the ticking of the clock, she wondered what might have happened if George had arrived at the cemetery hours or days earlier. He would have seen it all. The murderer, the girl, perhaps the act of violence itself. It was time that separated them from one another. Time that had delivered the girl into the arms of the killer.

But, then, perhaps the girl had been doomed from the start. Maybe she had been flirting with danger until the inevitable finally happened. Elizabeth didn't want to think about that now. It was enough that she had dreamed it.

*　　　*　　　*

It was so still, so silent, that she heard him even before he came into view. The sound was unmistakable. He was right outside. There was no time to change, no time to compose herself. Without pausing, she walked to the door. When she opened it, she saw the motorcycle parked in the driveway. The sky had turned orange. He moved forward bringing the orange inside with him.

He was just as she remembered him. The light played on his shoulders. He seemed very tall, taller than last night. He held out his hand.

"Hello again. I hope you don't mind me dropping in this way, but I didn't know your phone number, or even your last name."

"Kern," she said, still startled to see him standing there when she had just been imagining him.

"May I come in? Is this a bad time for you?" Without thinking, she nervously moved her hand across her breasts. She could smell the scent. It was the same one she had inhaled last night on the motorcycle. Not a perfume, but an essence. Something she had heard about but had never actually experienced. He filled the room. He looked as if he belonged here, as if he were returning to a place he had visited once before.

"I got the flower," she said. "What kind is it?"

He eased into a kitchen chair. Glancing at the sink, he spotted it immediately. "It's a wood lily, and we don't have much time left."

She breathed him in. Dark hairs curled along his forearms. There was something about his presence that made her unable to look away. He draped his jacket over the back of the chair.

"Time left for what?" she asked. She was experiencing an unfamiliar warmth. Everything was as if in a dream. Perhaps she had never fully awakened.

He was holding the flower. The red petals burst from his perfect hand. He gently touched the damp stem.

"The flower lasts only one day. When the sun sets it closes up."

"And dies?" she asked.

"Yes, but while it lives it's lovely, don't you think?"

"I've never seen one like it."

"They're difficult to find," Gary said. He was looking at her now, watching as she tried to avoid his eyes.

"Well, then thank you for the gift. Would you like a glass of wine?"

"Maybe tea," he said. "Would that be too much trouble?" For no reason at all she felt foolish. She had offered him wine and he had asked for tea. Why did that make her feel uneasy?

"Of course not. It's no trouble at all."

He watched her as she placed the kettle on the burner. She was unaccustomed to being so closely scrutinized. She wondered for a moment if he could see the outline of her breasts beneath the loose-fitting sweatshirt, if he could tell she was naked under her jeans.

"What sort of photographs do you take?" she asked, hoping to distract him while she regained her equilibrium.

Gary smiled. "All sorts. Nature. People. Anything I get assignments for."

She swirled the tea bag into the cup of boiling water. Moving close to his chair, she placed the cup in front of him. It was unlike her to feel so shaky, so entirely out of control. Was this what she had experienced last night? At the time, she had attributed it to the motorcycle. They were here now, yet everything felt the same as it had then.

She wanted him to touch her. She could feel her nipples stiffen as they rubbed against the sweatshirt. It would be crazy. She would never see him again, and she would wake up with that sad, empty feeling. She sipped her wine.

"Do you mind living here, almost in the forest?" he asked.

"I like it. It makes me feel safe. When I look out the window I know no one is looking back. For a long time when I lived in the city, I had shades on my windows and bars too. It's a free feeling here."

Gary smiled. "Last night I slept in a meadow. That's where I found the lily."

"Did you have a tent or anything?"

"Sure, I carry all sorts of equipment in the boxes on the back of my bike. The tent is fairly large, but it folds up into a little square. It's amazing when you think of it."

Elizabeth tried to picture him beneath a square of canvas, tried to imagine him naked and asleep.

He stretched out his legs. They were long and muscular. His boots showed the wear and tear of the road.

"It's good that you feel comfortable in nature," he said. "Someday I'll show you how I take photographs in the forest. If you have the patience, it's something you'd enjoy."

"How do you do it?" she asked.

Gary told her about the blind, about how he stood for hours behind a drape that blended in with the scenery. "It's the only way," he said, "to remain undetected. And that's how you get to learn about the secrets."

Through the window she could see that the orange was turning a deep gold. The warmth of the sunset filtered into the room. She had never seen a man quite so beautiful. And he was here, so close she need only reach out and touch him. Yet Elizabeth was unable to move. Frightened she might scare him away, and embarrassed by the intensity of her feelings, she did nothing.

He stood up. She scraped her chair across the floor as she rose to meet him.

"I've got to be going," he said.

The heat moved upward, spreading from her belly to her throat, until her face was flushed with warmth. She looked away, hoping he wouldn't see her disappointment.

"Well," she said, "I guess we'll bump into each other some time."

Gary laughed. His lips parted as he touched her face.

"Let's not leave it to chance. Can I call you?"

She wrote her number on a scrap of paper towel. He glanced at it before folding it neatly into his back pocket.

Was he really leaving? She wanted to say something that might make him stay. But he had already put on his leather jacket.

He opened the door and the gold rushed in to meet him. Without thinking, she stood on tiptoe until she touched his lips. He kissed her fingertips before he said goodbye.

In an instant the gold of the day vanished. She heard the hum of the motorcycle engine. Standing by the door, she watched as he moved farther away from her. When she could no longer see him, she walked back into the kitchen.

Sitting alone in the dark, she saw the last rays of sun disappear behind the treetops. Instinctively, she glanced across the room. It was just as he predicted it. The red flower had closed up its petals and died.

16

HE WAS CAMOUFLAGED AGAINST the night. Blending in with the darkness, he sped down the dusty road that led away from Elizabeth's house. He knew she had been unprepared, startled by his visit. There were no poses. She had had no time to arrange her face, the furniture. No time to conceal her secrets.

Gary knew she had been naked beneath the sweat-shirt and jeans. He could tell by the way she carried herself. The nervous, unsure movements. Now that he had seen her like this, she excited him. It would be hard to find her that way again. She had been struggling to regain her balance. Next time she would be more steady.

The motorcycle purred beneath his groin. Without his helmet he could feel the sensations as he plunged deeper into the darkness. The night was closing in. He had left her just as the sun began to set. It had been the perfect time. Between day and night. Uneasy and candid, Elizabeth had had a delicate and beautiful quality. He never wanted to see her in her day world. Under fluorescent lights and surrounded by office things, she would become someone else. Her face would harden into a controlled and impenetrable mask. If he were to see her again, it would have to be like tonight. And if he were to photograph her, she would have to be asleep.

Gary thought back to the afternoon. He had shot two rolls of the police officer asleep in his patrol car. He was anxious to develop them. This had been an idea of his for a long time. First, he had taken stills of unmade beds. Dream depositories bereft of their dreamers. Then he had spent months shooting empty motel rooms. Anonymous beds, beds made up, waiting, ready for strangers.

He had hoped to find something in these photographs, something true and revealing. But the photographs had not pleased him. They had not given him what he sought—entry into the forbidden world of unfamiliar dreams.

So he had returned to his older, more primitive method. Without his camera he took a different sort of picture. His vision was not confined to a flat square. Tonight he had seen Elizabeth, photographed her in a way he never could have had he used a camera. He had briefly glimpsed her most private self. This was what he wanted—to get behind people's faces, to crawl inside them, to capture a moment that was at once astonishing and real.

He kicked slowly through the gears of the motorcycle until he brought it to a gentle halt. Balancing the Harley artfully between his legs, he stopped to stare into the darkness. He was having the thoughts again. Thoughts that told him he would always be on the outside of things, that he would never photograph what he longed to see.

He had an impulse to walk blindly into the forest, to close his eyes and move in a waking dream through the pine needles and fallen leaves. This was something he had done many times before. He had spent nights beneath a canvas tent, passed days searching for wildflowers or looking for a particular bird or butterfly. Gary was obsessed with seeing, but sometimes he had to look away. Sometimes trying to see became staring, and staring brought on the numbness.

But tonight was different. He had, in that short time with Elizabeth, made tentative contact. She had warmed him and the numbness had begun to thaw. He took this as a good sign—a hopeful one.

And then there were the undeveloped rolls of film in his saddlebags; a subject captured sleeping in a car parked alongside the road. If he was beginning to see again, if at last his vision was to be restored, he could not risk losing it.

He glanced downward, watching as the Harley devoured the road beneath its wheels. He seemed to be moving in a direction north of Bakersville. The route was a familiar one. At the end of the scenic seventy-mile stretch there was a town, Crescent Springs. On a quiet side street there was a boarding house with an empty apartment on the top floor. And, most important, there was a darkroom where he could pay by the hour.

He was anxious to see the images he had shot of the policeman; the man with his revolver and his badge, a symbol of control and authority, drifting off into a deep and vulnerable sleep. There were times when Gary felt the intensity of his obsession with photography. At other times he felt only the numbness and the hunger to stretch the limits of his vision. Danger fueled his art. Walking the thin line between the possible and the unthinkable excited him. Gary believed risks were necessary. There was nothing safe about the worlds he wanted to explore, nothing ordinary in the forbidden portraits he longed to create.

He leaned the bike into a turn. The road responded as the Harley kicked up a wake of pebbles and sand. Every photograph was an adventure—a journey into the private world of a stranger. When those journeys became impossible, when his eyes ached from staring, he looked away.

But tonight he felt ready to begin again. He had liked the way Elizabeth moved, the way she touched things, the unfamiliarity she had felt in her own home. Perhaps she sensed that he had been there. If that were true, then the seduction had already begun.

He knew he would go back. It would be impossible not to see her again. Had she wanted him to stay? He thought she had. But he wasn't ready. Physical contact would have destroyed the tenuous connection. He wasn't even sure if he could have made love to her, not when his mind was so filled with images.

Gary stared into the darkness. It spread itself around him. He was speeding now, driving hard, eager to reach Crescent Springs. And he was thinking about touching Elizabeth. There would be a time, he knew, when he would get closer to her. That would be the danger. Right now he had the edge. He had already watched her when she thought no one was looking. He had seen the secret places. But Gary knew those were only things, artifacts. Getting closer might mean losing his own balance. But that was part of what he wanted, part of the risk.

Her telephone number was still folded neatly in his pocket. If he called her, the magic would be destroyed. It would have to be like it had been this evening. Unplanned. Unexpected.

He moved his hand into his pocket. The small piece of paper unfolded in the wind. He released his fingers. For a moment he watched as the paper fluttered into the blackness.

Now the only thing that was real was what he imagined. The portrait he was considering excited and disturbed him. Like the sleeping cop, she must never be aware he was observing her.

He would make love to her. He would sleep by her side. He would allow himself moments of carelessness. The danger energized him.

Within seconds, the energy turned into a gnawing, ravenous hunger. It had been hours since he'd eaten. There had been the cup of coffee in Peg's Diner and a quick sandwich later on. He was twenty miles from Crescent Springs. Judging by the blackness of the sky, he figured it was well after ten o'clock.

There was a place on the outskirts of the town, an all-night restaurant he had photographed years ago. He had liked the name, the New Chicago Lunch. There was nothing new about the small restaurant, and upstate New York was far from Chicago. When he had asked the owner about the odd name, the man had only grumbled that it had been called that by the previous owners, and it had seemed pointless to change it.

Gary liked the restaurant. It had a sinister, seedy atmosphere and catered to an odd crowd of locals, a regular gang of bikers, random travelers, and an occasional road-weary family.

The bike ground to a slow halt in front of the dimly lit restaurant. It had been nearly two years since he stopped here. The route from Crescent

Springs to Bakersville was one he had only recently begun to travel.

Inside, it was exactly as he remembered it. Long, low tables lined up neatly in front of a glass counter. Behind the counter a tired chef with a stained white apron ladled out food as customers scraped their plastic trays along stainless steel runners. He ordered a huge meal of soup and stew and a small loaf of bread. After paying the cashier, he walked toward a rear table. Noticing a folded newspaper, he picked it up, and placing it beside his tray, he began to read.

The photograph was the first thing he saw. A headless, handless mannequin wearing a paisley skirt and worn sweater. A gold chain bearing a small cross hung from her neck. The rawness of the image shocked him.

Pushing his food away, he stared at the grainy snapshot. The words became a jumble. Black print floated incomprehensibly between spaces of white. Unable to read, he leafed through the paper until he came upon the next photograph. The blond cop was standing beside the mannequin. A caption read "Lieutenant George Murphy, investigating officer."

Gary pulled a penknife from his zippered side pocket. Glancing around to make sure the owner of the paper would not return, he slowly cut the two photographs from the pages. The words "Princess Doe" were printed beneath the mannequin.

Gary studied the two photographs in the dim light of the New Chicago Lunch. At the table beside him, a woman in a worn party dress lined up the crumbs she had gathered from beneath her tray. She watched Gary as he folded the two thin squares and placed them between a thick layer of napkins.

After he had left, she slid wordlessly into his seat. His dinner remained warm and untouched. The newspaper with its two empty windows carried the headline UNIDENTIFIED TEENAGER MURDERED IN BAKERSVILLE CEMETERY. ASSAILANT SOUGHT.

17

IT WAS 9:15 P.M. George had already drifted into a restless sleep when the phone rang. He struggled to emerge from a cottony world of half-formed dreams.

The voice was unfamiliar. "The patient passed away at approximately 8:45 this evening."

He had asked to be notified. Now the image of Mason Kiley, pale and perspiring, leaning helplessly against a tree, returned to him. At precisely what moment had he begun to die? Was it as he walked through the weeds and undergrowth, smelling the rotting flesh, anticipating the corpse? Or was it moments later when he saw the murdered girl twisted in the branches behind the shed? Had the sight killed him or had he simply been ready to die?

George rolled over in bed. He traced the outline of a figure in the wrinkled sheets. When Tina had lived with him, everything had been clean and smooth. At night, when he pressed his face against a pillowcase he could smell the laundry detergent and the scented fabric softener. He wondered now, as he sat staring at the outline that still clung to the sheets, what she would have said had she been here. Tina had hated being married to a cop, and her family had hated having a cop for a son-in-law. It had been a ten-year tug-of-war, and they had finally won. Tina took Sheila and returned to New Jersey, where her family had welcomed her with open arms.

He knew it was a knee-jerk reaction to think of calling her. But here in the semidark her face floated behind his closed eyes. After the divorce she had not simply vanished into the past as he had expected she would. Sometimes he wondered if he would ever be free of her.

They had barely talked since the final papers had been signed. She was curt, polite, and coolly distant. It had been easy for her, ensconced in the protective bosom of her family, to forget the nights he had held her close to him, the nights she had cried and shivered in his arms. The night when, at 2:00 A.M., she had awakened him as the first contractions of her labor began.

He had stayed with her all the way—from those initial stirrings right through the long labor and the delivery. And he had been there to hold his daughter when she was only minutes old.

Nights like this made him sentimental. It had not been a perfect marriage, but he had expected it to be permanent. Ties like these endured. They could not be severed by a divorce decree. It would be a long time before he could stop thinking of Tina as his wife.

He ripped the sheet from the bed and dialed the number he still knew by heart. George told himself it was Sheila he wanted to talk to, but when he heard Tina's voice he was momentarily transported. She sounded so far away. He could almost imagine that nothing had ever happened, that he was calling her during one of her frequent visits to New Jersey. He wondered, as he watched a mist of light gather beneath the single bulb of his bedside lamp, had he done everything he could to keep her? Had he given up too easily?

The feelings that should have died seemed unmistakably alive.

"Hello George," she said coolly.

Tina still had the knack of making her resentments felt. The tone of her voice. The way she said his name. The strained pauses between words.

Immediately, he returned to the present. "Is Sheila around?" he asked.

He heard sounds in the background. He could envision the scene. Tina pointing to the receiver and silently mouthing his name. Her mother, Antoinette, wringing her hands, looking worried and concerned, as if any phone call, any contact whatsoever, might trigger a reconciliation.

They would hate that. The whole Nunzio family had worked long and hard to get Tina to return to them. But in the same way they believed that garlic hung over the door kept away evil spirits, they believed that a husband possessed enough magic to win back his wife.

"She's in her room, studying. Do you want me to get her?"

It was the type of question that said more than it asked. Tina knew he was calling about the weekend. She had probably told Sheila not to set her heart on seeing Daddy when he said he would be there, because police work always came first. Tina would never come right out and say he was a selfish bastard. No, that wasn't her style. Instead, she'd insinuate until the point was gently and subtly hammered home.

"Yes, I'd appreciate it if you'd call her. It will only take a minute."

"Hi Daddy," Sheila said. "Are you all right?"

Her voice was a smaller, more high-pitched version of her mother's. Despite what had happened between them, Sheila would always remind him of what they had once shared. They had been husband and wife. A family. It was inescapable.

"Of course I'm all right," he answered. "How's school?"

"Fine except for math."

"That's too bad, honey. Maybe I can give you some special help when we get together."

"This Sunday, right?"

"Well, that's why I'm calling. I have an important case I'm working on here and I just can't get away. I know how disappointed you must be, but it's very important. Top secret."

The secret policeman routine wasn't working on Sheila. Not anymore. Not since she had moved in with her grandparents.

There was an odd silence.

"Listen, baby, I'm going to call you during the week. I want to set up another time when we can be together. I miss you."

"I miss you too, Daddy." She blew a kiss into the phone before she hung up.

George gazed into the refrigerator. The dim light flashed and a shapeless bright spot moved against the opposite wall. A stale odor leaked from the plastic vegetable bin. He grabbed an open can of soda. The liquid was flat and tasted of tin. The loneliness was like a knife, sharp and sure. It cut deeply. George rubbed his hand across the old scar. It had become a habit, a reminder that his deepest wounds were not visible.

There was still time to call Elizabeth. He hated feeling this way. Needy. Empty. Wanting the kind of comfort he could only get from her. He just couldn't sleep alone tonight. He couldn't face the solitude, the ache, the sound of his own heartbeat. He realized how much Elizabeth had become part of his life. She filled the emptiness. He needed her. And then there was the business of contacting Kiley's daughter. Elizabeth had all that information. He told himself he would have to call her anyway, so why not now?

She had been sleeping. He could tell by the thick, dreamy way she said hello. He asked if he could stop by. At first he hesitated, thinking that for some reason she didn't recognize his voice. "It's me, George," he said.

"I understand," she answered. "Sorry, I just dozed off. Come on over."

By the time he reached her house he felt calmer, more composed. He wasn't going to say anything about his conversation with Sheila. He wasn't going to talk about a family that should have ended, but hadn't. Not quite yet.

She still looked sleepy. Her eyes were puffy, the way they got when he woke her early in the morning, or when she had been crying.

"I guess you're beat too," he said as he slumped into a kitchen chair.

"Well, this hasn't exactly been an ordinary day. Can I get you anything? How about a beer?"

He waved his hand in the air, creating an opening that didn't exist.

"I hate to lay this on you, especially after what I put you through this afternoon. But you're going to know tomorrow anyway, so you might as well hear it from me."

Elizabeth sucked in her breath and leaned against the refrigerator.

"Kiley died tonight."

"God," she said, exhaling, "I thought you were going to tell me you caught the murderer."

"Sorry to disappoint you."

"Listen, don't get angry, it's just that I was expecting something *really* horrible."

"You mean someone dying isn't horrible enough for you?"

"George, you know what I mean."

"Yeah, I know what you mean. It's lousy luck, don't you think? Here this poor woodchuck grave-digger comes upon a dead body, gets terrified, and dies of a heart attack. Probably would have lived ten more years if he hadn't been in the wrong place at the wrong time."

"You don't know whether that's true. He could have died peacefully in bed at exactly the same time."

"I'd sure like to believe that. It would make my job a lot easier."

"Then believe it," Elizabeth said as she poured herself a glass of milk. "What now?"

"Now we notify the daughter and hope she comes in to arrange for a funeral."

"I wouldn't count on that. She didn't even want to call him. Sounds like she's got her hands full already."

George shrugged his shoulders. He reached over and touched Elizabeth's hand. It was a signal they both understood. They sat silently in the kitchen, and then they moved automatically, by unspoken agreement, toward the bedroom.

George settled himself on the unmade bed.

"I feel like shit," he confessed as he pulled her down beside him. "Two deaths. No leads. And I can't even see my own daughter this weekend."

"Did you talk to Tina tonight? Is that what's got you so upset?"

He could tell by the tone in her voice that she was threatened. It was not an unusual reaction for her.

He ran his fingers through his hair. He couldn't go through this again. Not tonight.

"All in all it's been one terrific day, don't you think?"

Sensing both the irony and the desperation in his words, Elizabeth backed down. "Maybe you just need a good night's sleep and a sympathetic shoulder to cry on. I'd like to say that it will seem better in the morning, but in this case, I'm not sure it will."

George hadn't planned it, but he began to make love to her. It was a sudden, almost violent need. And he was surprised when she responded. He was aware that recently the passion between them had waned. After what he told her about Kiley, and after mentioning that he had spoken with Tina, he fully expected her to recoil from anything more physical than a good-night kiss. But he was wrong. As the moonlight seeped through the open windows and the evening turned into night, she reached out for him. Her body was warm, ready—as if she had been waiting. This was how it had been when they first met. He nibbled her fingertips, ran his tongue along the curve of her neck.

God, he had missed her.

They made love silently, two lovers dancing a well-choreographed routine. She stroked him slowly, gently. He felt the ache subside. There was an ease, a grace in their familiarity. When he entered her, he closed his eyes and the past disappeared. He didn't whisper her name, but he longed to. She wasn't completely his, and although he wanted to love her, he was still not free of the memories.

Afterward, she stared at his profile in the dark. He kissed her. She moved her fingers over his face, memorizing him.

Together, they lay listening to the stillness of the country night.

18

THE POSTCARD was right there waiting for her. Peg stared at the scene of the desert in a place called Borago Springs. Strange white flowers grew out of fat green cacti.

> Having a terrific time. Spent the day here in the desert. It's not like I expected. No sand dunes, only funny plants and a hot sun. Miss you.
>
> Love, Jamie

She had written the word "hot" with short wavy lines, so that Peg could almost feel the heat rising from the postcard. She looked once again at the scrubby landscape, finding it hard to believe her daughter could be so far away. She longed to hear Jamie's voice, but it was clear she and Herb were moving around. Wasn't that just like him? God forbid he should prepare meals like a responsible father. They were probably eating in filthy little roadside places or, worse, living on potato chips and cola.

But Peg knew she could no longer keep her daughter all to herself. Herb had wanted to spend this

summer, Jamie's final one before high school graduation, with his daughter. And Jamie had begged to
go. After all, he was her father. It wasn't right to
keep them apart.

Herb had been sending Jamie postcards since she
was a little girl. Like any adoring daughter, Jamie
read and reread each one before she put them away
in a shoebox. Nights when Jamie fell asleep with her
radio blasting and Peg came in to turn it off, she
would see the shoebox open beside her bed.

Herb traveled constantly. He was a fabric salesman who loved being on the road. In the end, that's
what had broken them up. Herb gone weeks, months
at a time and she all alone with a baby and no friends
in a strange town. After three years Peg decided to
stop waiting. She began to work at the diner. At
three o'clock she'd pick Jamie up from day-care or
kindergarten and spend the remainder of the afternoon baking, cleaning, and playing with the child
who became her only love.

When she had found out about the other woman,
it hadn't even come as a shock. He was gone more
than he was there. All Peg had to show for her
marriage, besides her daughter, was a box filled with
postcards and a plain gold band.

The other woman was named Sylvia. It had been a
clear autumn day when the call came. The woman
was crying. She made hard, choking sounds that
alarmed Peg. Sylvia said she was pregnant. Herb had
promised to marry her. She had no idea he already
had a wife somewhere else. It had only been by
accident, when she was preparing his clothes for the

cleaner, that she found the address and phone number. When he didn't come home that night, Sylvia couldn't help herself, she called Peg. While Sylvia choked and sobbed over the phone, Jamie played happily in the small front yard. Peg felt sorry for the woman, but she couldn't lie. She told Sylvia that she and Herb had been married for four years and they had a child.

After that, Peg had no use for Herb. She erased him from her mind. Since there was no way to contact him, she simply slipped off the gold band and declared herself divorced. Two years later when a court made it official, Peg felt nothing. She had already slept with three other men, and the box of postcards had long ago been discarded.

Herb's sudden desire to spend a summer with his daughter had thrown her. For years he had only visited sporadically. But the postcards always came: Chicago, New Orleans, Los Angeles. He still thought these little messages were enough. Peg knew she had been a fool to go along with him. Jamie made a fan of postcards in the corner of her mirror. When new ones arrived, she put the old ones in the box. Peg pretended not to notice. She pretended not to see herself in her daughter.

She surveyed the busy diner. Evelyn had everything under control. The grill was already sizzling, and the early morning locals had given way to the late morning regulars. It was 8:00.

When she had first moved here from Brooklyn, Peg had called everyone a hick. People who got up with the sun and were asleep by nine were strangers to her. But as the years passed, the locals forgot Peg was a city girl. She was on their schedule now, and when she finally saved enough to mortgage the diner from the former owner, everyone thought it fitting that she should rename it "Peg's."

Peg spent more time at the diner than she did at home. After school Jamie would come and sit in the back booth by the jukebox and do her homework. Sometimes she brought friends, loud-talking girls who wore too much makeup and danced until the linoleum was covered with thick black heel marks. But Peg didn't argue. It was all happening here under her nose, and it was innocent fun.

This morning the counter was a mass of cups and plates and leftover toast. Bernie, the busboy, was leaning against the only empty stool and listening to a conversation.

"Says here she was beaten beyond recognition. Look at that photograph, don't it just chill you?"

Edgar Rice, the used-car salesman who had sold her and Herb their first car, was pointing to the morning edition. The headline read WHO IS THE MISSING PRINCESS? This was more than front-page news. The entire edition of the *Democrat* was devoted to the case. Local reporters had interviewed everyone from a distant relative of Mason Kiley to three teenagers who had made an abortive attempt to run away more than two years ago. There were photographs of the gravedigger's shed, the cemetery, and Lieutenant Murphy pointing to the mannequin dressed in the now-familiar sweater and paisley skirt. There was a story about a psychic who had found a missing child in Crescent Springs five years ago, and one about a kidnapped girl who had turned up in New York City.

Peg had heard about the case the day before. She had been frightened to think Lieutenant Murphy might have made some connection, however tentative, between the body and her Jamie.

Peg remembered her own pregnancy, the giddy anticipation she felt the first time Jamie had kicked inside her. To think that somewhere a mother who had felt those same stirrings was waiting to hear—to be told—that her daughter had been killed was too much to consider.

"Have you seen this?" Edgar asked as Peg looked for a spot over the cash register to tack up Jamie's postcard. He waved the gruesome photograph of the mannequin in her face. She had to hand it to Lieutenant Murphy. He certainly had a flair for the dramatic.

"Yeah, I saw it, and I hope I don't have to see it again."

"Then maybe you don't know what else happened," Edgar said. His mouth was filled with food as he spoke. A shred of dried egg yolk clung to the stubble around his chin. He didn't wait for her to answer.

"Kiley dropped dead last night. Fright did it. Finding that body crushed and beaten took the life right out of him."

Peg stared at the plates all piled up on top of each other. "Are you sure about that?"

"Heard it over the radio just this morning. Died right there in the hospital last night. Never had a chance to regain consciousness. Might even have seen something, but now we'll never know."

Peg motioned for Bernie to get moving and start working on the mountains of china that covered the counter and the one empty table. Kiley had been here the morning he discovered the body. She had poured him the coffee herself. He stood right there and smiled at her. The old guy had had his share of troubles. First there was the drinking. It had made him wild and mean. After his daughter left and married some stranger, his wife had passed away. Then Kiley went from being wild and mean to being small and meek. She could still see him smiling at her as she wrapped his danish in waxed paper.

By the time George Murphy came in for his breakfast, the place had all but emptied out. Peg stood at the counter, wiping her hands on her apron as he sipped his coffee. She wanted to say something but couldn't figure out what. Certainly "congratulations" wasn't the right thing.

She had always liked George, found him easy-going, nice to talk to. Why that stuck-up wife had left him, she'd never know. But she was sure of one thing. Lieutenant Murphy was better off without her. It was the girl, his daughter, he probably missed—a sweet, quiet child a year or two younger than her own Jamie.

She wanted to ask him about Kiley and how he died. She was anxious to find out if there were any leads in the case. She liked the way he had named the girl Princess Doe. She wanted to say a lot of things, but the words just wouldn't come out.

Bernie came flying out from the kitchen and patted George on the back. Peg watched as the lieutenant squirmed uncomfortably in his seat. It was clear he had waited for the crowd to thin before he showed up. Bernie was asking a million questions, and she could tell George was trying to be polite. He wasn't talking. Even Evelyn, who usually minded her own business, moved over to the end of the counter to eavesdrop.

His coffee was only half-finished when Lieutenant Murphy stood up and walked over to the cash register. Peg motioned to Bernie to move his backside into the kitchen. She mustered a smile as she counted the change. But, still, she couldn't say anything.

Peg stared out from the door as George slipped back into his patrol car. His being there made her feel the way she did when someone she knew lost a loved one. They had that aura of sadness, a wall that nothing, not words nor expressions of sympathy, could penetrate. She had been behind that wall the first time Herb left her. It was as if he had died, and in a way he had, since after that time he was lost to her forever.

She saw George stop and talk into his radio before he drove off. She wondered what was really going on. Maybe they already knew who the girl was and who had killed her. Peg was glad Jamie was out of town. If there was a madman on the loose, it was better she only had herself to worry about. She picked up George's cup. Too bad you couldn't read the future or the past in leftover coffee. She sure would like to know what was coming. But then there was something else she wanted to know, something that had already happened. It was the same question that had been in the back of everyone's mind that morning.

Peg wondered how it felt to be George, to pull the mangled body of a child from a riverbank. How could it possibly have felt to stand and watch as the coroner cut apart the body of a child, a child close in age to George's own little girl? And she wondered how he could sleep at night, how George could keep the horror from seeping into his dreams and filling him with dread.

19

GEORGE WAS GONE. Elizabeth stared sleepy-eyed at the vacant space beside her. She remembered last night enough to know that when they had made love she had not been completely honest. It wasn't really George she was thinking about. The sex had been good, but she had been only partially there. The parts that weren't in the bed were floating in the darkness, dreaming of the man who had visited her earlier that night and who had left before she had wanted him to.

Elizabeth buried her face in the pillow. She didn't want to face what today had in store for her. There were phone calls to make, clients to see, and the brutal reality of a murder that had, in all probability, become the focal point of the entire town.

Bakersville would be buzzing. In every bar and restaurant, on every street corner, and in every home, the case of Princess Doe would be a major topic of conversation. There would be wild speculation and even wilder accusations. People would begin to suspect their neighbors. An innocent hole dug to plant potatoes or to unearth a shrub would become a possible burial sight. Angry husbands who shouted at cowering wives would be considered potential murderers. Children who stopped to play at a friend's house or who were late returning from a ball game would become the object of hysterical fears.

Elizabeth knew that the murder would trigger a kind of madness in the small town. Things were done slowly in Bakersville. On winter days Elizabeth found herself stopping by the local pharmacy, not really to purchase a box of tissues or some cough medicine but to chat, to make human contact, to avoid the nights when blackness arrived by five and she felt as though she were sealed in a dark, solitary cell until the sun rose over the frozen snow.

When the weather warmed and the ground thawed beneath the last layer of ice, people were eager to get out and about. There would be talk of spring planting, bass fishing, and the best way to break beaver dams. Human gossip was rare and treasured. A local farmer who finally quit drinking, a dog warden who shot a rabid German shepherd and a young woman who had taken up with someone else's husband became stories that were passed from friend to friend, neighbor to neighbor.

Except for William Steed, who at ninety-four had wandered off and been found dead, probably of exposure, in the woods, there had never been a mysterious death in Bakersville. People here were more likely to meet their ends conventionally, in hospital beds, crushed automobiles, or peacefully in their own beds.

There weren't many surprises in Bakersville. Just as the seasons rolled predictably into one another, the behavior of its citizens seemed to respond accordingly. Elizabeth knew as she stared at the clock that the discovery of the body would upset the natural order of things. It wasn't that tragedies hadn't happened here. They had. But there had always been something to do, some communal action to take.

If a local girl had died, there would be talk of taking up a collection or organizing a bake sale. But in this case there was no bereaved family, no one to offer consolation. The crime itself was unnatural, an alien thing. It was something that happened in big cities. And that disturbed her.

Elizabeth knew there was no such thing as a safe place, but Bakersville came close. Sometimes she forgot to lock her front door or she left her pocketbook on the counter of the diner or on the front seat of her car. Nothing was ever taken, no private space ever invaded. As a child she could remember skipping down dirt roads as the sun set or walking alone through town on her way home from a party or dance. There had been an innocence about that sort of freedom. People looked out for one another here. Lives overlapped.

When she had first left Bakersville, she had been glad to escape. The town had become claustrophobic. She found it exhilarating to live in a place where no one knew her history; where her cousin hadn't married the person who sold her a dress or a car; and where she could go into a restaurant without people asking about her family. But after a few years the exhilaration turned to loneliness. Elizabeth began to think more and more about the town where cultural events consisted of a 4-H club exhibition of pottery or a band concert in the park; where the library housed fewer books than a small Manhattan bookstore; and where schools closed the first three days of hunting season. She missed the friendly familiarity, the simplicity, and the security of small-town life. As soon as she returned she knew she had not made a mistake. It felt good to be back. Everything here was scaled down to human terms. It all had been manageable—until now. And that's what she resented most. Whoever had murdered the girl had violated Elizabeth's memories. He had shown her that there was no place to hide; he had warned her that even in Bakersville she was no longer free to walk alone in the dark.

Elizabeth was aware of the possibility that another body would be found, and then another. She tried not to think as she got up and walked toward the bathroom that she was a woman living alone, a prime target for a murderer who had killed only a few miles from where she slept.

The phone rang as she stepped from the shower. For an instant she caught her breath, thinking he might be calling and that last night might not have been more imaginary than real.

"I read everything in the paper. I saw the mannequin. This is awful. How is George?"

It was Celia.

Elizabeth studied the wet footprints she had made in the pale carpet.

"Well, now you know. I didn't want to tell you all the details yesterday. George is George. He's coping. He was here last night."

"And?" Celia drew out the word so it effectively implied more than it directly requested.

"And nothing. He looked like hell, slept over, and left before I even woke up."

"Is this all you're going to tell me?"

Elizabeth checked the time. She had half an hour before she left for the office.

"What else do you want to know?"

"There must be more about this murder. Stuff you're not telling me."

"The stuff I'm not telling you is mostly in my head. Like the fear I have that this whole town is going to go berserk or that the murderer is lurking in the shadows waiting for his next victim. I think you can figure out the rest."

"Sounds like you're scared to death."

"Funny," Elizabeth said. "We always talk about fears and fantasies as if we imagine most of the demons in the world, but this is one of those times when the outside world is more terrifying and brutal than anything I've ever imagined."

"Maybe you want to come down to visit for a few days until things calm down." Celia said.

"Thanks for the offer, but you can't believe how complicated this all is. I don't know if you've heard yet, but Mason Kiley, the gravedigger who first discovered the body, died last night. George was right there when it happened. Now we have to get the daughter down here and have a funeral without causing more panic. It's not like New York. Everyone knows everyone here. People are going to be terrified."

"I'm terrified for you," Celia said. "After I read the papers I gave Elsie another one of my don't-talk-to-strangers lectures. The poor kid is afraid to leave the house. She read the paper when I wasn't looking. She's worried too."

"I'm all right, really. In all probability George will be able to identify the girl in a day or two. Then it's only a matter of time until the rest of it falls into place."

"You mean until you catch the bastard who did it?"

"I guess so." Elizabeth didn't believe a word she was saying and hoped Celia wasn't catching on. She decided to change the subject. "That guy came over here last night."

"Who?" Celia asked.

"The motorcycle man. You remember."

"God! that seems like a million years ago. Sure, I remember. But I thought you said George slept over."

"He did. Gary, that's his name, only stayed for a little while. He made me uncomfortable. I can't put my finger on it."

There was a silence on the other end of the phone. "Celia? are you there?"

"I'm thinking. Maybe you should be a little careful now."

"Nothing happened. He stopped by, refused a glass of wine, drank tea, told me he was a photographer, and disappeared in a cloud of dust."

"This continues to sound very romantic. Am I right?"

"I think so. I know I'm a little off right now, but the man has a definite appeal. I probably would have asked him to stay, but I was afraid."

"Of what?"

"That he'd say no."

"That's a switch. Men don't usually visit women they intend to reject."

"Maybe. But why did I have this distinct feeling that although he was interested, he definitely did not want to stay?"

"I've had that same experience. There's only one explanation."

"What's that?"

"He's married."

Elizabeth frowned. "I just can't believe that this guy has any earthly ties, nothing so ordinary as being married. He drives around with everything packed on the back of his motorcycle. How could he be married?"

"Elizabeth, you've been living in the country too long. He probably rents the motorcycle and has a station wagon with fake wood paneling, a house in the suburbs, three kids, and a wife who's eating her heart out wondering where the hell he's disappeared to."

Elizabeth laughed in spite of herself. "You're unbelievable! Here I meet this mysterious, handsome stranger, and one minute you're worried that I'm not being careful, and the next minute you tell me I'm being conned by a runaway husband."

"Stranger things have happened."

"Seriously, I wish you could have been here. But probably if you were here it would have been different. It was this eerie feeling. Like he knew I wasn't wearing underwear."

"Were you?"

"No. But that's really beside the point. It's something I can't explain."

"Were you scared?"

"No, not at all. I was—tentative."

"Maybe you were turned on and that made you uncomfortable."

"Exactly."

Elizabeth anticipated Celia's next question. But it wasn't only guilt that had made her feel so uncomfortable, so hesitant. After all, she and George had slept together. It was true that the sex had been better than it had been in a long time. But, still,

Elizabeth was aware that something was missing. She longed for the passion they had shared at the very beginning. She wanted to experience something deeper, a physical sensation that went beyond everyday lovemaking. Maybe that wasn't possible. Besides, this was a difficult time for George. Although he never actually said it, she had known that he was frightened. And she could feel the fear, even as he made love to her.

As Celia talked, asking her details about the murder, confiding her fears about missing children and her own daughter, Elizabeth studied every detail of her bedroom. She recalled the idea she had had that something was different, out of place. Now, as she surveyed the room, she realized everything was perfectly in order. Had it all been an illusion?

"Celia," she said, "do you think that something like this, something so violent can affect your perceptions?"

"About what?"

"For example, yesterday I felt uncomfortable in my house, like something was misplaced or missing. I checked and nothing had been touched or stolen, it was just a feeling."

"That's understandable," Celia said. "Fear distorts reality. Remember when you were a kid and at night a favorite doll, or simply a coat thrown over a chair, took on monstrous proportions? That's what happens to kids in the dark when they're alone and they're frightened. I'm sure with all that's going on, you might be experiencing something like that."

Elizabeth thought back to the times when, as a child, she lay alone in her bedroom. Sometimes, if she put her ear to the wall, she could hear her older brother Steven breathing. They were heavy rhythmic breaths that often lulled her into a deep and dreamless sleep.

But on nights when Steven stayed out late, or when she couldn't hear him, she watched the faces in the wallpaper. In the darkness the simple rose and tulip pattern became a living collage of twisted features: noses that protruded from the flat space, eyes that rolled in bloody sockets, lips that snarled and curled back in horrible grimaces. She remembered sitting up in fear, calling for her mother, and waiting anxiously until the nightlight was lit and the familiar voice spoke her name.

Those were the times Elizabeth wished she had a father, a strong man with a hairy chest who could chase away the nightmares.

Her father's death, the result of a car accident in which he had been the driver, took him from her when she was three years old. Her mother, who never remarried, devoted herself to Elizabeth, but her presence was never enough. After years of therapy, and years of training for her profession, Elizabeth believed she had accepted the loss. Now, she worried that the nightmares would return.

"Do you really think that's it?" Elizabeth asked Celia.

"What do *you* think?"

Elizabeth recognized the familiar pattern their conversation was taking. Celia was answering her question with another question. Sometimes they did that with one another, behaved more like therapists than friends. Perhaps it was an occupational hazard, but at the same time, it was, Elizabeth knew, the best way to force her to look inward.

"I think I feel guilty that I made love with George and all the time I was fantasizing about another man." Elizabeth was surprised by her sudden honesty.

"And this frightens you?"

"Maybe this man, Gary, frightens me."

Celia was silent. Elizabeth knew she was trying to sort through the confusion of their conversation.

"You and George made love, right? Maybe what frightened you, and what continues to terrify you, is not some fantasy about another man but the possibility of real intimacy with George."

Elizabeth sensed what Celia was getting at. For a year now she and George had been engaged in a game of approach/avoidance. They grew close; they panicked and separated. She felt threatened by his ex-wife; he was terrified of getting close enough to be hurt again. It was an old story, a familiar routine.

"In this case," Celia went on, "I would say that the man of your fantasies is safe. He's unavailable. He comes and goes. There's no chance of commitment. George is what's frightening. He's real."

Elizabeth stared at her wet footprints, which had now begun to dry and disappear back into the carpet. Celia's logic was impeccable. But there was something here that defied logic, something that didn't fit.

After she promised Celia she would be careful and call in a day or two, Elizabeth placed the phone back on the receiver. She watched as her footprints dissolved.

On some level, Elizabeth accepted what Celia had said as being true. But in the same place where she had locked away the terrors of her childhood, there existed another kind of knowing. There, where flowers could be transformed into hideous faces and where nighttime held a special fascination, anything was possible.

And it was this knowing that troubled Elizabeth —this knowing that made her sense with a dark certainty that she was slowly slipping, moving closer and closer to something that was more dangerous than anything she had ever imagined.

20

PEG STARED AT THE SOFT mound of earth that rested beside the coffin. The sky was dull gray and the slow-moving clouds seemed to threaten rain. It was a good day for a funeral.

Everyone was there. People who had barely known Mason Kiley now stood looking forlornly at his grave.

Peg wasn't sure exactly why the whole town had shown up. She suspected it was probably for the same reason she had. Curiosity was only part of it. There seemed to be a need to do something.

For two days now there had been no news on the case. Parents were walking their children to and from school. Women were going out in pairs, local farmers were patrolling deserted country roads. Mason Kiley was the only victim the town really knew, and they had come out today as much to comfort themselves as to mourn him.

Lieutenant Murphy wore a crumpled trench coat. He looked somber and tired. Dark rings had formed beneath his eyes. He hadn't stopped by the diner since the morning after Kiley's death. He had been avoiding everyone. Rumor had it he was working double time: disseminating photographs of the mannequin, calling police departments in other towns, trying to find some shred of evidence that would help him move forward with the case.

Elizabeth stood to George's left. Peg noticed how she repeatedly glanced sideways at the young woman dressed in black. People were saying that that was Annabel, Kiley's only daughter. Peg couldn't be sure. It had been several years since the then sixteen-year-old had run away with a stranger. Everyone thought she'd marry a home boy, someone she'd known all her life. That was how it was in Bakersville. Childhood sweethearts got married right out of high school, settled down, had kids, and seemed to get old before their time.

Peg hoped something different was in the cards for Jamie. She was determined to send her daughter away to college. The state university and its lecture halls filled with small-town kids with small-town ideas wasn't good enough. Not for Jamie. Maybe she would go out West, or down to New York City. Some place where her mind would be challenged and where she would learn not to make the same kind of foolish mistakes her mother had.

They were lowering the casket slowly into the freshly dug hole. Peg wondered if she were the only one thinking how ironic it was—the gravedigger being buried in the same cemetery where he had worked, the same cemetery where he had made the terrible discovery that cost him his life. Edgar Rice had said just that morning that no one should think of it that way. Kiley's number had been up. That was it. Pure and simple. Finding the body of the girl had nothing to do with it.

Peg had wondered as she cleaned the counter how a used-car salesman could have such definite ideas about the nature of life and death. She wanted to ask Edgar if he thought that the murdered girl's number had been up as well. But Peg had been in the restaurant business long enough to know not to stir up the customers. And these days everyone was stirred up plenty.

Elizabeth moved back and away from George. She stood beside Annabel Kiley Morgan. Elizabeth had been astonished when the young woman said she would come back to arrange for the funeral. She had been so adamant about neither visiting nor calling her father as he lay dying. Now she was weeping.

There was something here, some bond between fathers and daughters that Elizabeth would never be privy to. She hadn't had an opportunity to properly mourn her own father. As she watched Annabel, she felt a curious envy. Perhaps because she had never known her father, she had had to live with the nightmares. She wondered if this funeral would trigger something she had not anticipated. She wondered if burying Mason Kiley would unearth the ghosts that had haunted her childhood.

Surveying the crowd, Elizabeth noted that almost everyone who was active in town affairs was there: shop owners, the local supervisor, members of the school board, even the regulars from the diner. Peg, whom she had come to like, stood beside her helper, the prim, tight-lipped Evelyn. Edgar Rice, the loud-mouthed car salesman, hovered in the background.

Elizabeth knew this was going to be an awful day. The hunkering gray clouds were only part of it. There would be more urgent inquiries; mothers calling when their children were ten minutes late.

Jean, the dispatcher at headquarters, was working overtime. Now many of the calls were coming into Elizabeth's office. Eventually, every child in Bakersville was accounted for. No one was missing. No one else had been murdered, and there were no new leads.

She wished Celia were here with her. George hadn't been by since the evening they had slept together, though he called every night. Exhausted, angry, frustrated, he told her she was better off sleeping alone. All He did was pace the floor and smoke cigarettes. He was back at his desk, back at the phones by six every morning.

Elizabeth knew he was probably right, but besides being her lover, he was her only close friend in Bakersville. There would be time, she knew, to make more friends, but she needed someone *now.*

Peg would be good to talk to. It was just a feeling, but Elizabeth sensed there was something there, some sad wisdom in those blue eyes. But the diner didn't seem the right place to start a conversation. It was a place to trade gossip, news, jokes, and the typical rural small talk that Elizabeth had only now begun to appreciate. But it was not the place for a woman to open her heart.

If Celia were here, she'd know what to say. Or she would embrace Elizabeth in a protective silence. That's how it was with good friends. Sometimes not saying anything was more comforting than words.

Christ, George thought, I hope they don't start with that "he was a good man" crap. In all probability Kiley didn't have one real friend in the unlikely crowd that had gathered for his funeral.

He thought back to all the times he had found Kiley lying shit-faced in a ditch beside the road. One time he came upon him hanging on a fence surrounding the Cunningham farm. Lyle Cunningham didn't give a hoot about the man whose cheeks had been pierced by barbed wire. All he wanted was compensation for his fence.

Not once in the dozen or more times George had driven Mason Kiley to the slammer to dry out had anyone expressed the least bit of interest. And now this. The whole goddamned town shows up for his funeral!

George shook his head. It was morbid curiosity. The same kind of curiosity that had led Billy Grenson at the garage to ask him about the dead girl's body. He had been disgusted. Did anyone really expect him to tell some greasy mechanic about the naked body of the murdered girl?

Chief Norris was standing beside the town superintendent. There was plenty of pressure brewing. George was sure of it. Since all the publicity, there had been an outcry to solve the case.

"Find out who the kid is," Norris had told him. "And find out soon."

George wanted to reach out for Elizabeth. He wanted to tuck her hand into the crook of his arm and feel the soft coolness of her palm. But even if she had been his wife, even if she had been Tina, he wouldn't have done that now.

One thing was clear, though. Elizabeth had been dead wrong about Kiley's daughter. Annabel was weeping uncontrollably. That's how it was with family. You could hate them and not see them, but when they were gone for good you cried your eyes out. It comforted George to think of Sheila. She was a good kid. He hoped she'd never have to run away like Annabel had. If things ever got bad at the Nunzio's, he'd take her in. Somehow he'd make the time.

Someone was whispering about how Kiley had been a victim and how the murderer had killed him just as sure as he had bludgeoned that poor little girl. George pretended not to hear. He pretended not to notice when Edgar Rice shot him a searing look. Shit! He was doing his best. He had tried everything.

Today, after this funeral, he was going to hit every fast-food joint within a fifty-mile radius. The autopsy had shown she had died with undigested food in her stomach. That meant she had had to eat somewhere around here. He was going to show the photograph of the mannequin to every counterperson he could find. Hopefully, someone would remember having seen her.

He glanced around at the group of mourners. It occurred to him that he should say something to Kiley's daughter. In some small way he felt responsible for the old man's death. It was the very least he could do.

Annabel looked younger than he had expected. Up close, the gray light revealed only the tiniest lines in the corners of her eyes. Other than that, her face was smooth. She could have passed for a teenager.

"I was with your father when he had the heart attack. I'm sorry," he said.

Annabel spoke in a low voice, almost a whisper.

"Are you the cop?"

"George Murphy," he said, holding out his hand. Her palm felt fragile in his. She looked like a frightened child.

"Did he say anything before he died? Did he mention me?"

"It all happened too fast," he said, wishing he could comfort her. "He never knew what hit him."

Annabel nodded. "I really didn't think he was going to die. When that lady called, I just thought he had gone off on another bender. That's how it used to be. There was no way I could have known." She paused to dry the tears that streamed down her cheeks. "He never even got to see my kids."

George stared past Annabel at the open grave. A sudden gust of wind startled him. He looked into Annabel's eyes. His words seemed to come to him from a great distance. He was surprised to hear his own voice.

"Sometimes fathers and daughters lose each other, for all kinds of reasons."

It was almost as if he hadn't spoken at all. The words formed themselves. But at that moment, George knew he had uttered something true about himself, about Sheila, and about the child whose body he had pulled from the riverbank.

Annabel nodded sadly as she moved back toward the remaining cluster of mourners.

George grasped her hand one more time. Old man Kiley had died before he had had a chance to settle things with Annabel. Unfinished business. It was something Annabel would have to resolve on her own, if she could.

"If there's anything I can do," he said. "You know where to contact me."

Annabel gazed at the encroaching rain clouds. "It's like you said. We lost each other. I won't be back. There's nothing here to come back to."

George turned to see where Elizabeth had gone. She was moving to the edge of the crowd, getting ready to make a hasty retreat. It was a good idea. Peg had invited everyone back to the diner for coffee and cake. He never could understand why funerals made people hungry. But they did. He could use some of that coffee himself, but he knew better than to appear before a jury of local big mouths.

Everyone had ideas. Everyone knew how he should do his job. Right now he was thinking that, except for Elizabeth, everyone in Bakersville was a jackass.

The rain started just as the crowd began to disperse. Small droplets of moisture came slanting down, making it hard to see. But even through the rain, George was sure he spotted it. The black Harley-Davidson, the same one that had passed him a few days before. It moved, crawled almost, along the periphery of the cemetery. But when George looked away to turn up his collar and shake the hand of the local minister, the bike was gone. Maybe he had imagined it. Today was a day when nothing seemed very real anyway.

*   *   *

Elizabeth found herself walking beside Peg as they passed through the large iron gates of the cemetery. She kept her head down against the driving rain. Somewhere in the distance, she heard the revving sound. Looking up, she caught a glimmer of black and chrome. The Harley-Davidson seemed to drive directly into the woods.

"Did you see that?" she asked Peg.

"See what?" Peg responded just as the motor-cycle disappeared into a sky-high forest of fir trees.

21

GARY OBSERVED A LONE MAN walking around the perimeter of the grave. He watched him tilt his head slightly to the right, as if there were something, some message he was just not receiving. It would have made a perfect picture. But when he brought the lens up to his eye and pointed it through the slanting rain, the man moved suddenly, as if he could feel Gary watching him. He let the camera drop against his chest.

The grayness coated the sky like a thin smear of watercolor. Gary stood motionless by the edge of the forest. He allowed himself to relive a moment that had changed him. The moment returned to him now as the man blinked his eyes, forever abandoning the dead body to the wooden coffin and the damp earth.

It had been three months before his ninth birthday. He remembered because he had been riding the old blue bicycle, the one with the thick wheels and the flecks of rust along the handlebars. When the rain came, he rode up on the shoulder of the highway, seeking shelter beneath a cluster of maple trees. Leaning the blue bicycle against the tree trunk, he watched the ground for signs of life. Time passed. The rain turned into a thick, steaming mist.

Standing beside the bicycle, wondering what hour it was, he noticed the brown van. Two men emerged carrying a rope noose that dangled at the end of a long stick. He recalled the texture of the tree bark as he moved behind it. Sensing a nameless danger, he prayed for invisibility.

The dog seemed to appear magically from the center of the mist. It was thin, mangy, and it propelled itself forward with an urgency reserved only for the hunted. The dog was surefooted; it ran carefully through the moist and slippery grass. The men moved in different directions. There was a silence, a noiselessness that made Gary aware of his own breathing, his skin, and the pulsating sensation in his wrists and neck.

The two men converged on the dog, coming closer than they should have. The animal, cornered and terrified, rolled back its upper lip, exposing a flash of pointed teeth. Yet it stood its ground, refusing to dodge or run at the men. It seemed somehow frozen to the spot.

There was a signal. A nodding of heads, imperceptible to the dog. In an instant the noose was artfully slipped over the dog's neck. Held at the end of the stick, growling and twisting, the animal was dragged through the rain-soaked grass. While one man held the stick, the other opened the door to the van. Gary could see the metal cage inside.

But then something changed. This time there didn't seem to be a signal. Or maybe Gary was too busy watching the stick that controlled the snarling dog, a stick that reminded him of the strings attached to a wooden puppet. But he did see the revolver. Drawn from a black leather holster, it appeared only briefly in the gray mist.

The sound of the shot lingered in the air, splintering the scene into a thousand images. Gary clapped his hands over his ears. Too late. The sound waves moved through the tree. He felt the unmuted vibration. The dog lay on its side in a patch of flattened weeds. He never saw the men's faces, never noticed if there was another signal, another wordless communication.

The doors of the van slammed shut.

When the men left, Gary walked out from behind the tree. It had not been a dream. The dog was there—silent and unmoving. It was then, at that moment, that Gary took his first picture. Making a circle with his thumb and forefinger, he clicked the image: the dog, the grass, the thickening mist. It had been a perfect murder, and Gary had been the only witness.

Remembering the picture had been easy. All his first pictures had been that way. Seared into his mind. Impossible to forget. Like the marks his mother made on the wall behind his bedroom door as he grew, they were traces of his own history. When he finally began using a camera, he lost the need to remember. The photographs themselves were real. But the images were what mattered to Gary. And those first images—the ones of the dog that had

been cornered and executed for a nameless crime—
remained the most powerful he had ever captured.

*   *   *

The rain was coming down harder now. It pelted
against the back of his jacket and threatened to seep
in between the metal teeth of the zipper. If he stayed
here in the cemetery, more pictures would come
back to him. He could shelter himself beneath the fir
trees. But if he left, he might find Elizabeth. She
might be in the house. Alone. Gary was sure he had
seen her glance at him as he drove into the forest.
Already, she was sensing his presence.

It had been three days since he was last here. He
had remained in Crescent Springs, calling his reps,
taking care of business. And he had developed the
photographs of the cop. In the darkroom he rented
by the hour, he had watched the images swim up
from beneath a bath of chemicals. Underwater, the
outline of the man had been blurred and dreamlike.
Pulling it from the liquid, Gary noticed that the face
of the cop was partially obscured by his arm, which
rested against the open window. The photograph
had been unremarkable.

But now the cop had a name. Lieutenant Murphy.
Gary had saved the photographs. They were scenes
in a story. And Gary was excited about what might
come next.

He was not unaware that something dramatic,
something unexpected had gripped the small town.
Walking aimlessly through the damp and empty
cemetery, Gary resolved that this time he would not

merely be a silent witness. This time he would be a player. Even if his part were only a minor one, he would no longer be an unseen presence.

He knew that a girl's body had been discovered and that the cop he had photographed and had seen visiting Elizabeth was investigating the case. This funeral today meant something too. Elizabeth had been there and so had Lieutenant Murphy. There was a connection, something he could probably discover by reading the newspaper.

But that would mean setting himself outside the drama. No, he would find out by playing his role. As Elizabeth's lover he would become part of a cast of characters. Not knowing the ending made it all the more interesting.

There were only three places she could be. Although the unusual had happened here, Bakers-ville was still predictable. There was her office, her home, and the diner. It occurred to him that she might be at the police station or even at Murphy's house, but he thought it unlikely. If they were having some sort of relationship, it was one of those on-again-off-again things. That would make it easier for him, and it would add an unexpected twist to the plot.

He pushed the Harley out of the mud. The rain had thinned, becoming a moist shower. He liked riding in this weather. The light rain made every-thing seem ethereal, as if a soft-focus lens had been lowered from the sky. It was going to be easy not to take photographs today. Remembering that first picture had disturbed him. It reminded him of a life spent outside—watching, waiting, never acting.

As he hit the kickstand and revved the engine, Gary smiled to himself. Today he was going to become part of a story that included Elizabeth, the cop, and a dead girl—a girl who, apparently, had died among strangers.

22

IT WAS AN AFTERNOON for ghosts. Elizabeth could feel them welling up inside her as she rode aimlessly along the unpaved road. An eerie mist filtered through the thick clusters of trees. She listened as small loose pebbles bounced against the sides of her car.

There was no sense returning to her office, to the desk piled high with a mountain of senseless paperwork and to clients who demanded an empathetic listener. She could no more listen than she could talk.

Her head was filled with a rush of voices. She could still hear the murmurs of the crowd at the funeral; familiar faces etched in dark lines and somber shadows against the soft gray morning. There had been whispers about Kiley dying because of the horrible shock of what he had seen and whispers about the dead girl, her murderer, and the possibility of more victims.

As she drove through the countryside, the whispers became a chorus. Someone was out there.

He had killed once, and that murder had set off a chain reaction. When George had told her about Princess Doe, even when he had brought the garments spotted with dried blood into her home, she had not fully understood. Elizabeth had seen the clothes, she had touched them, but the girl who once wore them was not real. She was George's creation: a column in the newspaper, a few minutes on the evening news, a photograph that would yellow with time.

But right now everything was very real. The enormity of what had happened descended upon her with an impact she could not have anticipated. The chorus became a high-pitched wail. Suddenly, Elizabeth could see the girl, her head split open, her skull beaten until it fell in upon itself. It was not only the violence that stunned her, it was the awful finality. She saw, for the second time that morning, Mason Kiley's coffin. Death had a color, a smell, a pounding rhythm.

She thought of George. He had stood there as they revealed the secrets of the child's body. He had watched as they took her apart, organ by organ. He had taken the child's hands away in a bucket. Then he had slept by Elizabeth's side, and all the time she had been unaware of the images and the sounds he carried with him.

Everything was moving closer. She felt an awful, suffocating feeling. The voices in her head became an incomprehensible drone. She stopped the car, and stretching through the open window, she let the thin rain fall on her head, her arms and her out-stretched fingers.

Ordinarily, she would have walked through the moss-covered forest, but she was frightened. And it was a fear she could taste inside her mouth, a fear so real it shook and trembled until she curled up in the front seat of the car.

Listening to the steady sound of her own breathing, Elizabeth allowed the fear to ebb and swell. She inhaled and exhaled with deliberate, exaggerated thrusts. It was just a feeling, she said to herself. But her words were soaked up by blackness. This was the same stuff from which her childhood nightmares had been made: a dark, nameless terror, a chilling emptiness.

Elizabeth pressed her throbbing temples against the steering wheel. Her hands searched automatically through her handbag until they found one of the small pills she kept for emergencies, and swallowing hard against the dryness, she let the chemicals release their magic into her blood.

When she awoke, she felt a hand on her throat. Struggling against the cottony feeling, she fluttered her eyelids. The light seeped in, bringing with it the greenness of his eyes. Her lids parted just enough to reveal his face as his fingers anxiously felt for her pulse.

"Are you all right?"

The eyes moved closer. The forehead, wrinkled with concern was directly above her. The lips were moving. A warm breath passed between them. Gary completely filled the square tissue of light that shimmered in the drugged haze.

Her mouth felt stiff, unable to shape the familiar sounds.

"Open the door," he said. "Let me inside."

The door was unlocked. She pushed it open and slid along the smooth vinyl seat. He sat beside her and pressed his hand against her forehead.

"What's wrong? What are you doing here?"

Elizabeth stared at the dusty dashboard of the car. She felt herself emerging from a heavy sleep.

How had he found her? By what strange telepathy was he able to come upon her when she was most vulnerable?

"What time is it?" she asked, shocked by the raspy sound of her own voice.

Gary grasped her wrist and turned it toward her. Looking at her own watch, she saw that it was well past two o'clock.

"God, half the day is gone."

He brushed a stray hair from her cheek as she reached for her car keys.

"Driving isn't a good idea right now."

"I'm okay, really," she said. But her voice shook. He must know she had taken something.

Placing her car keys above the dashboard, he leaned forward and peered out the window.

"It's a nice day for a bike ride."

The gloom of the morning had lifted. The sun floated across a pastel sky. Elizabeth wanted to be outside in the warm summer afternoon. A bike ride sounded good.

"Can I go like this?" she asked. She looked down at the wrinkled cotton skirt and suit jacket she had worn to the funeral this morning.

"Why not?"

*   *   *

They were flying. The motorcycle was moving so fast she could only see impressions of trees, flashes of road. She glued herself to him, feeling the sun on her back and inhaling all the scents that rushed at her. It was like eating the air, like breathing in a thousand sounds at once. She closed her eyes. It didn't matter where he was taking her. The last sticky residues of sleep blew into the wind.

She was fully awake now but at the same time aware that the afternoon had taken on a dreamlike quality. She almost never took tranquilizers. She wanted to explain that to him. She wanted to excuse herself and detail the circumstances that had caused her to swallow the pill. But he had never asked. And, truthfully, it had been a relief. The fear was gone. Now there was only the terrific speed of the motor- cycle as it sliced through the summer day.

She pressed her cheek against his back. She was aware that he was accelerating. The wind was sharp now, moving up her sleeves, snaking in under the thin cotton skirt she had tucked beneath her legs. Nothing was familiar. At this speed the landscape became a blur of colors. She tightened her arms around his waist, feeling that at any moment she might fly off the seat and disappear into the thousand shades of green that shot past her on either side.

They were off the paved road. The motorcycle revved and sputtered and she bounced hard against the seat. He was slowing down. They were in a meadow. The long grasses were flecked with the blues and yellows of summer wildflowers.

"We were going pretty fast there," he said as he leaned the bike at an angle so she could dismount.

That feeling again. Those vibrating sensations.

"How fast were we going?"

"Over eighty, but I figured you needed to wake up."

He kicked down the stand and hung their helmets on the handlebars of the motorcycle.

Now that the ride was over, Elizabeth felt embarrassed. Her clothes were oddly out of place in the sunlit field. Gary reached down and picked a small purple flower. He crumpled a leaf between his fingers and held it beneath her nose.

"Here, smell."

The leaf smelled sweet, familiar.

"What is that?"

"It's wild basil. Not as strong as the cultivated variety, but it's delicious."

"What's that?" Elizabeth asked pointing to a clump of tiny orange trumpet flowers.

"Jewelweed." He broke off a piece of stem and showed her the liquid that dripped from the cut end. "Hold out your wrist."

Without thinking she put her wrist in his outstretched hand. He rubbed it with the clear juice from the jewelweed.

"If you ever get poison ivy, this will clear it up. It works better than most things I've bought in the store. See that little bead of moisture in the center of the leaves? That's the 'jewel' in the weed."

Elizabeth stared at the glistening drop of liquid. She had walked through meadows like this one all her life, but she had never noticed a sparkling jewel or tasted a wild herb.

"How do you know all this?"

Half-smiling, Gary turned to her. "I guess you could say it's my business. I used to spend a lot of time outside taking photographs."

"And you don't anymore?"

"Not as much, no."

Elizabeth realized this was the first real conversation they had had. She was accustomed to asking people questions. It occurred to her that she knew very little about Gary. Where was he from? Where did he live? Yet she felt uncomfortable asking. Maybe the answers would come without having to force the questions. She touched the place on her wrist where he had rubbed the plant juice.

"Are you all right?" he asked.

His face showed a genuine concern. It was hard to look away. Here in the bright light he was just as handsome as he had been that evening in her apartment. She ran her hand across her hair. She probably was a mess.

"Maybe we ought to sit down. I've got some lunch."

"Where?" she asked.

He was laughing now. His eyes crinkled into two green slits.

"We'll sit on a blanket and the lunch is in that bag on the side of my bike. Are you sure you're okay?"

She nodded as he rummaged through the luggage boxes and the saddlebags that were arranged behind the passenger seat of the Harley. Maybe the tranquilizer was still in her system. She was feeling so unsure, shy almost.

They were sitting on a heavy wool camp blanket. The fabric was rough against her skin. Gary had placed a loaf of bread, a triangle of cheese, and a thermos of juice between them. He pulled a knife from his back pocket and cut the bread and cheese. His hands moved with graceful certainty. She watched silently, as if the sound of her own voice would transform the moment. She still hadn't told him what she had been doing in the car, and, surprisingly, he hadn't asked.

"I went to a funeral this morning. A local gravedigger, who discovered the body of a murdered girl, died of a heart attack."

The words hovered over the wildflowers before they were sucked into the sky. She heard her own voice but still could not believe what she had said.

"Did you know the man?" Gary asked.

"I did. But that's beside the point. The whole town was there. They came out of some morbid curiosity."

"You too?"

Elizabeth had never thought of it before. Why had she gone? Then she remembered Annabel, the daughter. She had gone out of a sense of professional responsibility. And she had also gone to be with George. But they had neither touched nor spoken.

"I'm not sure," she said, rubbing her hand across the coarse wool of the blanket. "I work for the division of social services, so I'm sort of involved in all this."

"What were you doing in the car when I found you?"

"The funeral upset me. I took a pill. Believe me, it's not something I usually do."

Gary looked out over the field. "I read about the murder. Seems like a lot of people are doing things they don't usually do."

Elizabeth nodded silently. The world had suddenly tipped. Nothing drastic, just a small, almost indiscernible change in position. Enough for her to feel a shudder move through her insides, enough for the fear to rise again.

Gary offered her the thermos. When he looked at her, it was as if he could see right inside to where the fear was reforming.

"You'll be okay," he said. He pulled her toward him.

She rested against his chest. His flannel shirt was moist and smelled of the road. She closed her eyes because now everything was moving again. He spoke in a steady voice, telling her about the field. He described the spotted knapweed, the burdock that was edible, and the thousands of tiny mushrooms that popped up in the dark, moist areas. She didn't have to look at all. He had already seen it for the both of them. He brushed her cheek with his lips. The fear dissolved, until all she could feel was desire. He covered her with his shirt while she slipped out of the clothes she now imagined smelled of death.

*   *   *

It was not like anything she had ever done before. The afternoon was turning a muted orange. Gary traced the outline of her body with his hands. His lips moved across her face, her breasts, between her thighs. When he covered her mouth with his, she felt herself moving toward a flame. It didn't matter that they were in the meadow, that she hardly knew him. The warmth traveled in waves, sweeping her in ever-widening circles.

He moved slowly, gently, as if she were the first woman he had ever seen. He rubbed her nipples between his fingers. He licked her breasts until they glistened with his saliva.

She ran her hands along his body. Naked, he was more beautiful than she had imagined. His lips, his tongue, his fingertips—every place he touched her was seared with the burning. She was ready for him. Moist. Aching. She wanted the fire inside. But something was wrong. When she reached down to guide him, she did not feel the hardness. He was unwilling, or unable, to enter her.

His voice was soft as he touched her eyelids with his fingertips.

"Let me make love to you."

Elizabeth opened herself to him. She spread her legs as he plunged his tongue deep inside her, blowing his own warm breath into her body. She held nothing back. Feeling herself rise and fall with excruciating pleasure, she let him explore until, finally, the heat exploded and the cool evening blanketed them in darkness.

"Sleep here with me," he said.

She wore his flannel shirt, which hung nearly to her knees, as he pitched his tent.

The warmth was still there, it lingered in the places he had touched her. Although she knew she should leave, she made no attempt to go.

He lay the sleeping bag on top of a plastic tarp and pulled the tent up around it. Inside there was room enough for two.

"When was the last time you slept under the stars?" he asked.

"I can't remember."

He slipped his hand inside the shirt, caressing her shoulder.

"I'm sorry about what happened, but sometimes when I'm with someone new, and it's unexpected, I react slowly. I hope you weren't disappointed."

There was a burning where his hand had been. Was he apologizing because he hadn't made love to her in the usual way? His honesty surprised her. No one had ever touched her with such intensity.

"I wasn't disappointed. It was a beautiful afternoon."

Gary smiled. He kissed her eyelids, her cheeks. The kisses linked into one another until his mouth was on hers. She was sinking into him, traveling downward into a tunnel of darkness.

This time he responded. His penis was hard in her hand. She caressed it, tracing the shape of him with her fingers, holding him until he throbbed in her palm. The desire thickened. He licked the moisture from her vagina. Then, pressing his penis against her, he mingled their scents. She tasted herself in his kisses.

Finally, he entered her, moving slowly, then quickly, then slowly again. She arched her body as she rode with him, pounding the rhythm deeper, louder, more violently. She felt his strength, the power of his body, the yearning he was no longer able to contain. She couldn't be sure if the noises came from her mouth or his. She licked the sweat from his shoulders and let the taste linger on her tongue. She buried her face in his chest, inhaling his flesh.

He opened the tent flap and the night breeze cooled the burning. It was well past midnight. He smiled at her. It seemed as if they had been making love, not for hours but for days. She had imagined it from the first moment she had seen him. But there was no way she could have known this.

He covered her with a thin blanket. Holding her face in his hands, he kissed her eyes closed. She had never been able to sleep in a strange place. But tonight, as she lay beside him, she breathed the dark until the night entered the tent and enclosed her in a dreamless embrace.

*   *   *

It was very early when she awoke. The mist had formed a web of moisture over the field. Gary was already up and dressed. He was outside, gazing at the meadow.

She opened the canvas flap and watched him. His thumb and forefinger were pressed up against his face, forming a circle.

"What are you looking at?" she asked.

He seemed startled. "I'm not looking. I'm trying to see."

"See what?"

He turned and faced her. Suddenly, she felt self-conscious. She had no idea what she must look like. She hadn't combed her hair, bathed, or changed her clothes since yesterday.

"How about coffee?"

He had a small pot already brewing on a portable gas burner.

She ran her fingers through her hair and buttoned up the flannel shirt she had slept in. She felt awkward now after the intensity of the night before. It was always like this the next morning.

"Feel better?" he asked. "You look great."

"Really? I must be a wreck."

"Want me to take a photograph?" He pretended to pull a camera from the bag that lay open beside the tent.

It was 6:00 A.M. and she was laughing.

"I'm usually pretty grouchy in the morning."

He handed her a cup of coffee. The steam formed a cloud of warm air.

"You seem okay to me. Want something to eat?"

"I never eat breakfast."

Gary crouched down in front of her. "Last night was terrific."

She hadn't expected him to say that. Before she could reply, he winked and handed her clothes to her.

"Whenever you're ready, I'll take you back to your car."

The clothes didn't seem to fit her now. They were limp and old, a second skin she had shed and left somewhere among the tall weeds.

Gary took down the tent and rolled it up into a small packet while she rearranged herself. She wanted to say something, to tell him how beautiful everything had been, but she felt clumsy standing in her funeral clothes. The warmth returned, spreading between her legs as she watched him bend and move and straddle the motorcycle.

He drove slowly this time. Elizabeth could see the scenery. The meadow, which had seemed to exist on another plane, was just outside the town, directly north of the diner and not at all far from her house. She recognized all the familiar landmarks, and gradually she fell back into herself.

When they got to the car, she was stiff and uncomfortable.

She looked down as the heels of his boots dug into the ground, steadying the motorcycle.

"Will I see you again?" She hated herself for asking, but the words were already out there, floating in the predictable morning after.

"Of course you'll see me again. I have some business in New York and some developing to do in Crescent Springs, but I'll come back. How can I leave you now?" He smiled as he brushed her cheek with the back of his hand.

When he had gone she chided herself for not asking him more. Where did he live? What sort of business was he doing? When exactly would he return?

Elizabeth gazed at the clumps of grass that had burst through the dust and shale of the road. She stared at her feet, her hands, the body that she had believed held no further surprises. Reaching into her handbag, she searched for her car keys. Always careful, Elizabeth habitually tucked the keys in her purse for safekeeping.

As the sun rose higher in the morning sky, a flash of silver glinted through the car window. It was then that Elizabeth realized she had forgotten to lock the car. The keys, which Gary had taken from her shaking hands, remained in plain sight over the dashboard, exactly where he had left them.

23

THE CAPS HAD PLENTY to talk about this morning. Peg smiled at them as she wiped the counter with a damp rag. The caps were always here by 6:30. They were a predictable assortment of working men. Locals. Woodchucks. She nicknamed them after the hats they wore. It had become a private joke between her and Evelyn. The men's hats were red or yellow—polyester numbers with a band and a hole in the back to make them adjustable. They bore brand names like "John Deere" "Caterpillar," "Exxon," or "Cat." The caps were farmers or mechanics—the unemployed and the retired. None of them had attended yesterday's funeral. Although Mason Kiley had been one of them, and despite the fact that they had all, at one time or another, gotten drunk with him, they had not gone to see him buried.

Peg knew it had nothing to do with lack of respect or with bad feelings. There were invisible lines in this town. Lines most folks didn't cross. The men who were gathered around the counter this morning, drinking coffee and eating oversized portions of ham and eggs hadn't gone to the funeral because it had been a town event. The supervisor had been there, so had members of the town council and several outstanding citizens. Workingmen didn't mix with that set, not if they didn't absolutely have to.

It was true even here in the diner. The caps came in early, and except for a few stragglers, most mornings they were gone by 7:30. That left Peg just enough time to smoke a cigarette, exchange a word or two with Evelyn, and rattle off a quick list of supplies to Bernie, who would leave immediately after the second breakfast wave had come and gone. Peg and Evelyn called the second wave of men, (and a sprinkling of women) the collars. They worked in banks and offices. Some of them wore suits and ties, but mostly they were distinguished from the group that preceded them by their bare heads and smooth hands.

Funny thing was, the collars did the same work the caps did, but only on the weekends. Most of them, born and bred in Bakersville, knew how to fell a tree, split a log, and skin a deer. Some had forgotten, or chose to forget. When that happened they hired a local to do the manual labor. After the job was finished, they shared a beer, a few snippets of gossip, and went their separate ways, careful to draw the boundaries of class up around them.

Peg observed all this maneuvering with interest. Her diner was the one place where all roads converged. On a busy morning, caps and collars, manual laborers and office workers might briefly sit side by side. But whatever camaraderie they might share was only an illusion. They were worlds apart.

Today, Lyle Cunningham was retelling the story everyone had heard many times before. It was all about the time Mason Kiley had fallen drunk into his barbed wire fence.

"His face was all cut up. Like nothin' you ever saw."

Peg clipped another order on the string of clothespins that hung over the square opening that led to the small kitchen. Lucian Milk was asking if Kiley's daughter had been at the funeral.

"She was a wild one," he said. "Ran away and nearly broke her daddy's heart."

Several of the men shook their heads in agreement. Bucky Vassmer, a recent widower, rubbed a grime-encrusted hand over his eyes.

"Don't know what you have, till you lose it," he said to no one in particular. "Talk says she was at that funeral, crying her eyes out. And all them bigwigs was there. Reporters too. Old Kiley got a hero's farewell. That true, Peg?"

Lucian searched her face for the answer he knew was forthcoming.

"Annabel was there all right," Peg said as she filled his half-empty cup. "And a lot of people who didn't give a damn also showed up. Your friend Mr. Rice tell you that?"

Lucian smiled up at her. For a cap, he wasn't bad looking. His eyes were clear and his skin hadn't yet taken on the hardness of too many winters and too much booze. But he was young yet. As time passed it was inevitable that his good looks would fade. She had seen it many times before.

"Now what makes you think I've been talking to Edgar?"

Lyle Cunningham let out a hearty laugh.

"You talk to that wheeler-dealer every chance you get. Since your last pickup died on you, you'd think you'd know better. Rice'd sell his own mother a lemon."

Lucian blushed. It was true that Edgar was sought out by many of the locals. He ran the only used-car dealership in town.

Office workers preferred to buy their cars new, on time. But men like Lucian couldn't get bank financing. Cozying up to Edgar Rice, passing time on the lot, and even running little errands for him sometimes paid off. The green truck Bucky had bought eighteen months ago, when it was over seven years old, was running like a top. It had been a special deal from Edgar Rice. No one could say for sure, but rumor had it Bucky did some work around Edgar's house to make sure he got first pick. That was how things got done in Bakersville.

Men like Bucky and Lucian felt there was something shameful in this. They kept it quiet, maybe because they couldn't pay up front. But, the way Peg saw it, trading labor for services was honest barter.

By 7:30 only Bucky, Lucian, and Art Wheeler, a logger who had injured himself in a chain-saw accident, were still drinking coffee and reminiscing about Kiley.

Evelyn poked her head out from the kitchen. She rested a chipped white mug on the ledge that led from the counter and grill to where the refrigerator and microwave were located. Peg talked as she poured.

"Seems Lucian's already talked to Edgar Rice about the funeral. Makes me feel bad for Annabel. Here she comes back to her hometown, expecting a quiet little funeral, and all of a sudden her father, who's always been a good-for-nothing, has become a local hero."

Evelyn shook her head. "Don't see as he's any hero. All he did was discover what someone else was bound to find anyway."

"You'll never make that bunch see it that way."

Evelyn nodded. Her first husband had died when he fell from a roof he insisted on repairing during a rainstorm. Her oldest son was killed in a flaming wreck at the Bright Lake speedway. And as much as she had mourned, Evelyn knew that nothing she could have said would have changed things. "No sense talking to men who won't listen," was what she said. Slowly, Peg was coming to agree with her.

At 7:45 Roy Miesner and Emerson Newhouse, both employees of the New Valley Bank, joined the men at the counter.

"Anything new on the murder?" Roy asked.

"Yeah, we heard she was kin to one of them VP's down at the bank. Seems he was so hardassed he wouldn't give his own cousin a loan. She wandered off in the woods and was ravaged by a bear." Lyle laughed as Roy looked at him, shocked.

"That ain't funny," Lucian said. "No telling who that girl is."

Edgar Rice slipped into a seat at the end of the counter. He waved his cup at Peg. She took her time, walking slowly. There was no love lost between them. When Herb had left her, Edgar had been the first man she slept with. He was married, but she hadn't cared. She had felt so lonely and hurt, she would have done anything. And Edgar knew that. He had been right there, practically on her doorstep, as soon as he got wind of the news that she and Herb had split for good.

He had taken her to a motel called the Pines. It was way out on the Brisco Road, a sleazy place that had made Peg uneasy. Somehow, she got the feeling Edgar was comfortable there and she was not the first woman he had checked in with. Afterward, he acted as if he didn't know her, as if nothing had happened between them. That was a long time ago, but Peg wasn't one to forget.

"I heard the girl was a hooker. Some runaway from New York City who was turning tricks on Forty-second Street."

"Where'd you hear that?" asked Roy.

"I have my sources," said Edgar as he gazed around the diner. "Anyone seen George Murphy?"

"He's not showing his face 'til they find out who that girl belongs to and who finished her off. My guess is it'll be a cold day in August before we see Lieutenant Murphy again." Lyle laughed as he pushed his plate across the counter.

Bernie rushed to clean up after him. "What do you think, Bernie?" Lyle asked. "Think that girl was bad?"

Bernie didn't answer. No one really expected him to. For years he had been the butt of cruel jokes. A gentle guy, slow and fat, he took more ribbing than he deserved.

"I'm telling you," Edgar insisted, "the kid was a tramp. Why else would she be out alone like that? Why hasn't someone claimed her? If you ask me, her folks know very well where she is. In some drawer in the morgue. They're probably glad to be rid of her."

Emerson Newhouse cleared his throat, dropped some change on the counter, and made a quick exit.

"What's he so sensitive about?" asked Rice. "You'd think he knew her or something. I hear she was built too. Maybe it was those boobs that did Kiley in."

Lucian looked into his coffee. Peg could tell he thought Rice had gone too far, but he wasn't going to say anything in defense of a stranger.

"Anyone read the paper this morning?" Rice asked. Peg pushed the house copy of the *Bakersville Democrat* across the counter. Maybe that would shut him up, she thought. But Rice was on a roll.

"Did you see those reporters crawling all over the place?" he asked, staring right past Peg. "They wanted to interview me, but I told 'em to go talk to Murphy. Let him explain how a kid wound up dead in the cemetery. Not that I couldn't have given 'em an earful."

"Just what are you saying?" Roy asked. "You saying you know something?"

"I've been around," Rice answered. "Good girls don't just get beaten to death for no reason. She was probably asking for it, maybe got herself involved in one of those prostitution rings. Murdered by her own pimp."

"You've been watching too many television shows," Roy said as he rolled his newspaper up under his arm.

"Time will tell," Rice said smugly.

Lucian and Lyle whispered something to one another. Peg was sure she heard the name "Maggie." Maggie Rice, Edgar's niece was a friend of Jamie's. She was a nervous kid who bit her nails down so far she had to bandage her fingertips. Her father had passed away a few years ago and her mother worked the day shift at the canning factory in Crescent Springs.

Maggie liked to spend time at the diner. Peg liked her and had been concerned when just this past spring she had run away. But her uncle had found her and brought her home. Peg figured it was probably the only decent thing Edgar Rice had ever done. Thank goodness there was no cause to worry now. Maggie had stopped by the diner only yesterday to say hello and read Jamie's latest postcard.

"Gotta be goin'," Lucian said as he handed Peg a few bills and some extra change.

"You just keep away from that TV," Art said to Rice. "Those rays can rot the brain."

"Woodchuck!" Edgar said in disgust as the two men swaggered out the door.

At 8:30 the diner was filled to capacity. All the regulars were there. All except Lieutenant Murphy and the social worker, Elizabeth. Peg wondered about that woman. Yesterday, after the funeral services, she had asked Peg the strangest thing. Something about seeing someone in the woods. Probably it was the strain. Elizabeth was sleeping with George Murphy. No doubt she knew more about the case than anyone outside the police department. As Peg prepared the last order of ham and eggs, she wondered how that must feel, to sleep with a cop.

"Shut up, Rice," someone was saying. "You've been running your mouth off all morning. If you know so much why don't you go out there and catch the guy who did it."

Edgar got quiet.

"Maybe he's guilty himself," said Ray King, owner of King's hardware.

A chorus of uncomfortable laughter broke out at the counter. Peg sensed everyone had heard enough. They could joke all they wanted to, but the murder couldn't be laughed away. Someone might just be biding his time, waiting for another victim.

By 9:00 only Art Wheeler, who had nowhere else to go, sat on a stool reading the paper. Peg leaned over and lit a cigarette for Evelyn.

"Everyone's sure hot under the collar about this one. It's probably the biggest thing to hit Bakersville since the hurricane in 1958."

Evelyn smiled. "I believe Princess Doe will put us on the map."

When the door swung open, neither woman bothered to look up. It was about time for Bernie to return with the list Peg had handed him half an hour ago. So when the woman sat down at the counter, no one rushed forward to take her order. She must have sat there silently for a good ten minutes before Evelyn saw her.

"What can I do for you?" Peg asked, wiping her hands on her apron.

The woman twisted a handkerchief between her hands. She pushed a photograph of Princess Doe across the counter.

"This is my daughter," she said.

24

THE BOY BEHIND THE COUNTER at the Chicken Roost wanted to know why Princess Doe had no head.

"She get her head cut off?" he asked.

"This is a mannequin," George said. "What I want to know is if you remember seeing anyone dressed like this in the last week or so. She had long brown hair."

"With no face, it's hard to tell. What happened to her face?"

George was losing his patience. He had been to every fast-food joint from Bakersville to Crescent Springs. So far, the kids who worked behind the counters, the cooks, and the busboys were unable to identify the clothes or the cross he had found on the dead girl.

The kid rolled his gum around in his mouth. "There's lots'a people comin' in here. If I knew what she looked like; if she had a face, maybe I could tell ya."

George nodded and slipped the photograph back into his pocket. He was beginning to wonder if things would be any different if he did have a face to show. Whoever she was, Princess Doe had managed to leave home, travel, eat in places like the Chicken Roost, and then, with the abruptness of a nightmare, meet up with a murderer—all without being noticed or remembered.

George asked the kid for a black coffee, and sinking dejectedly into a vinyl chair, he tried to assess the progress of the investigation.

So far, no one, not the ticket-takers at the bus station, the clerks at the roadside motels, or the fast-food employees had been able to help him. And the pressure was building. After Kiley's funeral, Chief

Norris repeated what George already knew: the case had attracted statewide attention. Feelings were running high. People needed to feel safe.

The scar on his chest was throbbing. He had tried to reach Elizabeth last night. By 11:30 he had given up and fallen asleep with his clothes on.

George could feel his life slipping away. He and Elizabeth were becoming distant from one another. He was throwing himself into this and it was siphoning off his energy. He hadn't seen his daughter in two weeks. Last night he hadn't been able to speak with Elizabeth, and that had left him feeling restless and uneasy. Like eating and sleeping, her presence sustained and nourished him.

Crumpling the Styrofoam drinking cup in one hand, he tossed it in the garbage and headed out to the car. There were no more fast-food places to hit unless he returned at night for the late shift. He was considering it when he heard Jean's voice over the radio. She was calling him back to Bakersville. He knew it probably wasn't important, but he was eager to leave the Chicken Roost behind him. As he turned the key in the ignition, he glumly concluded that it had been an altogether futile morning.

On the drive back, George listened to a DJ from Crescent Springs play a trivia game with listeners who were jamming the phone line with calls. He wondered why people prided themselves on remembering the names of obscure television personalities but failed to notice important details in their own lives. He was sure that the boy in the Chicken Roost would rather memorize the names of

Bruce Springsteen's records than tax his brain trying to recall seeing a young girl in a brown sweater
and paisley skirt.

As he drove down the Briscoe Road, it occurred to
George that the clerk in the Pines Motel would
sooner call in an answer to a trivia question on the
radio than tell him about a teenager who, on a
moonless summer night, may have checked into a
room with a stranger neither of them would ever lay
eyes on again.

It was odd for Peg to be away from the diner in the
middle of the day. But there she was, still wearing
her apron, at the station house door. George realized
he had become accustomed to seeing Peg behind the
counter, from the waist up. She had been at Kiley's
funeral, but he had been too preoccupied to take
more than a cursory notice. She wasn't a bad-
looking woman. When she touched his shoulder, he
jerked back unexpectedly.

"There's this woman," she said breathlessly, as if
she'd been running. "She came into the diner about
thirty minutes ago. She's in a bad way. From someplace in New Jersey. She's been driving around for
hours, got lost, and came in and told me the girl you
found is her daughter."

George tried not to show any emotion. He knew
there had to be people who would claim Princess
Doe as their own. He had been expecting this, but
now he felt a hopeful anticipation.

"Where is she now?"

Peg wiped her hands nervously on her apron. "She's inside. She won't talk to anyone but you. I told her to wait. She's pretty upset."

George saw the woman huddled in a chair beside his desk. Someone had made her coffee, which sat untouched and steaming next to the photograph of Sheila.

He held out his hand. "Lieutenant George Murphy. What can I do for you?"

It was almost as if she didn't hear him. She continued staring straight ahead. Standing beside her, looking down, he could see the dark roots poking through the bleached blond hair. She was in her midforties but looked older. Her hands were red and raw. She wore a thick gold band on the third finger of her left hand.

"This is my child," she said, pointing at the photograph, which had been torn from a newspaper.

George sat down, pulling his chair closer to hers.

"Why don't you tell me all this from the beginning."

"She's been gone two months. Nothing. I've heard nothing. The cops gave up after a few days. Said she was a runaway. This cross. I gave it to her on her fourteenth birthday. This is my daughter's cross."

"Can you tell me your name and your daughter's name?" George asked.

"Lola Kane. My daughter is Terri Ann Kane."

The woman was exhausted and distracted. It took George nearly twenty minutes to learn that Lola Kane was from a small town in Warren County, New

Jersey. Her daughter had indeed disappeared nearly two months ago. Parental kidnapping had to be eliminated since Mr. Kane, an invalid, lived at home. The family was supported by the wife, who waitressed by day and cleaned K-marts by night.

Terri Ann was eighteen years old. She had auburn hair, blue eyes, and an appendectomy when she was twelve years old.

When he heard this, George felt his hopes begin to fade. But when Lola Kane asked to see the cross, he could not refuse her.

"This is it. Real gold just like she wanted."

"Mrs. Kane," George said, remembering what Elizabeth had said about the chain, "is this the chain your daughter wore?"

She fingered the beads as if by doing so she could conjure up a vision of her child.

"I can't remember," she said.

George persisted. "Look closely. Notice those beads. Do you remember your daughter wearing them?"

The woman was crying now. Softly. George knew she was desperate.

"Tell me, did Terri Ann have any unusual dental work. Any caps, fillings, crowns, root canals?"

Lola Kane shook her head. No doubt she had been through all this a dozen times before.

"What about wisdom teeth? Did she have any of them removed?

"She had all her teeth. Every one of them. Made her real proud. Her daddy and I, we've had trouble all our lives. Terri Ann had the most beautiful smile."

George knew without looking at the pathologist's report that Terri Ann Kane and Princess Doe were not one and the same. During the autopsy it had been established that the teeth numbered 1, 16, and 32—the wisdom teeth—had been missing. Another one, number 8, had been dislodged when the child's skull was crushed. That and the appendectomy made it pretty clear that wherever she was Terri Ann Kane was not in the morgue, at least not in Bakersville.

George continued to question the woman. More and more he knew that this was a mother so anxious, so filled with guilt and fear, she would rather discover the worst than continue to wonder.

Lola Kane didn't recognize the clothes, and she had no idea what her daughter might have been doing in Bakersville. Terri Ann had disappeared one night without any warning. She had taken her clothes and some money from her mother's purse. The local authorities assumed she had run away. They checked the usual places but had come up empty-handed.

George tried calling Elizabeth. If she could be here and talk to the woman, it would make his job easier. Her supervisor said she had come in late and had taken an early lunch break from which she had not yet returned. George tried not to appear puzzled. He frowned as he took out a pad and wrote down all the details Mrs. Kane had given him.

Terri Ann sounded like the classic runaway. She had not been kidnapped. The fact that she had taken personal possessions pointed very clearly to a planned exit. Lola Kane seemed oblivious to this. Dry-eyed and calm now, she insisted that her daughter was a "good girl" who would never have left without calling.

As the woman continued to talk, George wondered how far off the mark she really was. Clearly, Lola Kane could not imagine her child ever leaving of her own free will. He speculated if it were possible to really know another person, even your own flesh and blood.

"Terri Ann was seein' this young man. He lived somewhere close to New York. His name was Richard something or other."

George continued writing. He didn't doubt for a minute that the girl had fled with her boyfriend. The fact that she hadn't notified her mother was surprising but not entirely unusual. According to Lola Kane, the family was a close one. Her husband, who had been injured in an automobile accident seven years earlier, took a great interest in his daughter. As the woman spoke, she twisted a handkerchief between her hands. Terri had just graduated from high school. She had a C average. Mrs. Kane said her daughter was looking for work. What sort of work she didn't say, but George guessed that Terri was probably looking for a way out.

Everything about Lola Kane telegraphed desperation. The work she did showed on her hands. The poverty was evident in her clothes, her voice, the tentative, obsequious way she moved. If he closed his eyes, George could conjure up the third-floor walk-up over a hardware store where the Kanes lived. There would be fake wood paneling in the living room, a chipped sink in the kitchen, and thin sheets of clear plastic stretched over the bedroom windows.

George had lived here in Bakersville and had been a cop long enough to know what that kind of life did to people. It made them dream of better things, and if they couldn't run away to find those dreams, they'd do something terrible to try and forget them.

"I appreciate you coming all this way, Mrs. Kane," George said, "but there is no evidence that this girl and your daughter are one and the same."

George explained to the woman that Terri Ann was older than Princess Doe. She also had all her teeth and an appendectomy scar—proof that she was not the child found in the cemetery.

"But what about the cross? It looks just like my girl's."

George squirmed. He was beginning to feel hungry. Or maybe it was just the realization that Mrs. Kane had proved to be one more dead end.

"This isn't an unusual article of jewelry. You yourself weren't sure about the chain. Am I right?"

The woman shook her head and began to sob. Her shoulders rounded into a soft curve. George noticed that her thin raincoat was nearly threadbare.

"I don't know what else to do. Where else to go."

George nodded. "I can understand your situation. But you live in another state. Even if I wanted to help, it's out of my jurisdiction."

The woman ran her hands through her hair.

"Is that your child?" she asked, pointing to the photograph of Sheila.

"Yes, it is."

"Then you must know how this feels. To raise someone, to have them be part of you, and then not to know. It's a pain that just gets worse. Sometimes it hurts so, I wanna do somethin' awful just so it'll go away."

George looked from the woman to the photograph and then back again. He remembered what he had said to Annabel Kiley the morning of her father's funeral. He thought about the lost girl and the father who sat home—waiting.

So when Lola Kane begged him to help her find Terri Ann, when she told him it didn't matter what he found, or where he found it, just as long as he could stop the wondering; when she told him she'd die if he didn't help her, he took her hand and promised he'd try.

25

THERE WAS A MESSAGE on her desk that Lieutenant Murphy had called. Talking to George was something she had hoped to avoid. She hadn't thought about him at all yesterday. He hadn't existed in the field or in the tent. But today he was real.

Elizabeth didn't like lying. She prided herself on a certain forthright honesty. But in this case, she wasn't sure. Now when she thought about it, she realized that in all probability Gary would be a one-time thing. He said he would call, but that was a pretty standard line. If it hadn't been for the tranquilizer, she probably would never have made love with him. And that must have distorted the sensations. Elizabeth was not inexperienced, but yesterday had been different. She was still trying to figure it all out.

She called Celia before she called George. Celia was with a patient and would be busy for another hour. Reluctantly, she dialed George's private line. It wasn't as if they were married, but Elizabeth knew that a certain trust had been established. Sometimes it wasn't necessary to promise something out loud.

"Where the hell have you been?" George asked without waiting for her to answer. "Something's come up here, and if you have time later, maybe we could meet at the diner and talk it over."

She could tell by the tone in his voice that a phone conversation wouldn't do. They agreed to meet at 4:30. That, George said, would give him time to attend to paperwork and report to Chief Norris. It would also give Elizabeth time to sort out her feelings.

When she reached Celia, she had more or less figured out what had happened with Gary. Her reactions had been caused by a combination of factors: the funeral and the feelings it had stirred up, her involvement with the murder case, and, of course, the tranquilizer. Celia wasn't so sure.

"Part of me is envious of that kind of passion," Celia admitted, "but another part of me wonders how this is going to affect your relationship with George. What does it mean, sleeping with one man when you're involved with another?"

Elizabeth had been asking herself the same question all morning. She told Celia it had been a fluke, that it would never happen again.

"How do you know it won't happen again? You didn't think it would happen the first time?"

Elizabeth admitted that although she hadn't thought it would happen, she had imagined it. She confessed to a certain restlessness. Although she and George had what was commonly called "a relationship," it was fraught with problems. His ex-wife for one. And her own ambivalence about a more permanent arrangement. At least she wasn't having an affair with a married man, she told Celia.

But deep down Elizabeth knew that George was the next best thing, a man who was half-married. In the year they had known one another, Tina had always been a silent third presence. George was still smarting from the way she had left him. It had been Elizabeth's observation early on that the wound George had suffered at the hands of an unknown assailant was, in a way, a real-life enactment of the symbolic one Tina had inflicted when she had walked out. She had told Celia all this before, and when she realized she was repeating herself she became annoyed.

"I've always seen myself as someone in control," she said. "It frightens me to think that I could get swept away like I did."

Celia didn't offer any easy answers. Elizabeth confessed that she thought a passion that strong would probably burn itself out anyway.

The two women decided that for now Elizabeth would just try and collect herself and let the intensity of the experience diminish. Probably, in a few days, she would have forgotten the whole thing, or else it might seem embarrassing or foolish, but surely it would not seem as vivid as it did right now.

After she hung up with Celia she didn't feel any better. It was still the morning after, and as much as Elizabeth hated to admit it, she was having all the typical regrets. At the same time that she was hoping never to see Gary again, she was wondering if she would. It was an odd juxtaposition of feelings, and it left her in a turmoil of guilt and confusion.

As she prepared to leave her office for the diner, she mused that yesterday at this time she was making love with Gary.

*   *   *

George was facing the door when she walked in. The way he looked her up and down, she wondered if he knew. But when he smiled and stood up to kiss her lightly on the lips, she realized that the look just meant he had missed her. He took both her hands in his, a show of affection he rarely displayed in public. She glanced around the diner and noticed Evelyn was behind the counter. Peg and a woman whose back was to her were huddled in a booth in the rear.

"God, it's good to see you," George said. "I tried calling you last night, but when I didn't get an answer I fell asleep. I could have used your company."

It wasn't an accusation, or even an inquiry, but Elizabeth felt obliged to answer.

"I took a late walk," she said, hating herself for lying.

George smiled. He was used to Elizabeth's moonlight strolls. Sometimes she even cajoled him into joining her.

"I've got a little problem here," he said, indicating that the previous conversation had been resolved. "A woman came to me today and claimed Princess Doe was her daughter. Turns out it's impossible. But the kid's been gone for two months now. The woman's at the end of her rope. She's from New Jersey and the cops there have let the case go inactive. She's asked me to help her, but it's out of my jurisdiction."

Elizabeth studied George's face. His blond hair fell across his forehead, and the tiny lines around his eyes and mouth seemed to have deepened since she saw him last. She felt drawn to him as he explained the case of Terri Ann Kane.

"So what can be done?" Elizabeth asked, staring at the back of the woman she now knew to be Lola Kane.

"I promised to do something," George said. "But with this Princess Doe case, I've got to be careful. It can't be done on department time. For one thing, I'd be stepping on the toes of the New Jersey authorities; for another, I'd be in hot water with the chief if he ever got wind of this."

Elizabeth nodded. She understood George's predicament. Lola Kane was in trouble. It was George's obligation to do what he could. And she shared that obligation. There was no question in her mind that she would help. What she wasn't sure of was exactly how.

"You can start by interviewing her. Find out as much as you can about her and the girl. I've got all the basic facts, but the more we know the easier it will be."

"You know what it sounds like to me? It sounds like the girl took off with her boyfriend."

"I think you're right," George said. "And if that's the case, it's only a matter of a few phone calls and some minor legwork before we locate the kid, and maybe bring her home."

"What if she's better off where she is?"

"Then we'll notify the family and leave it up to them. The girl is eighteen."

Elizabeth felt relieved. She needed to be busy; that way she wouldn't think about what had happened yesterday. Working with George on something important like this was bound to improve their relationship. She wondered if that had had anything to do with George's decision to search for Terri Ann Kane. It was possible, but in all probability he would never admit it—not even to himself.

"Do you want me to talk to her now?" Elizabeth asked, checking her watch. It was already past five, and there was no reason for her to return to the office.

"It will save you the trouble of traveling to Warren County. The woman works two jobs. She lost a day's pay to come out here. I'd hate to ask her again."

Elizabeth stood up and gathered her things. George handed her her briefcase.

"Can I see you tonight?" he asked. He seemed oddly formal. Usually they got together at the Nugget or he called before stopping over with some take-out food.

"Since when do you have to ask?" she said as she reached over and hugged him.

George watched as Elizabeth slid into the seat opposite Lola Kane. He waited until he heard her voice, soft and steady, asking questions and pausing long enough for answers.

Of course she had come, he thought. The vague uneasiness he had felt all day dissolved. Elizabeth was here. Working on this case meant she would be involved with him, with his world. Unlike Tina, Elizabeth understood his job; she respected it. She was his partner as well as his lover. George wondered just how far that partnership could go and how much it could endure. He wanted it to work. But he had been burned once. And although he reminded himself that Elizabeth and Tina were different women, he still felt the impulse to pull away every time he got closer to admitting his love for her.

He looked back over his shoulder as he left the diner. All three women were chatting like old friends. George envied the easy intimacy women seemed able to establish. It was always so difficult for men. But he wasn't complaining. Tonight he was feeling lucky—lucky to have Elizabeth back by his side and lucky that Lola Kane had walked into his life just when he needed her.

26

SHE WAS DESPERATELY GLAD to see him. He had remembered to order pepperoni for her side of the pizza. The box was still warm as he placed it on the kitchen table. His being here like this, the aroma of the freshly baked pizza, it all reminded her of the first months of their relationship. In those days, they made love first. Afterward, they'd linger in bed talking about their work, exchanging bits of gossip, sharing secrets. Sometimes they took turns massaging one another. She loved the way George warmed the oil between his palms before rubbing it into her skin, the way his strong hands kneaded her flesh, the way he kissed the spot behind her knees and ran his tongue along the arch of her foot. Tonight she remembered that there had been evenings when they made love a second time. Later, they would reheat the pizza and split a bottle of wine.

That seemed like a long time ago. It had been before she realized that George was still preoccupied with his ex-wife. And it was before she had let another man touch her.

As he ripped away at the cardboard box, being careful not to make a mess, she told him about the interview. Mrs. Kane was indeed at the end of her rope. Elizabeth was experienced enough to see all the warning signs. She was out of hope and out of luck. Her life, as she described it, was an unending grind of work and worry.

Survival was the keynote of the Kane household. Paralyzed from the waist down, Bill Kane had also suffered recent strokes that had left him with slurred speech and a fragmented memory. Terri Ann was an only child, conceived during the early days of the marriage. After that, it had been sexual estrangement and periodic unemployment punctuated by bouts of alcoholism for both Lola and Bill Kane.

"Not a pretty picture," George said as he picked a mushroom from Elizabeth's plate and placed it on his own.

"And I think she was trying to make it sound better than it really was," Elizabeth said.

"Any violence? Wife-beating? Child abuse?"

"No, I don't think so. I can usually tell with these women. They tend to hold things in so much that when they do start talking, it's difficult for them to stop. For what it's worth, Bill Kane sounds like an ordinary guy. According to Lola, he worshipped his daughter, and even after the accident they were very close. Lola swore he never once lifted a hand to her or the child. She made a point of telling me he's a slight man. He had wanted to build up his arm muscles after the accident, but they couldn't afford the therapy."

George pulled out the photograph of Terri Ann that Lola had given him.

"Look at this kid. Too much makeup, an overdone hairdo, but you can still see that she's pretty."

"And she probably dreamed of becoming a model or a movie star. Someone who would move to Beverly Hills and tell journalists about her humble beginnings."

George sighed. "Yeah, and God knows where she'll wind up. Where half of them wind up—on Forty-second Street or in the morgue."

"Or right back where they started. Living over the corner store, working the night shift, pregnant by nineteen, and abandoned by twenty-one."

George tipped his chair against the kitchen wall. Elizabeth picked at a loose circle of pepperoni. There was nothing left to say. They both knew the story. They knew how it began and how it would end. It was a conversation they had had countless times before. George complained about the endless paperwork and the bureaucracy. Elizabeth wondered if what they did made any difference at all.

Tonight they were content to sit together in the silence.

George was first to speak. He told her about his afternoon interviewing kids at fast-food joints.

Hearing about a day of grueling police work made the fantasy of her encounter with Gary seem surreal, almost as if it had never happened at all.

George's voice was reassuring, steady. She knew him. Unlike the man who had made love to her yesterday, George was real. There's no way, she thought to herself, that this man is going to disappear, to walk out of my life without a trace. But as much as she reassured herself, she still had doubts. It would be easy to love George completely. And it would be devastating if he were to leave her.

He was the one who suggested they go to bed.

Still dressed, he stretched out beside her. He stroked her hair as he told her about the conversation he had had with Mason Kiley's daughter. She cuddled up to him, hoping they would make love and that it would be the way it used to be. She wanted to forget Gary. She wanted to prove to herself that it was all within her control and that she could experience that same passion with George.

Staring at the shapeless shadows moving along the wall, Elizabeth realized that George had stopped talking. He was snoring softly—small, puffy snorts that came and went at irregular intervals. He must be exhausted, she thought. Lovingly, she removed his socks and his trousers.

As she unbuttoned his shirt, she ran her hand over the scar. It seemed as raw and red as the first day she had seen it. His body was spotted with various little knicks and bruises: childhood wounds that had never correctly healed. She knew the history of every scar and bump. Learning about them had been part of their intimate life together.

She stared at the slash that ran through the coppery hairs. And, at that moment, she thought of Gary. His skin had been so smooth, his chest and arms completely unmarked. No, that probably wasn't an accurate observation. Everyone had some small distinguishing feature, some scar or peculiarity. Gary had only seemed that way, she thought. No one could be that perfect.

Elizabeth folded George's clothes and put them beside his gun belt, which rested on her dresser. She was used to seeing his service revolver here. At first, the sight of a gun in her bedroom had been unsettling. But now it comforted her. Despite herself, she enjoyed feeling protected. But she worried that she would come to depend upon that protection, even to count on it.

She shaped her hand around the handle of the revolver. She tried to imagine what it must feel like to carry such a weapon, to have at her fingertips such a potential for destruction. It was something George wore every day. Even off duty, he was required to be armed. She wondered, as she gripped the gun, if George could ever really kill anyone.

Elizabeth slipped into bed beside him. She studied his sleeping face. George had never done anything but police work. She knew that in some way the danger energized him, yet he seemed aware of his limits. He rarely took risks or unnecessary chances. She admired his control, and she envied his unwavering belief in the system.

At the same time, she acknowledged that what had attracted her to Gary was his recklessness. He seemed to play with control. She thought of the way he had balanced the huge motorcycle between his legs, how he had pitched a tent in a moonlit meadow, and how he had touched her in ways she had never thought possible.

Awake in the room filled with shadows, curled up in her own bed, Elizabeth felt herself torn between the two men. But even as the shadows faded into blackness, she realized that her conflict had less to do with George and Gary than with two very different aspects of herself.

27

A FLY BUZZED IN A SQUARE of sunlight. Peg moved the rag along the empty counter. She was thinking about Lola Kane. She was also thinking about Terri Ann. It all seemed so impossible, and yet she believed everything Lola had told her. Terri Ann had taken her clothes, and she had stolen money from her mother's purse. But she hadn't really meant to run away. She may have thought about it, but surely she would have come back. Or called. Terri Ann had disappeared. She had fallen into the hands of some maniac. A cult. A pimp. God knows what else.

Peg knew Lieutenant Murphy hadn't believed the woman. But that's how cops were. They always suspected the worst. Besides, a man couldn't possibly know how a woman would feel. A mother always knows her child. Sure, there are some surprises and disappointments. But it's a different kind of knowing. The kind of knowing that told Peg there was more truth to Lola Kane's story than a cop could ever understand.

The patch of sun dissolved and Peg watched as the morning melted into afternoon. Elizabeth had believed Lola Kane. Or else, she acted as if she had. She had a funny way of asking questions, sort of turning statements in on themselves. Like when Lola Kane had said, "You can't imagine how I felt when I woke up in the morning and my baby's bed was empty," and Elizabeth had answered with a question, "Tell me, how did you feel?" As if anyone needed to ask such an obvious thing. Maybe that was part of being a social worker. Peg couldn't know for sure. It might just have been a peculiarity of Elizabeth's. Like the way some people finished your sentences for you.

Evelyn passed an empty mug through the opening, and Peg filled it for her.

"Still thinkin' about that lady? Still wonderin'?"

"I'm not wondering," Peg answered. "I'm sure she was telling the truth."

Evelyn shook her head. "Can't understand why a child wouldn't call home."

At that moment, it occurred to Peg that Jamie hadn't called in almost three weeks. But the cards kept coming. More regularly now than before. It was enough that the girl wrote every few days. There was really nothing to say on the phone. The trip was special. Something between a father and daughter. Peg was afraid Jamie thought she couldn't understand that. Or, what's worse, that she would resent it. But she *did* understand. She had been a daughter once herself. The resentment part was there all right, but Peg was fighting it. Herb was the girl's father. And he had rights.

"Any of your kids ever stay out and not call?" Peg asked Evelyn.

"The boys, sure. But that's their nature. Out there getting wild, doing who knows what. But the girls, we kept a close watch on them. I never woke up to an empty bedroom."

Peg nodded as she pulled out the old coffee filter and dumped it into the plastic container under the counter. Jamie's bedroom had been empty for too long. Peg felt a longing, a pain she called her mother's ache. It moved from her breasts, down deep to where Jamie had once lived inside her. Yes, she believed everything Lola Kane had told her. How could she possibly doubt a woman who had been willing to claim a dead body as her own child?

*   *   *

George stared at the plastic paneling in his tiny office. He was making lists. Lists of things to do. Lists of people and places. Princess Doe was his first priority, but it was not his only responsibility. Chief Norris had reminded him of that this morning, when he informed him he had sent two other men out to question employees on the night shift at the bus station and the fast-food joints. George had smelled a trace of booze on Norris' breath. And it had only been 8:00.

There had been a call about a break-in in a garage on Chestnut Street. A chain saw and a gas can had been taken. And then there was the Jefferson woman down in Gardner who had swallowed ninety Tylenols with half a quart of scotch. This was her second attempt. Three strikes and you're out, George thought as he tapped his pencil along the desk blotter.

Routine small-town police work wasn't doing it for him. This case was all he could think about. And all he could do was think.

George hated being inactive. Tina used to accuse him of squirming in his seat during dinners that lasted more than forty-five minutes and movies that lasted more than two hours. But George was a cop because he liked action. If he had wanted to spend his life sitting, he would have become an accountant or a lawyer. Not being able to go out there and *do* something made the tension build.

He reached for a cigarette. Damned if he could figure it out. A kid is found and no one comes to claim her. No one, that is, if you discount Lola Kane. He had expected more crackpots, more mistaken identities. But so far there was only this Kane woman from New Jersey. Shit, George thought, how could someone not inquire? The photograph had been plastered in every newspaper in the tristate area. Even the big papers from New York City had given the story some play. No one had recognized the clothes, and the fingerprints he had insisted upon had not matched anything on file.

There was one possible answer here, but George didn't want to consider it. It had occurred to him early in the investigation, but he had pushed it away. Repressed it, as Elizabeth would say. He hadn't even told her. Somehow, even thinking about it quietly to himself made him feel ashamed. But there was one explanation that fit so neatly it wouldn't budge. An explanation that would account for the fact that the girl had not defended herself and had not been claimed.

The smoke from his cigarette made the air in the small room thick—almost suffocating. As he stood to open the window, he glanced at his daughter's photograph. It was unthinkable, yet he had been a cop long enough to consider it. He had seen everything: teenage hustlers, child abusers, wife beaters, kidnappers, murderers, junkies. Why, then, did the thought of a father killing his daughter, dumping her body, and ignoring the news that she had been discoved make him feel so oddly uneasy? Sure, it was a horrible crime, but it was possible. And more and more, it was looking very probable.

George knew he wasn't in the psychology business. As a cop he had been trained to figure out motives, reasons why people committed crimes. But there was a difference between understanding a motive and comprehending the complexities of human behavior. Sometimes when he listened to

Elizabeth discuss a client, he got a glimpse of just how wide the gap was. And this morning he was staring it right in the face. Sure, he could explain some sort of motive for a father murdering a daughter, but he could never understand it, not enough to visualize it, not enough to really believe that was what had happened.

George pushed aside the lists. He emptied his ashtray and piled his *New York Statutes with Forms* and the *Prosecutor's Sourcebook,* volumes 1 and 2 in a neat pile on the edge of his desk. He took his daughter's photograph and wiped it with the cuff of his sleeve. It was time he got his act together. He was going to see Sheila this weekend, no matter what. The hell with everything else. The hell with Princess Doe. The hell with Tina. Sheila was his kid, and he was going to spend time with her.

*   *   *

Elizabeth wrote the name. Richard Darby. It had been easy to find; a few phone calls, her softest voice, and she had found out all she needed to know about Terri Ann's boyfriend. Lola Kane had only known his first name. She had been vague about everything else. But Terri Ann had friends. And when Elizabeth used her special, tell-me-everything tone, it had worked like a charm. She had only said she was a close friend of the family and that she had a gift for Terri Ann and was anxious to locate her. That was something she had learned from George. Never play the cop. Never show your badge.

Elizabeth smiled as she underlined the name. George would be proud of her.

One or two of the girlfriends had been questioned by the New Jersey PD, but not all of them. Probably too much trouble for what seemed an obvious runaway. And Terri Ann was no longer a minor. She was out there on her own. But now that the excitement had worn off, the friends were anxious to talk. Eager. No one knew where the girl was, but they had known all about Richard. He was twenty-three, tall and skinny, with dark brown hair, a fuzzy moustache, and a rebuilt 1974 Chevy van. He worked in a coffee factory in North Jersey. A quick glance through the phone book, a few questions, and Elizabeth was able to locate a Maxwell House factory in Hoboken. Not bad for a morning's work.

She leaned back in her chair and contemplated the ceiling. It had been fun sleuthing around in Terri Ann's life. Unlike the work she usually did, this entailed gathering information secondhand. It was interesting and in many ways a lot safer.

Now it was George's turn. He would probably want to drive down to Hoboken alone. But she wanted to go along. There wouldn't be any danger involved, just finding a young man and asking him a couple of questions. George had a gun. What could possibly happen? They could make a weekend of it. Maybe find the boy, find Terri Ann, reunite the daughter with her family, and spend Sunday happily ever after.

But Elizabeth knew it wouldn't be that neat. Nothing ever was. What if they couldn't find the boy? Or what if they did and Terri Ann wasn't with him? Then there was George's continuing obsession with Princess Doe. It was doubtful that he'd take time off to be with her when the investigation was stalled like this.

Elizabeth gazed out of the window. It had been two days and she hadn't heard a word. If she called Celia again, everything would become obvious. They would discuss it, and together they would come to the same conclusion: going away with George was one way to escape from what was troubling her. It would take her mind off the waiting.

At that moment Elizabeth was absolutely sure she would never see Gary again. She was sure the hours they had spent together had been a mistake. A slip. It was a fantasy that would not hold up under scrutiny. There couldn't be a second time because it could only be a disappointment. She was back in her life now, and Gary had no place there.

Elizabeth stared at the name she had written on the pad. She tried to imagine Richard Darby. She closed her eyes and attempted to conjure up an image. But there was only one face that came to her—one body, perfect and unmarked. Gary had no place in her life, but, stubbornly, he refused to fade from her fantasies.

*   *   *

The photographs he had taken of the funeral floated like suspended moments in the developer. He moved them around in the chemicals. They were immobile—frozen. All the characters were assembled. There was the cop, buttoned-up and stern-looking, and the woman who worked in the diner.

Then there were shots of Elizabeth. He hadn't expected them to come out, he had been so far away. But even in the rain, the telephoto lens had captured her image. Grainy and blurred, he could still make out her face. She had been standing on the edge of the crowd, staring straight ahead, as if she knew she were being observed.

Gary leaned back in the small folding chair. The odors of the darkroom were comforting. When he closed his eyes he could see her spread out before him, naked and eager. Elizabeth had been hungry. But he wasn't sure now, as he looked at her blurred image swimming beneath the soup, if she was responding to him or to something within herself.

He hadn't anticipated having sex with her. Perhaps that's why his body had not responded the way he had hoped it would. Yet she had been so child-like, so open and entirely his, that he had found pleasure in making love to her. His own reactions hadn't mattered, not to her or to him. She had entirely lost herself in the moment, and he had been able, for the short time they had shared, to see behind the mask.

Gary slipped the prints into the stop bath and then the fixer. He hung the squares with the images of Lieutenant Murphy, Peg, and Elizabeth on a clothesline he had stretched from one corner of the darkroom to another. Squinting into the dim light, he examined their faces. Ordinary people trapped in an extraordinary moment.

He wondered if it had been a mistake to throw away Elizabeth's phone number. It had been two days and he had promised to keep in touch. But events had detained him. There were these photographs to develop, and then there had been the article on the orchid.

The art director from *Botanical Magazine* had sent it to his post office in Buffalo, and they had forwarded it here to Crescent Springs. This time the orchid had definitely been located.

A farmer on the southwestern coast of Australia had come upon it purely by accident. The rare species, known as *Rhizanthella gardneri*, grew entirely underground. Beneath a surface of dead leaves and other debris, the farmer had found the spetacular flower pushing upward.

But Gary knew the orchid would never show above the surface. Somehow, the underground flower obtained its nourishment from dead or decaying matter. Unlike all other plants and flowers, it did not require sunlight for photosynthesis.

For as long as he could remember, Gary had dreamed of photographing the orchid. But a *Rhizanthella* had not been located for more than thirty years. When he had first heard about the flower, he had been intrigued. It was proof that everything was not obvious, that there was something alive, something worth seeing below the surface.

Gary thought about the flower. The assignment was his if he wanted it. The photographs would prove that there was a dark side to everything—even beauty.

He considered all this as he opened the envelope in which he had placed the newspaper photograph of Princess Doe. Unclipping the damp prints from the clothesline, he moved the images into position. First the cop, his face, tense and stern, looked out of place on the headless torso of the mannequin. The woman from the diner looked too old, too weary. Next, he moved Elizabeth's head onto Princess Doe's body and was momentarily stunned by how familiar, yet how frightening, it looked there.

Gary swept the damp squares onto a sheet of white paper. He stared at the small pieces of reality he had captured in his lens. The decision was his. He could go to Australia and photograph the orchid, something that drew its life from the dead, or he could remain in Bakersville with Elizabeth and feel alive.

28

FOR REASSURANCE GEORGE TOUCHED the .38 snub-nosed revolver that was strapped to his ankle. The sun baked into the brick tenement, and he could feel his own perspiration form circular stains beneath each armpit.

Terri Ann Kane was in that building.

The foreman at the coffee factory had been a talker. He had not asked for identification when George had told him he was a claims adjuster for an insurance company. When he added that Richard Darby had a check coming, the foreman had given him the address right then and there. It had been a lucky break. He never had to show his shield, and the foreman had forgotten to take his name.

Darby lived in fifth-floor walk-up in Jersey City. The air was heavy with the stench of gray fumes. The streets were lined with an endless procession of attached buildings. Tenants sat on stoops drinking beer, waiting for an occasional breeze to move through the relentless heat. Women stared from open windows, and a distant chorus of bleating car horns vibrated into the sun.

This was just the kind of place he had imagined Terri Ann would come to. Ironically, it was almost identical to the place she had run from.

Elizabeth motioned to him from her car. Against his better judgment, he had let her come along. But he had insisted they take separate cars. If anything happened, he didn't want her to be involved. She had objected. They had argued. He had stood his ground; it would be his way or it wouldn't be. Reluctantly, she had agreed.

What George hadn't told her was that he intended to visit Sheila after they had found Terri Ann. They would need two cars for that. One so he could go on to his ex-wife and daughter, and another so Elizabeth could return to Bakersville alone. He had told himself that she would understand and that it would be okay. But now, as she smiled at him from the open window, he could see the look of expectation in her face.

He had wanted her to become involved in this case and she had. The past few days had drawn them closer than ever. But he had not been completely honest with her. He still felt a lingering loyalty to his former family, yet at the same time he couldn't bear the thought of losing her. Now, he had made his decision, and it was too late to change it.

"I want to come with you," she said. "If the girl is in there, it will be easier for her to talk if I'm with you."

"We agreed you would talk to the girl," he answered, "but I've got to check that building out first. This Darby character could be anyone. He could be dangerous."

"How will I know?"

George pointed out a window on the fifth floor. It was open but a shade was drawn, sealing it from the blistering sun. "That's Darby's apartment. I'll motion to you when you can come up."

Elizabeth nodded. She touched his hand as he turned to go.

From the outside, all the tenement windows looked the same. Some had small electric fans whirring in half-opened windows. Others had patched screens and torn curtains. There were no names on the bells in the hall. An old man sitting on the front stoop, fanning himself with a newspaper had told him where Richard Darby lived. Now the man looked away as George entered the building.

*   *   *

The hallway was dark and suffocating. A dim light bulb cast an irregular shadow over the cracked plaster. George inhaled the stench of cooked vegetables, rotting garbage, and mildew. The walls were covered with the sprawling script of urban grafitti. He felt the gun against his ankle as he walked up the first flight of stairs.

He was more aware now than ever that he did not have the protection of his uniform. This place, these people were out of his jurisdiction. He was putting his career on the line for a girl he didn't know.

By the time George reached the third floor, he felt the familiar fear. He had experienced it first as a young cop walking a beat. It had returned that rainy night when he had approached what he thought was a disabled car by the side of the highway; it was the same fear that had surfaced as he dragged the body of the murdered girl from behind the gravedigger's shed.

Then he felt the rush—an equal mixture of terror and excitement.

He walked silently, cautiously, down the hallway.

The fifth floor was pitch black. Strains of music filtered into the deserted hallway. Putting his ear to the door, he heard only the muffled sounds of a radio. There were no voices. If Terri Ann was in there she could be sleeping.

She could be drugged.

She could be dead.

He thought of his own daughter as he considered the risks. It wouldn't take much to dislodge the door. But even in the blackness George could see the boundaries between a violent act and a tactful one. He was alone. Only Elizabeth, waiting patiently five floors below, knew of his whereabouts. But she was inexperienced and unarmed. He had to proceed carefully. There was no one to back him up if he made a careless move or an error in judgment.

Although he had no idea what to expect, his balance was steady as he approached the door to apartment 5F.

He knocked twice before retreating into the shadows. Then, waiting in the silence, he watched expectantly as the door opened.

The girl stood motionless in a circle of light. She was barefoot and dressed in shorts and a halter top. She stared into the darkness.

"Richie?"

He could tell at once it was Terri Ann. She seemed younger than the photograph, but the resemblance was unmistakable. Her face was upturned, as if she were expecting a familiar greeting.

George moved toward her.

"Hello, Terri Ann."

"Who are you?" she asked as the light shot through the shadows.

"I'm a friend of your mother's. She's been worried about you."

Terri Ann walked back inside the apartment, leaving the door open. George took this as an invitation and followed her.

The place was cluttered and filthy. A half-eaten meal had hardened in plastic dishes on the card table in the kitchen. There was only one other room; it was filled with a fold-out couch, a radio, and a small portable television. Bruce Springsteen was singing something about a freight train running through his skull.

There were two joints, neatly rolled, on the kitchen table.

"I've never seen you before," she said. "How do you know my mother?"

"She came to me because she was worried about you."

"You some kind of detective or something?"

"I'm a friend. That's all. Have you been here all along?"

"Sure I've been here. Me and Richie are just waiting until we can drive out to California and see the Pacific Ocean."

"Terri Ann, why haven't you called your parents? They've been worried sick about you."

The girl glanced down at her chipped nail polish, then up, beyond him.

"Who's she?"

George turned around. Elizabeth was standing in the doorway. Perhaps she had suspected that he wouldn't signal her until he had gotten the answers he needed.

"She knows your mother too. We came here together to find you."

Elizabeth moved wordlessly into the room. Terri Ann avoided meeting their eyes. It was clear she was becoming uncomfortable. George knew she didn't have to answer their questions.

"I didn't do nothin' wrong. I'm eighteen."

"No one's said that you've done anything wrong, Terri Ann," Elizabeth said. "But your parents are terribly concerned. They miss you and had no idea where you'd gone."

"I was gonna call. I just forgot. That's all."

"It's been a long time. Didn't you think that after two months they might be frantic?"

"Two months?" Terri Ann gazed at them in disbelief. "I guess I lost track of time. Me and Richie have been workin' on his van at night. Days are too hot and there's nowhere to park. Nights we go down to the Grand Union parking lot. We're almost ready now. I was gonna call them from California to surprise them. You know, sorta like, here I am. I made it to the Pacific."

"Is that why you ran away, to go to California with Richard?" Elizabeth asked.

"Richie and me didn't run away. We left, that's all."

"Were you unhappy at home? Was anything wrong that made you want to leave without telling anyone?"

"I was *gonna* tell them," Terri Ann insisted. "I just wanted to wait 'til we got to California."

George watched as a roach crawled up the side of the sink. The ancient refrigerator groaned and sweated in the heat.

"What about your father? You know he isn't well. Weren't you concerned how your leaving might affect him?"

"He's all crippled up," Terri Ann said. "He don't even know who I am half the time. He just sort of sits there and drools. Mom says he can understand everything, but I don't think so. Richie says he's brain dead."

George shuddered at the image Terri Ann's words conjured up. Where was the loving closeness Lola Kane had talked about? It was clear there was nothing more he and Elizabeth could do. Except for one last thing. He owed that much to the woman who had begged him to find her daughter.

"How about calling your mother now? It's Saturday and she'll be home."

"We ain't got no telephone." Terri Ann waved a skinny arm toward the room with the bed and the television.

"There's a public phone booth on the corner across the street," Elizabeth said. "Why don't we go there now?"

Terri Ann looked like a little girl as she rubbed her bare feet across the curling linoleum. George couldn't be sure if she was frightened, or high, or both. From the blank expression on her face there was no telling what she might do. And there was no way he could force her to do anything.

"Okay. But I don't have no money."

"You can call collect," Elizabeth said.

Terri Ann slipped her feet into a pair of rubber beach thongs. Leaving the apartment door ajar, she followed George and Elizabeth downstairs.

It was only a few hundred feet from the brick tenement where Terri Ann lived to the phone booth on the corner. It had taken her two months to walk those few hundred feet. George tried not to think of Lola Kane, waiting by a phone that never rang. He tried not to think of the thousands of kids who left home, meaning to call, but who never quite got around to it. Terri Ann had been lucky. The girl whose skull had been smashed before she was dumped in the Bakersville cemetery had not done so well.

After they heard Terri Ann greet her mother, George and Elizabeth returned to the car that remained parked across from the red brick tenement. They had not waited to hear the rest of the conversation. Neither of them wanted to hear Terri Ann reject her mother's pleas to come home.

Elizabeth inhaled the cigarette George lit for her. He watched as the smoke melted into the sweltering stench of the afternoon.

"I could use a drink," Elizabeth said. "Something long and cool, in a dark bar with soft music."

"Jesus, it's hot here," George said. He took off his jacket and loosened his tie. Even the seat of his pants was damp with sweat.

Elizabeth nodded. She longed for the cool breezes of Bakersville. Here in the city, the heat seemed to seal itself into the cement. There was no relief.

"I could barely breathe in there. I have no idea how she can stand it. The filth and the heat."

"And the roaches," George added.

"It was pretty much what we expected. Only seeing it made it worse. More real."

George nodded. He wanted to tell her she shouldn't have come up there like that—alone, unexpected. She should have waited for his signal. But it was senseless to mention that now. This would never happen again. He had made a mistake letting her come along.

"Well, how about that drink?"

As he turned to her, George knew he was about to make another mistake, but that too was inevitable.

When he told her about his plans to visit Sheila, she merely nodded. No, she assured him as he left for his own car, she wasn't angry. Just disappointed. He planted a kiss on her cheek as he waved goodbye.

Elizabeth watched him until he turned the corner. She sat in the parked car for some time. Studying the window of Terri Ann's apartment, the answers finally came. Suddenly she understood what before she had been unable to comprehend. She understood how people could have wildly different perceptions of the same situation.

She had misinterpreted every message George had sent this afternoon. She had led herself to believe that they were in this together and that they formed an unbreakable bond. She could no longer deny how much she wanted that and how sure she had been that he felt the same way. But instead of remaining by her side, he had returned to his family. She had trusted him enough to follow him, to let him take the lead. And he had betrayed her.

It became clear to her how the situation between Terri Ann and her mother could happen. Because

this afternoon, she too had waited for a signal that
had never come.

29

THE HIGHWAY GLISTENED in the afternoon light.
Like a snake, it slithered up the mountains, curling
and twisting toward its destination. Elizabeth followed the white line that ran up its back. She drove
automatically, barely noticing as cars passed in
either direction.

The anger had formed a heaviness in her chest.
Everything about this day had been an illusion. She
had allowed herself to believe George's excuse for
taking separate cars. She had trusted him when he
said he would motion to her from the tenement
window. Like Terri Ann's mother, she had deluded
herself into believing only what she had wanted to
think was true. It had been easier for Lola Kane to
assume her daughter had been murdered than it was
for her to see the facts; Terri Ann had run away and
had not cared enough to call. And George had
pretended to need Elizabeth. Now she knew all of it
had been a lie.

When would she ever learn? Gary. George. Lately
she hadn't been careful. She had allowed herself to
be misled. Celia was right; love was a kind of madness. She wanted to get past that now. She wanted
to numb the feelings and regain her equilibrium.
No more fantasies, no more illusions or mysteries.
Elizabeth wanted to feel the earth firmly beneath

her feet. She could no longer afford to be swept away by her feelings.

The ride seemed much longer now. Without the anticipation, the road rolled slowly beneath the car. The hot sun made the highway ripple and shimmer until it looked like the sea. Waves of pavement melted into the steaming landscape. Just an illusion, Elizabeth thought as she drove through each watery mirage.

Eventually, the highway narrowed, four lanes becoming two. The wide lanes gave way to dusty country roads. A certain coolness remained trapped in the forests that had been blasted and bulldozed to make way for larger thoroughfares. It escaped now through the spaces between the trees, and Elizabeth inhaled the sweetness of the day.

Jersey City with its heat and roaches was far away. Terri Ann was no longer real; a figment of her imagination, Elizabeth could blink and forget her forever.

*　　*　　*

Elizabeth sensed him before she actually saw him. It was as if his presence could be felt, intuited; or maybe her longing actually produced him. But there he was, doing figure eights in her driveway. The wheels of his motorcycle ground against the dry shale, kicking clots of dirt into the air. As she got closer, she could see the intense concentration that had settled in the lines of his forehead. His body guided the machine, forcing it into tighter and tighter circles.

Was he waiting for her, she wondered, or simply passing time?

He stopped when he heard her car door slam. Remembering her promise to herself, she stared past him, fixing her eyes on the door, hoping not to get trapped by looking too closely.

She was tired and hot. Her blouse stuck to her back; sweat made the insides of her thighs damp and clammy. She longed for a cool shower, a glass of wine, a few hours to be alone.

"This isn't a good time," she said as she walked toward him. "You should have called first."

But he refused to go. Still straddling the motorcycle, he shifted it back and forth between his legs. A rectangular lozenge of light glinted off the handlebars and spread across the driveway. Elizabeth glanced down at the light and pretended not to notice that he had set the motorcycle on its kickstand.

"Please," he said.

She left the door open behind her, neither inviting him nor turning him away.

When he was inside, she could smell his scent, a pungent earthy smell that brought back all the memories of their lovemaking. Despite her resolve, she felt the beginnings of desire. She glanced at his hands and remembered how they had moved over her body.

For a moment, she felt herself slipping, momentarily losing control. It was almost as if he had cast a spell in the empty shadows where they now stood.

"Look, what do you want?" she said, snapping back into herself, angry at her temporary weakness.

Gary said nothing. He stood motionless, a still life in dust and denim.

"Why are you always showing up like this? Who do you think you are? I don't know anything about you." Her anger freed her. The rage strengthened her resolve. There was no more room in her life for mysteries.

When he spoke, his voice was soft, almost pleading. He had not meant to seem evasive. Hadn't he told her his name?

He slipped, uninvited, into a chair. His complete ease in her home startled her. He seemed to belong here. There was none of the awkward discomfort she herself experienced in strange environments. And he looked so disarmingly at ease, as if the brief, physical intimacy they had shared in the field had been preceded by a different kind of knowing—something she had sensed before, something that made her feel exposed.

Gary shifted in his seat. He crossed his dusty boots at the ankles. Smiling shyly, he began to talk. His name, he said, was Gary Rolf. The Rolf was a shortened version his grandfather had concocted when he immigrated here from Poland.

"You're Polish?" she asked, incredulous that the man she had envisioned as an enigmatic stranger could have such mundane origins.

"Fifth generation," he said, smiling. "Born and raised in Buffalo, New York. Biggest Polish American population in the country.

She loosened her blouse from the waistband of her skirt, knowing that such an intimate gesture underlined the fact that they had been lovers. This small act of control pleased her. She was aware that he too must feel self-conscious.

He continued talking, as if telling her the story of his life would deepen their brief past together.

"I was an only child. Grew up in a town owned and run by a steel plant. The air always stank of chemicals. The windows were permanently gray. No one ever hung wash out to dry. My dad worked at the plant; my mom stayed home and tried to keep the dust from settling. I went to school there, at the university. Got a BA and an MFA, and swore I'd spend the rest of my life breathing fresh air."

"Ever get married?"

"Nope. You?"

Elizabeth shook her head.

"Will you show me your photographs?"

"Do you really want to see them?"

It was the last remaining piece to the puzzle. His photographs, if they existed at all, would tell her more than the bare facts of his life.

"Yes. Have you got any with you?"

Gary motioned toward the Harley that stood gleaming in the late-afternoon sun. "Got lots of stuff in those boxes behind the seat. Sometimes I think my whole life's in there."

"But you must live somewhere."

"Sure I do. I rent a place in Crescent Springs. There's a darkroom there where I pay by the hour. And I still have a small apartment in Buffalo. When

I'm in New York or out West, my reps put me up
with friends or get me a sublet. Elizabeth, I don't
live in a tent."

She laughed. For the first time, she began to
doubt herself. He was a real person after all. Not
someone she imagined, not a mirage that would
disappear.

She watched him from the bathroom window as
she showered. He unlocked the big luggage box to
the right of the seat. There must have been a great
deal inside. He rummaged through things until he
found a black portfolio. Glancing up at the window,
he made a point of relocking the box.

The cool water ran down her back. Pressing her
face against the tile, she let the heat and disappointment of the day wash away. None of that mattered
anymore. He was here. And she had asked him all
the questions. Now he was going to show her his
work. Maybe she could begin to know him after all.

*   *   *

She poured herself a glass of white wine mixed
equally with seltzer. Holding up the bottle, she
offered him a drink.

"Nothing for me," he said.

"Don't you drink?"

"Not much. It dulls the sight."

"But you're not taking pictures now."

"But I'm looking. I'm always looking."

The photographs he showed her were remarkable:
close-up shots of flowers, insects, tiny glowing
worms; broad sweeps of fields in the purple light of

late summer. The pictures all had a haunting emptiness. There were no people, no faces. No sign of anything human.

"Don't you ever take photographs of people?"

Gary leaned over the portfolio. "These are old shots. I try to do people, but as soon as they sense I'm shooting, they get self-conscious, posed. They smile and grimace and hide the thing I most want to see."

Then he explained about the other kind of pictures.

"As soon as the shutter snaps, the subject dies. Its essence is stolen. In that instant everything changes. It disappears. Once I develop a photograph, the moment I've caught is gone for me. Other people can see it, but for me it's over. Gone. So when there's something I want to capture and keep, something I want to stay alive, I use *this* camera."

He made the circle with his thumb and forefinger.

"Click. Elizabeth caught unaware, not pretending. Elizabeth without the mask."

She sipped her drink slowly, trying to understand everything he had told her. The photographs he had shown her, the ones she had asked to see, weren't important to him. They were moments he had destroyed when he captured them on film. She wasn't sure she understood, but the intensity of his voice, the choice of his words made her tremble. Perhaps this was the way artists spoke. She couldn't be sure. But she felt herself drawn to him once again.

Only it wasn't just his physical presence. This time it was more.

"You see, these pictures," Gary said as he pointed to the photographs beneath the plastic sleeves, "these are all surface. They're just moments. Images of moments. To be successful, a photographer has to be invisible. He has to get beyond the surface, to break through to the secret."

"What sort of secret?"

"The split second when the subject relaxes. There's a crack in the armor, and something unexpected is revealed. Like before, when I shot you through my fingers. If I had had a camera in my hands you would have gotten all stiff and tight. You would have hidden from me. A photographer is like a thief—only people don't miss the things he steals."

"What about these photographs? Does that mean you're finished with flowers and fields?" She wanted to say that the photographs she had been looking at were exceptional, ripe with colors and textures, reassuring in their beauty.

He reached into his pocket and took out the letter he had received from the editor of *Botanical Magazine*. He handed it to her. "Here's an assignment that interests me."

"Is this true?" she asked, looking up from the letter. "Is there such a thing as an orchid that grows underground?"

Gary pulled his chair closer to hers. His breath was warm against her cheek as he told her about the flower that never sees the sun. The petals, he explained, were almost fluorescent in their paleness, the tips were tinted purple.

"It grows in the dark and it's pollinated by tiny humpbacked flies that live on rotting vegetation."

"Are you going there?" she asked. Something about the underground orchid seemed macabre yet, at the same time, alluring and wonderfully exotic.

"I'm not sure. That would mean leaving this place. You."

His words stunned her. She was struck by the sudden intensity of his feelings. That afternoon in the field had meant something to him as well.

They were close now. An orange light lingered at the window, then descended, flickering across his face. Tiny particles of color collected on his lips. Feeling the desire twist and flutter inside her, she leaned toward him, aching to feel his hands on her body. A strand of damp hair fell across her forehead. He reached over, brushing it away. She knew then there was no turning back. All her reservations, her attempts at control, vanished.

When he kissed her, she felt herself drowning, sinking deeper into a dark, liquid space. He carried her into the bedroom and in an instant, he peeled away the last layers of her resistance. They slipped out of their clothes, and pressing herself against him, she left the imprint of her flesh on his. She moved her mouth across his body, licking the perspiration from his warm skin.

The memory of his perfection had not existed only in her imagination. He was smooth, scarless; veins twisted like thin ropes through his muscles.

She placed his penis in her mouth and felt it swell and harden against the softness of her cheeks. He moaned as she licked and sucked, moving faster and slower, trying to find the rhythm that would make him explode in her throat. Instead, he pulled away, and clasping her breasts, he kissed her until she slid obediently beneath him.

He caressed her thighs with his hands, entering her with his fingers until he was sure she was ready. She twined her hands around his neck, begging him to come inside her. He moved with a deliberate slowness, torturing her with his tongue, his hands. She was dizzy with the smell of him. He moistened the crease between her breasts. When she felt him hard, insistent—huge against her belly—she reached down and caressed him with her hands. She guided him into her. As she yielded this last secret, she felt herself unfold like the petals of the orchid.

30

HIS FOREARM WAS PRESSED against her throat. She found herself gasping for air. The slightest pressure and she might have suffocated. She removed his arm. He blinked, half-sleeping.

"Elizabeth?"

She brushed a dark curl from his forehead. The watery morning light spilled across the sheets. She still could not believe he was real and that he was here, with her.

He stroked her naked breasts and reached down to feel the moisture between her legs. Bringing his hands to his mouth, he tasted her scent before pulling her to him. The hours they slept had not been an interruption but merely a pause in their lovemaking. There was none of the discomfort, none of the morning-after feelings she had experienced before.

Last night they had become lovers in the true sense of the word.

It was nearly an hour before they left the bed. Sunday morning promised a whole day of lazy pleasure. There was no office to go to. She was free from papers and files and the pointless speculation about the murdered girl whose body remained unidentified in the county morgue.

Elizabeth was deliriously happy. Like Gary, she wanted to capture this moment, seal it forever in the circle of her fingers.

"Tell me how you do it," she said. "How you take those pictures without film."

Gary took her fingers and formed them into a circle against her eye.

"But you have to know how to see. Looking isn't good enough."

Elizabeth stared at his naked body as he sprawled sideways along her bed. She never knew a man could be so strong and delicate, could move with such natural grace.

"But I see you right now," she said. "I want to remember you just this way."

"You don't see me, not really. There's a difference between looking and seeing."

She traced the line of black hair that grew from his chest to his penis.

"What's the difference?" she asked.

"It's not something I can explain. Words don't do it."

He stood up, looking around the room for his clothing.

"Come," he said, "let's go take pictures."

They rode back to the fields. She wore jeans and this time she was able to maneuver her legs as she straddled the motorcycle. She felt joined to him as they leaned into the turns, swaying the machine with the force of both their bodies.

"Look out there," he said, pointing to the summer grasses, and the green and yellow splotches of color that stretched to the sky. "Describe it to me."

"It's a field. There's grass and flowers and the sky is cloudless."

"You've looked, but you haven't seen."

He reached down and pulled a blade of grass from the soft earth. A white, mucouslike substance clung to its underside. "Did you see this?"

"What is that stuff? It looks like spit."

"Exactly. It's called a spittlebug, and if you could see past this, you would see this." Gary wiped the mucous away to reveal a tiny black bug.

"This field is filled with a thousand dramas: a spittlebug clinging to the underside of a leaf, a monarch butterfly perched on a flower, a wood lily blooming only as long as the sun shines."

They walked through the field and Gary trained her eyes to see. There was so much. How could she have missed it all before? The place she had thought was simply dirt and weeds was alive with insects, plants, and flowers. He was right. Before she had only been looking. There was another level, something more beneath the surface of her most superficial vision.

The field became overwhelming. She could never see it all, not really. As soon as she noticed an iridescent dragonfly sunning its wings on a bit of goldenrod, her eyes lighted on a patch of delicate white flowers or a blade of timothy grass.

"Feeling dizzy?" Gary asked.

"How did you know?"

"That's how it is in the beginning. I remember walking through the streets of Buffalo, tripping over my own feet as I studied the light creep across a crack in the sidewalk."

"This could get dangerous," Elizabeth laughed.

A dark look passed across his face. "It can," he said. "It really can."

*   *   *

She spent the afternoon trying to see through his eyes. As they walked down the street, he pointed out subtleties of light and color, texture and shadows she would never have noticed before. He told her about his "sleep series," the way he believed that objects bore the imprint of their owners, and how empty rooms whispered forbidden secrets.

For the first time she understood what seeing was all about. It involved much more than eyes. It included the mind and the imagination. Seeing went beyond the five senses; it embraced emotions and fantasy, reality and dreams. They took hundreds of pictures that day, none of them with a camera.

"The camera changes everything," Gary said. "It numbs the photographer, replaces his eyes."

"But then how do you manage?" she asked. "If using a camera does that, how can you be a photographer?"

"I'm a photographer because I see pictures, whether I print them on paper or not. Art isn't a product, it's a process. It has to involve risk. You can't feel fear or excitement if you're frozen behind a lens or locked up in a studio worrying about f-stops and shutter speeds. That's technique. Any-one can take those kind of pictures."

Elizabeth tried to understand. She wanted to grasp what he was saying, but she wasn't sure. He seemed to possess such a remarkable gift. He was sensitive to the slightest shift in light, the tiniest details. Yet he seemed tortured with this "seeing," as if it were a fate he hadn't chosen.

"I want to take you someplace where we can look at faces," he said, "a place I've been going to for years. I'd like to shoot it someday."

They drove through the warm summer evening until they reached the New Chicago Lunch.

"What an odd name," Elizabeth said as she looked at the neon letters that glowed orange in the twilight.

"Everything about this place is odd," Gary said. "It's all black and white and grainy."

The minute they walked inside she knew exactly what he meant. The restaurant seemed drained of color. Long tables stretched from one end of the place to the other. Weary men in stained white aprons ladled food onto chipped plates. Two bikers straddled chairs as they wolfed down enormous portions of stew and potatoes. A pale young man with wild hair stared forlornly at a plate of spaghetti; an old woman in a party dress nibbled on a stale roll.

"Look at that old woman," Elizabeth said. "I remember seeing people like that in the Automat in New York."

"She's always here," Gary said. "Check out her hands."

Elizabeth looked. They were smooth and delicate, almost like a child's. She wore enormous gold rings on each pinkie.

"I'm afraid if I load my camera in this place," he said as he placed two cups of coffee and a slice of pie on the table, "I'll lose it forever. It just won't have the same feeling for me. Know what I mean?"

"I think it would make a wonderful series of photographs."

"Maybe, but a good photograph has to be more than wonderful, it has to make you want to look, sort of pull you in and force you to see. I'm not sure I can do that right now."

"Do you mean here, with me?"

"No, I mean now, so soon after what's happened."

"What's happened?" she asked, moving closer to him.

At that moment Gary wanted to explain everything. He wanted to tell her how standing behind the camera had plunged him into a period of darkness. He wanted to explain how he had become unable to separate himself from his photographs, how he had become trapped, lifeless, like the subjects he captured in his lens. But there would be time for that later. He had shown her some of his world today. Soon she could begin to understand.

"Us," he smiled. "We've happened." He kissed her fingertips. "I don't want to take dreary photographs of this place now. Not when you're here with me."

The two bikers stood up and pushed their trays toward the center of the table. She noticed how the light spread along the planes of their faces and how it gathered, darkening in the hollows around their eyes. She was sure that after today, nothing would ever look quite the same. She was noticing things now she had never seen before.

On the ride home, Elizabeth closed here eyes against the images. As she pressed her breasts against Gary's back, she wondered how it must be for him. So many pictures, a shutter constantly snapping in his mind; an endless whirl of visions, snapshots, portraits. She could understand for the first time the power of Gary's gift. It was exhilarating, but it was a burden as well. Nothing escaped his eyes. He spent his life as a spectator, watching shadows, scrutinizing faces, hands; waiting for the special magic when a moment was transformed and became a photograph.

Elizabeth wondered what Gary did when the magic failed. She wondered how he escaped the prison of his own sight.

It's enough to drive anyone mad, she thought as the motorcycle sped deeper into the last blaze of evening.

31

THE GIRL WAS REPORTED MISSING at 7:30 on Monday morning. Lieutenant Murphy, exhausted and filled with regrets, took the call himself.

Maggie Rice had gone out with friends Sunday afternoon. On Monday morning, when her mother returned from the nightshift in the canning factory, she found her daughter's room empty. Her bed had not been slept in.

Aida Rice was hysterical and barely coherent. No, she assured Lieutenant Murphy, her daughter had taken no clothing, no money, no suitcase. It was as if the girl had simply disappeared into thin air. Yes, she told him, she had called all Maggie's friends. The last anyone had seen Maggie was 6:30 P.M. on Sunday. She had been walking home. Aida was convinced she had never reached her destination.

George took down every detail. He knew the girl himself, had seen her occasionally at the diner.

Edgar Rice was her uncle, and she sometimes did odd jobs around his office.

"We've got to notify the FBI," Aida Rice was saying. "There's a killer out there and he's got my girl."

George calmed the distraught woman. There was certainly no cause to think Maggie's disappearance had anything to do with Princess Doe. Not yet, anyway.

"Has she ever stayed out overnight before?" he asked.

"Of course not." Aida hesitated. "Once she did stay out a little late, but her uncle fetched her. It wasn't nothing."

"Boyfriends. What about boyfriends?"

"My girl doesn't even date. Just goes out with a group of local kids."

George thought of Terri Ann. The image of her barefoot and frightened, living in the filth and poverty of that apartment was fresh in his mind. Lola Kane hadn't thought her daughter had a real boyfriend either. Richard Darby had been just a name to her, just one of her daughter's harmless friends.

He stopped by Chief Norris' office and repeated his conversation with Aida Rice.

"This might mean something," Norris said. "And then on the other hand, the girl may show up tomorrow morning and make us all look like fools."

Appearances didn't matter to George. He wanted every resource the department could come up with. He wanted to find Maggie Rice alive.

"She's about the same age as our Jane Doe. Am I right?"

George nodded. Two young girls, both walking on a road in Bakersville. One dead, one missing. It could just be a coincidence.

Chief Norris shuffled a pile of reports to one side of his desk.

"Let's make this a priority. I'll call in the rest of the department. I'm putting you in charge, Murphy. I don't want any screwups. I want to know everything that kid did, every place she went, every person she spoke to in the last twenty-four hours."

George was already out the door. Despite what had happened, Bakersville remained a small town with a smalltown grapevine. He knew almost everyone, and those he didn't know personally he could find out about. If she was still here, Maggie Rice wouldn't be too hard to find.

As he drove toward the mobile home where the girl lived, George reviewed what he did know about her. Her father had died about four years ago when the semi he was driving hit a guardrail in an ice storm. The truck had fallen a couple of hundred feet down a ravine; they had had to pry his body out from the crushed cab. He had seen Maggie at the funeral. She was just an awkward kid then, biting her nails, staring down at the frozen ground.

Her uncle, who had no children of his own, had taken a proprietary interest in her. She worked at the dealership after school and summers. Edgar drove her to and from school when the weather was bad. It was about the only unselfish thing George had ever known Edgar Rice to do. He made a note to stop by and see him before the day was out.

The mobile home was out on Herd Road where land was cheap and the sites flat and easy to build on. George remembered how he and Tina had gone out there when they had first been married. Even on his policeman's salary, they could have easily afforded one of the corrugated tin homes, but they had both agreed to spend more on a real house in town.

George lit a cigarette. He had known this would happen. Just thinking about Tina made yesterday come back to him. It was a bad taste in his mouth, a bitterness that burned his throat.

It was over between them.

Yesterday, after he had left Elizabeth, he had driven the forty-five miles to the Nunzio's house in just under twenty minutes. He had been that anxious. But when he saw Tina, smaller, thinner, her eyes lined with dark concern, he realized how much she was still her mother's daughter, and how little being his wife had meant to her.

Tina was comfortable back in her parents' home. It was a pleasant refuge for her—a regression, an escape from the burden of independence. She told him she didn't date. Her family and her daughter were enough for her.

George wondered why he hadn't seen it before. Tina had never really grown up, never separated from her childhood. He had married her and taken her away, but it was inevitable that, like a lost child, someday she would return.

Sunday night when he got back to Bakersville, George had to face the repercussions of what he had done. He hadn't been truthful with Elizabeth. He had used her concern for the missing girl as a ruse to bring her closer. But then he had pushed her away, shut her out with his own ambivalence. He wasn't sure she would ever forgive him. And the irony was, he wanted her now more than ever. She was everything Tina could never be: a woman, not a frightened little girl.

As he approached the missing girl's house, he tried not to think what would happen if Elizabeth would not come back to him this one last time.

George drove up the gravel driveway and became a cop again. He stopped thinking about Elizabeth and concentrated on Maggie Rice. Aida greeted him tearfully. He asked to be shown to Maggie's room.

The bed was neatly made, with hospital corners and a pillow that had been left smooth and unmarked. The room was obsessively neat. A row of shoes was lined up against the side of the small closet. Inside, clothing was arranged by color, the slacks on one side, skirts and dresses on another. A full-color poster of Bruce Springsteen wearing a bandana and strumming his guitar hung on one wall. The other walls were bare. There was a postcard on the Formica desk. Instinctively, George picked it up. He had seen this before. Then he remembered that Maggie and Peg's daughter Jamie were friends. The postcard was from the San Diego Zoo.

"It's great out here. The boys are blond and cute and my dad is taking me to Malibu next week. Can you believe it?"

It was signed, "Love Ya, Jamie."

The postmark, already three weeks old, read "San Diego, California."

George placed the card back on the desk and looked through Maggie's room for something personal, something that might give him his first lead. But the place was like a cell. It was as if Maggie wanted to leave no trace of herself.

"Is she always this neat?" George asked Mrs. Rice, who leaned against the open door.

"Ever since she was a little girl. She got sloppy there for a while, but after her daddy died, she tried real hard. Even cleaned the bathroom and kitchen. Not many teenagers will do that, not without being nagged."

George nodded. He took only one item from Maggie's room. A small, blue address book. He wasn't going to make any mistakes. He was going to speak to every friend Maggie had. If there was a boyfriend, if she had run away, he would be able to prove it.

By 2:30 that afternoon George had talked to six of Maggie's closest friends. The seventh, a girl named Patti Suplicki, was the only one who gave him an inkling that something had been troubling Maggie, something serious enough to make her want to run away.

"This Princess Doe thing really bummed her out," Patti said. "Like, we're all pretty uptight, but Maggie took it sort of personal. If we joked about it, you know, just to make ourselves feel better, sayin' things like, 'she was probably a hooker' an' stuff, Maggie would get all red and upset."

"Did you ask her why?"

"Nah, I just thought she was scared, is all."

"When did you notice something might have been wrong?"

Patti snapped her gum and cast her eyes downward. George read this as a sign of embarrassment. It was always difficult talking to adolescents, especially girls.

"Well," Patti continued, "we didn't mean no harm. A group of us were talkin' about how maybe this Princess Doe had been raped. Maybe she fought the guy off and he killed her. Then Sue Tompkins said that she'd rather be dead than be forced to have sex."

George knew the girl was trying to get to something. He waited patiently for her to finish.

"Is any of this gonna be used against me?"

"Patti, there's been no crime that we know of. We just want to find your friend. We're concerned."

"Okay. I just wanna be sure."

"What happened after Sue said she'd rather die than be raped?"

"Well then Maggie got all angry and said Sue didn't know anything and that she was stupid."

"Is that all?" George asked.

"Sue said somethin' really mean then. She said that Maggie was sleeping with someone."

"Was that true?"

Patti flushed crimson. "I don't know. I never saw her with a guy. But, you know, there are some things you just don't tell anyone. Know what I mean?"

George nodded. "Do you know anyone Maggie might have confided in?"

Patti shook her head.

"Thanks," he said, flipping his notepad closed. "You've been very helpful."

"There was one more thing," Patti said as George turned to leave. A doorknob confession. It worked all the time.

"What was that?"

"Well, Sue said that that's what happens to tramps."

"What happens?"

"They wind up dead, dumped in the dirt, with their heads all bashed in."

"What did Maggie say when Sue said that?"

"She didn't say nothin', she just started to cry."

George knew he had to go back. When he returned to the cemetery, he was surprised to see that summer had continued, despite everything that had happened. The spot where he had first discovered the body of Princess Doe was soft and green. Small yellow flowers nodded in a breeze that swelled up over the riverbank. There was no sign of murder. Nature had taken care of that. It had healed the scars that had been made by human violence.

Left to itself, the once shocking crime scene had now grown lush and sweet. Light alternated with shadow, creating small patches of brightness that darted between the trees.

He hadn't expected to find Maggie Rice here, not really. But he felt that somehow the two girls were linked. It was almost as if they had known each other. As if Maggie's tears had been shed, not from rage or embarrassment but from something else, something deeper.

George considered this as he squatted in a shadow cast by a maple tree. He couldn't say how or why, but he was convinced that Maggie Rice was still alive. Whatever had happened to her, he was sure she hadn't met the same stranger who had murdered Princess Doe. But still, instinctively, he felt there was a similarity. The girls shared something. Maybe it was just their age and their circumstances, but he felt that if Princess Doe were alive, Maggie would have told her the secret she took with her when she disappeared.

32

PEG WOBBLED SLIGHTLY before grasping the counter for support. Lyle Cunningham was telling her he knew for certain. Had heard it himself down at the station house when he had gone to complain about someone trespassing on posted property.

Maggie Rice was missing.

"Now it's startin'," he said. "It's one of them serial murderers. A Jack the Ripper right here in Bakersville, U.S.A."

A vibrating sensation moved through Peg's head. She heard something high-pitched in her left ear.

"You all right?" Lyle's face was directly above hers. He looked blurred, out of focus. She could feel the cool linoleum against her bare legs. Evelyn was pressing something ice cold to her forehead.

The high-pitched sound became a low wail. She was freezing and sweating at the same time.

"Let her be," Evelyn was saying. She pushed Lyle's hand away. "Can't you see she's fainted?"

"It's just too damn hot in this place," he said.

"It's got nothin' to do with hot. Next time think before you shoot off your mouth. This here's a mother of a little girl, same age as Maggie Rice. A friend of hers too."

Lyle backed off. And, slowly, Peg felt the clammy feeling subside. She let Evelyn help her to her feet.

"You go lie down now. You'll have some splittin' headache if you walk around too much."

Peg let Evelyn lead her to an empty booth.

It couldn't be true. She was just thinking about Maggie the other day, remembering how she and Jamie had spent so much time together.

She couldn't be dead. Let it not be true. She just forgot to call. Like that girl Terri Ann the social worker had stopped by this morning to tell her about. Maggie had stayed out with a boy and had forgotten to call. Kids could be like that sometimes. But even as she drank the glass of water Evelyn offered her, Peg knew that wasn't true. Maggie Rice was a nervous child. She would never go away, not without telling someone.

"I don't know what this world's comin' to," Evelyn was saying. "First a girl found dead, then this mother comes here all lost and confused, now we hear one of our own is missing. Just don't know what's happening anymore."

Peg tried to get up. She had to call Aida Rice. What that woman must be going through. And George Murphy. She would call him too, and maybe even his social worker girlfriend. But her legs felt leaden. When she tried to stand, the buzzing started again.

"Do what I tell you," Evelyn said. "Sit there and put your head down between your knees. It brings the blood back to the brain. Do it."

Peg hung her head down until the noises seemed to fall out of her ears and her head cleared.

"Now you just set a while before you try to move."

Evelyn walked back and took Peg's place behind the counter.

She was standing there, pouring Lyle a second cup of coffee, when Lieutenant Murphy came in.

"Anyone here know where I might find Edgar Rice?"

Lyle and his friend Art Wheeler were the only locals in the diner. They stared into their coffee mugs, avoiding George's eyes.

"Ain't he in that car lot, rippin' some sucker off?" asked Lyle.

"Hasn't been there all day," George answered. "His salesman, Bill Stosh, said he had no idea where he was."

"Stosh wouldn't tell you even if ol' Edgar was hidin' under the table. He's a real good ol' boy."

Lyle and Art laughed as if George was stopping by to round up a couple of guys for a poker game, as if he wasn't a cop at all.

Peg motioned to George from the booth in the corner.

"Nice talkin' to you," he said to Lyle and Art.

They exchanged wiseass grins.

Damned woodchucks.

George sat across from Peg. He lit a cigarette.

"I know this girl," Peg was saying. Her skin had an odd greenish cast. "Maggie Rice is a friend of my daughter. If there's anything I can do."

"There're no secrets here, are there?" George asked, knowing full well the whole town must know by now. "Is there anything you can tell me about her, anything that might make her frightened enough to run away?"

Peg shook her head. "Kids do things. They keep things all locked up inside themselves. But she's a sweet girl, not like that Terri what's-her-name who took off like that."

"Like what?" George asked, pretending Peg was giving him some new information. But she was quick enough to call his bluff.

"Your Miss Kern was here this morning. She told me all about it."

"Elizabeth, here?"

Peg looked annoyed. "She comes here all the time. You ought'a know. You're usually with her."

George watched Evelyn sponge down the counter. He had tried calling Elizabeth last night. There had been no answer. Maybe she had let the phone ring just to spite him.

"She was lookin' real happy, like finding that girl really made her feel good. She's a nice lady."

George tried to hide his confusion. He would have expected Elizabeth to be fuming. Maybe he had read her all wrong. Maybe she had softened toward him somehow.

But he hadn't come here to talk about his personal life. This was an investigation. He crushed out his cigarette.

"Can you think of anywhere Edgar Rice might be?"

"Him, what's he got to do with it?"

"He's Maggie's uncle. He cared for the girl. She might have told him something."

Peg shook her head. "I can't imagine anyone, let alone Maggie, confiding anything in that sleazeball."

George detected a hint of something stronger than distaste in Peg's voice.

"What do you know about Edgar?"

"All I want to know, believe me."

That's when it clicked. Edgar Rice was gone. Absent from work in the middle of the afternoon. His assistant had no idea where his boss might be. Edgar was missing. Maggie was missing. This had to be more than a coincidence.

"If there's anything you can tell me, anything that might help Maggie, I'd appreciate it."

"It's nothing about the girl," Peg said.

George felt it coming. Just as he had felt it with Maggie's friend this morning. He waited.

"He sleeps around," Peg said, looking away.

"Edgar?"

"Yeah, Edgar. He's a regular Don Juan."

This didn't surprise George. Most of the married men in Bakersville had had their discreet and not so discreet affairs.

"And how might you have come upon this information?"

Peg looked him square in the face. Her brown eyes were flecked with hazel. "How do you think?"

Peg told him, in frank and graphic terms, of her brief encounter with Edgar Rice. The sex had been ordinary, nothing kinky or violent, nothing that would make George suspect Rice of anything worse than a little extramarital fling.

"Is that all?" George asked.

"Yes, that's all. Tell me, do you think he might have aything to do with Maggie's disappearance?"

"I honestly don't know," George said.

"God, I hope you find her. I'd hate to think of what this would mean . . ." Peg covered her face with her hands. She sobbed quietly, turning away from him.

He touched her shoulder. "We'll find the Rice girl. Don't you worry."

By the time George radioed Chief Norris, it was confirmed. Two patrolmen had been sent to Edgar

Rice's home. His wife hadn't seen him since yesterday.

George turned on his siren as he sped past the string of cars on Broadway. He was back in the station house in ten minutes flat. Chief Norris had his feet upon the desk. He was smiling broadly.

"Nice work," he said. "I think we've got our man."

"Wait just a minute," George said. "Exactly what are you saying?"

"While you were out talking to teenagers, I sent Hurley and Green out looking for Rice. Nada. The guy hasn't been seen for twenty-four hours. We've got a missing girl and a missing uncle. One and one makes two. In this case, three."

"Who's three?"

"Your Princess Doe. My bet is find Rice and you'll find out who she is."

It was sweltering in the station house. George felt as though he might stop breathing altogether.

"Rice is no murderer. He's a bastard, but he's no murderer."

"Not sayin' he is. Things may have gotten out of hand. A young girl, a summer night. It's been known to happen."

So the chief had already received information about Rice's sexual appetites.

"The pieces don't fit," George said.

"Make them!" Norris said, almost shouting. "We've got a full-blown panic on our hands. I say Edgar Rice is our man. Find him!"

There was no use arguing, no use saying that his police sense told him this was all wrong. Instead, he nodded. He would play it the chief's way, for now. But he knew in his gut that Maggie would be found and that Edgar Rice had never touched Princess Doe.

33

THERE WERE A THOUSAND surfaces in her office. It was a wonder she had never noticed them before. And the colors and shapes. She was seeing for the first time.

Elizabeth seemed oblivious to the commotion around her. The office was buzzing with news, rumor, and gossip. She closed the door to her private cubicle and, inhaling on a cigarette, watched the gray drift of smoke dissolve in a splinter of sunlight. She had been like this ever since Gary had left her last night, as if she had been temporarily transported. Reluctant to return, she allowed herself the luxury of basking in the day after.

Everything about her time with him had been so unexpected, so perfect. It was confusing, she thought as she moved a stack of files toward the center of her desk. How was she supposed to go back to being herself? Could she just slip into her old life as if nothing had happened?

She glanced down at her desk and, recognizing her own handwriting, read a note she had made to herself before she had left for New Jersey with

George. It was the address of the coffee factory in Hoboken. Beneath it was the name Richard Darby. There was no doubt she had written it, but she had been someone else then. The memory seemed fuzzy, blurred by the day and night that had transformed her. When she concentrated, the images came back to her, one after another, flickering behind her eyes like a silent movie.

She could see the window beneath which she had waited in the sizzling heat of the morning. She could see Terri Ann Kane looking confused and guilty.

Had all that really happened?

The anger she had felt so strongly seemed like a distant pain, a bruise that marked a once-vulnerable area. At that moment she wanted to believe that George no longer mattered and that she was finally immune. She hoped that after a while he would become part of her past, melting silently into her gallery of old lovers.

Elizabeth crushed the half-smoked cigarette into the ceramic ashtray on the corner of her desk. She had explained it all to Celia last night. After Gary left she had felt lonely and restless. She had expected him to go; it was Sunday night and it would have been awkward having him there as she prepared for work. He had wanted to return to Crescent Springs. He told her he had an assignment to complete. She had watched him from the window as he reattached her helmet to the motorcycle, waved, and sped away.

Later, talking to Celia, she had tried to describe what had happened between them. It had been more than making love. He had taken her into his world, shown her a secret part of himself. And he had taught her the difference between looking and seeing.

Celia hadn't said much. In her silence, Elizabeth thought she read disapproval.

A bird fluttered past her window, and for a moment she considered leaving Bakersville. It would be so easy. There would be no more confusion. She could escape with Gary, bringing only what would fit into the luggage boxes on his motorcycle. She smiled to herself, realizing for the first time the seductive lure of running away. Before she had considered it a childish fantasy, but today, trapped in her office, daydreaming about the possibilities of a summer's day, she saw how those ideas might shape themselves into reality. That's probably how it happens, she mused. In an instant the dreary predictability of your life is revealed. You long to erase your past, to disappear and start all over again.

She was so absorbed in thought that it took her a few seconds before she realized she was no longer alone. Her supervisor was standing in the doorway. Elizabeth saw the concern on her face and was struck by the urgency in her voice. But the actual words didn't register. She wanted to keep looking at the bird, the sunlight; she wanted to return to her daydreams.

"Maggie Rice has been gone since yesterday afternoon."

Elizabeth felt the breath catch in her throat. She knew the girl. This was not some anonymous child, someone to speculate about. She had met Maggie in the diner last autumn. Peg's daughter Jamie had introduced them. Elizabeth remembered watching the two girls whisper their secrets in each other's ears. She recalled how they had put their heads together and giggled in the back booth by the jukebox.

"It seems like a hundred years since I was a teenager," Elizabeth had said to Peg.

Peg had turned around and smiled at the two girls. "Right now they're the best of friends. I hope it lasts. Maggie needs someone. She's been awful quiet since her daddy died. A real tragedy that was."

Elizabeth hadn't known Peg very well then, so she merely nodded as if the entire story were familiar to her. Later, when she returned to her office, idle curiosity had prompted her to look through the agency files. There was nothing on any member of the Rice family. She'd had to ask George about Maggie's father and the circumstances of his death.

"What do you know so far?" Elizabeth asked her supervisor.

"Just that she's missing and the whole town is on the verge of hysteria. Let's hope we hear more this afternoon."

Elizabeth nodded. She glanced at the telephone. She could call George and find out what was happening. First Princess Doe, and now this. She wondered how he was holding up. Inexplicably, she wanted to be there with him. But only moments ago she was sure those feelings were gone.

Elizabeth knew all about the politics at the station house. It didn't take much to imagine the pressure George must be under.

She took a deep breath. No, she wasn't going to call him. There was really nothing she could do other than wait. Maggie Rice could turn up at any moment. It was an unfortunate coincidence that she had run away so soon after an unsolved homicide, but Elizabeth could not let herself believe there was any connection between the two girls. That would mean that Princess Doe was not a random victim, and not the only one.

She watched tiny particles of dust rotate in the brilliant sunlight. Elizabeth did not believe that people just vanished. There was always a reason; there had to be. A young girl walking down a country road takes a ride with a stranger, boards a bus, buys a train ticket to another town. A young girl who sees the somber inevitability of her life gives in to a moment of reckless longing. And the hope is always the same, that somehow she is being offered an opportunity to reinvent herself.

Elizabeth wondered who the girl George had found in the cemetery had longed to be and what unspoken desire had led her to her death. George had told her again and again that there had been no signs of struggle, no defensive wounds. Whoever had lured her away from home had not done so forcibly. But he had known. He had sensed her willingness, her eagerness for adventure. It had been apparent to him that she was dreaming of escape at exactly the moment he had offered it to her.

Then Elizabeth thought of Maggie Rice. What if, experiencing the same yearnings, she had met the stranger and had been swept away by the same fantasy?

An unsettling feeling, something physical, crawled across the surface of her skin. Despite the heat, Elizabeth felt chilled. It was a coldness that told her she was coming very close to knowing something. In the past, this knowing had always come to her unexpectedly in dreams: symbolic land-scapes that fell away to reveal powerful truths. In the inky blackness of her deepest sleep, that part of her mind that was not bound by fear and inhibition explored the forbidden thoughts. And, sometimes, when she awoke Elizabeth remembered enough to understand something that before had only been partially evident.

But this was daytime, and Elizabeth was not dreaming. Yet the sensation was just the same. She felt a truth trying to break through, past an icy barrier that she herself had erected.

There was a connection. Princess Doe, Maggie Rice, and herself. Elizabeth shivered. This was a knowing that was too dangerous. She felt frozen, numbed by a force she recognized now as her own fear. She wasn't ready. She let the coldness move through her, protecting her like the first fragile layer of ice on a winter pond.

Elizabeth knew her safety was only temporary. She knew the moment would come when, treading on a weak spot, she would slip, the ice would part, and there would be nothing between herself and the truth.

She could only hope that when that instant came, she would be prepared.

34

HE WAS DEFINITELY SWEATING this one out. He had run smack into a brick wall. No one was talking. Everyone, it seemed, owed Edgar Rice something. The locals who were in his debt claimed they knew nothing about his personal life. The other business-men only knew him as a regular member of the Rotary.

George sat at the bar in the Nugget and watched as Fred, the bartender, swatted flies with a rolled-up newspaper. A ceiling fan swirled the hot air around his head.

"He's been in here from time to time," Fred was saying. "Local bimbos. Nothing significant as I can remember."

George leaned forward, flicking a fly off the rim of his glass.

"Can you give me any names? Do you know anything about the women?"

Fred rattled off a list of first names. George had talked to them all, Bakersville women, some married, some single, who had had one-nighters with Edgar.

"He hasn't been here for a couple of months, not with a lady, anyhow. Sometimes he shows up with Roy or Bucky. Other times he just sits and drinks until I close the place down. Never gets stewed, though. Got to hand it to him, he can hold his booze."

It was becoming clear to George that Edgar Rice led a fairly predictable life. He slept around with different women, frequented the local tavern, and moved easily between the locals, who were his customers, and the Bakersville white-collar community, whom he considered his peers. Nothing indicated a reason for his sudden disappearance, if that's what it really was. And although he was known for his loudly voiced opinions, there was no evidence that he had ever been violent, not with anyone.

George had not been surprised to find the women, even the married ones, eager to talk. It was confession time, and they were glad to admit their indiscretions to a cop. But all their stories had been identical. Sexually speaking, Edgar was a real meat and potatoes man—quick, simple, and passionless. He never forced the women, though some admitted that a quickie with Edgar helped lower the price on the family car. Afterward, he preferred to pretend nothing had ever happened.

But as much as the women had been happy to reveal Edgar's secrets, his male acquaintances were unusually closed-mouthed. It was as if they all knew something and no one was giving it away, not for free. George was aware that their silence was part of the code. They were protecting one of their own, returning a favor with a favor.

"So tell me," Fred was saying, "do you think Edgar has something to do with that kid found in the cemetery?"

George shook his head. Fred was an old friend, a high school chum of Elizabeth's. He needed someone to talk to, so why not a bartender?

"Can't find any connection. The guy slept around. What else is new? If Edgar is a suspect, then so is just about every man in town."

Fred laughed as he poured himself a beer. "Yeah, but the guy's kid is gone, right?"

"His niece," George corrected him. "And we don't even know that for sure. Let me tell you, teenage girls stay out overnight all the time. When they get caught, they get scared, and then they're afraid to come home and face the music."

"Sounds plausible to me, except for one thing."

"What's that?"

"If she's not home, and she's not at any of her friends' houses, where the hell is she? It's not like Bakersville is a big city. The kid's got to be somewhere, right?"

"Well, that's why we're looking for Rice. He's her uncle. Them both being gone at the same time may mean something."

"Can't figure that one out," Fred said. "If Edgar went somewhere with the kid, he would have told someone. Then, on the other hand, maybe his not being around's got nothing to do with her."

George looked glumly into his Coke. Like his investigation, it had gone flat, fizzled out. There was something here, he was sure of it, and like the fly that buzzed past his face, it was so close he could touch it.

Shit. He had been on a wild-goose chase since the day he had found the murdered girl in the cemetery. The only satisfaction he had had was finding Terri Ann Kane. And then he had screwed that one up by leaving Elizabeth in order to visit his ex-wife.

George ran his fingers through his hair. He was wringing wet. "What happened to your air conditioning?"

"Something with the compressor. Want another Coke?"

He shook his head. What he really wanted was a drink, the same drink he had been wanting ever since Elizabeth mentioned it two days ago. There was a pay phone back by the pool table. He thought of calling her but decided against it. She must have heard about Maggie Rice by now. Maybe she had called headquarters and left a message for him.

"So if Edgar Rice isn't involved, who do you think killed that kid?"

Funny, George thought, everyone wanted to know who did it; no one seemed concerned with the victim.

"Beats me," George said. "There are hundreds of possibilities. Could be a stranger who drifted into town, could be an angry boyfriend, or an irate parent, could even be someone we both know, some-one we see every day."

Fred glanced toward the entrance of the tavern. Lucian Milk was standing in a jagged shadow cast by the partially open door. He seemed to be strain-ing to get someone's attention.

Fred was surprised to see Luke here in the middle of the afternoon. He usually worked days.

George got up to leave. Luke remained in his corner of darkness, almost hiding.

"Can I talk to you a second?" he said. Fred exchanged looks with George. It was clear that Lucian was here because he had seen a patrol car parked outside.

George dropped some change on the bar and walked toward the door. Lucian grabbed his elbow.

"I gotta talk to you."

"Here?"

"Over there." Lucian motioned toward the pool table. It was hot and George was tired. This had better be good, he thought.

"You know about Maggie?"

"I know her mother's looking for her, if that's what you mean."

"Well, I know where she is."

"So tell me." George wasn't playing games. If Lucian knew something he wanted him to spit it out. Right now.

"She's over at my place. The trailer. Been there all night."

"You're sure about this?"

"Sure I'm sure. She's been sleeping on my couch, eating my food. I ain't imaginin' it, if that's what you think."

"What the hell is she doing with you?" George couldn't see Lucian as a love interest for Maggie. He was more like a big brother.

"Won't say, but she won't go home neither."

"You mean you've had an underage girl living with you for over twenty-four hours, and you don't know why? Didn't you ever think of calling the police?"

"She ain't livin' with me. I said she was sleepin' on my couch." Lucian had flushed crimson. "She won't tell me nothin' and she said she'd run away if I called the cops or her mama. I don't want her hurt or nothin', but I figure someone oughta know."

"Good thinking. Let's go over there now."

"No." Lucian was insistent. "I promised her, no cops. She's terrible afraid of somethin'. She can see a cop car comin' down that road a mile away. She'll be gone out the back door before you get close enough to see what direction she's run to."

George was willing to take his chances, but he sensed Lucian had other ideas. Why else would he have come here?

"What do you suggest?"

"A woman. The kid won't talk to me. Says her girlfriends wouldn't understand. Her mama neither. I was thinkin' you might send Peg Moore from the diner over there. She's a real listener, that one. And Maggie and her girl are tight."

Lucian was probably right. George had talked to enough teenage girls in the last two days to last a lifetime. But he couldn't send Peg out there alone. This was still an official investigation. Elizabeth would have to go along. If Maggie knew anything, anything at all about her uncle's whereabouts, he had to know every detail.

"We'll take my car," George said as he put an arm around Lucian's shoulder.

Fred watched as the two men hurried toward the parking lot. A breeze slipped in through the open door, bringing with it the smell of rain. He thought about what George had said. Of course it had occurred to him before, but now it seemed real. It was possible that whoever had killed the girl, and whoever might be responsible for Maggie Rice's disappearance, was someone he knew, or had talked to, or was someone he had served a drink to. There was no way of telling.

Fred passed a damp rag across the bar. He half-closed his eyes, giving in to the heat and the droning monotony of the ceiling fan. He conjured up all the familiar faces, flipping through them like pages in a spiral notebook. Some of them were men he had known all his life, guys he had gone to school with.

There were strangers, too. Couples passing through on their way to someplace else, women alone looking for action, thirsty travelers stopping by for a brew and a chance to get out from behind the wheel. He was small-town, and up until now he had lived without big-city fears. Hell, he even left the keys in his ignition. Just the other night, he had urged Elizabeth to take a ride home with someone he had never seen before. And she had made it safe and sound. That oughta' prove something, Fred thought.

In the fading brightness, he surveyed the tavern. He couldn't talk himself out of this one, and drinking would only make it worse. He was sorry George had stopped by, because now he couldn't get it out of his head. The idea was there, and there was no getting rid of it. His hand shook as he brought the beer to his mouth. It was definitely possible. The man who had murdered Princess Doe, the man who might be involved in Maggie Rice's disappearance, might show up at the Nugget. If he hadn't already.

35

PEG STARED STRAIGHT AHEAD, watching for the bend in the road that led to Lucian Milk's trailer. Elizabeth sat beside her. She still didn't see why she had to come along. George had been insistent. She hadn't wanted to speak to him, but he had made it clear that their conversation was strictly business. She had done her best to seem disinterested. She thought about that now as she watched the clouds gather over the cornfields.

Lucian Milk lived way out on the western tip of the county. The roads were bumpy, and Peg's car had lousy suspension. The rural scenery unfolded, one picture postcard after another. The air smelled of rain and manure. It was hard for Elizabeth to believe where she was and what she was about to do.

"What kind of a guy is this Milk character?" she asked, hoping Peg could give her more than the sketchy information George had rattled off.

"He's a woodchuck, but okay. Youngish, about twenty-five. Works as a carpenter. He's a cut above most of them, but that's not saying a helluva lot."

Elizabeth wondered about Peg's connection to all this. It wasn't her job. She was more or less a volunteer. So her daughter and Maggie were friends. Jamie probably had dozens of friends. She realized there was a lot she didn't know, and that made her uncomfortable. There was no telling what she might find in Lucian Milk's trailer. For all she knew, Maggie might not even be there.

"What's your guess?" she asked Peg. "Why do you think Maggie is with him?"

Without moving her eyes from the road, Peg answered, measuring her words carefully.

"I know Maggie. If she's hiding, there must be a reason. I think Luke was just a warm port in a storm, harmless. Know what I mean?"

"What about the uncle? George told me no one's heard from him, not his wife, or his salesman—no one. Doesn't that seem odd to you?"

Peg wasn't sure how much George had told Elizabeth. She hoped he hadn't mentioned what she had told him about her affair with Edgar. Elizabeth didn't seem like the kind of woman to understand that sort of thing, even though there had been extenuating circumstances.

"Not really. Men around here aren't exactly reliable. He may be sleeping off a drunk somewhere. Who knows?"

Elizabeth nodded. George was convinced Edgar had nothing to do with the murder. All he wanted from Maggie was information to prove that. In her own way, Elizabeth hoped for a different outcome. Edgar Rice was a plausible suspect. If he was involved with the girl, if he did kill her, they would finally discover her identity and the case could be closed. George would have no excuse to keep calling her. She could tell him it was over between them.

As Peg steered down the winding roads, Elizabeth reminded herself that she had a life of her own, that homicides and missing children were work for the police department. She wasn't George's wife; she no longer considered him her lover.

But ever since he had brought those clothes into her house, she had cared. It was as if the dead girl had been there, sitting beside her; it was as if she were still there, inhabiting a dark corner of Elizabeth's life. The images had been powerful enough to force their way into her dreams, powerful enough for her to be here, in this car, driving into a situation about which she knew very little but suspected a great deal.

"It's down there," Peg said pointing to a small yellow trailer at the end of a dirt road.

The trailer was barely visible behind the maple trees.

"How did you know about this place?" Elizabeth asked.

"Oh, live here long enough and you know just about everything about everybody. Lucian bought this trailer from a cousin of my ex-husband's. I've even been inside. It's smaller than a sardine can."

This was the first she had ever heard about Peg having been married. But, of course, there was Jamie. Bakersville might be the kind of place where everyone knew everything, but more and more Elizabeth was beginning to feel like a stranger.

She had never even laid eyes on Lucian Milk.

The rain started just as they drove up to the trailer, small hard drops that stung their faces, making it difficult to see. Elizabeth wanted to turn around right then and there. But Peg grabbed her arm, and bending their heads against the rain, the two women ran together toward the trailer.

Peg was right, it was smaller than a sardine can, and suffocatingly hot. Maggie was sitting on a tweed couch in the one room that served as kitchen, living room, and dining room. There was a bedroom off to the left.

Elizabeth stood in the doorway, shaking her hair dry. When she looked up, Peg was beside Maggie, cradling the girls' head in her arms. Maggie was crying, and Peg whispered words of comfort as she stroked the girl's hair.

Elizabeth felt out of place, an intruder in an intimate moment. She poked her head into the tiny bedroom. Like the rest of the trailer, it was spartan, as if no one lived there at all. There were no decorations, no shades on the windows, and only a worn blanket on the bed. There was a small radio on what looked like a homemade dresser. A clock ticked beside a coatrack. Elizabeth wanted to stretch out on the narrow bed, to close her eyes, and disappear. She knew Maggie was here for a reason, and all her experience told her the reason was a lot more serious then a spat with her mother or a few bad grades in summer school.

"This is my friend Elizabeth Kern," Peg said as she dried Maggie's red eyes. "I asked her to come along because she's a good listener, and if you need help, she can get it for you."

Elizabeth had not expected Peg to be so comfortable, so easily in control of what was clearly a difficult situation.

The rain was coming down hard now, driving in slanting lines outside the small trailer windows. It pounded on the roof, creating a steady, almost hypnotic rhythm.

So far, Maggie hadn't uttered a word. Elizabeth wondered how long it would take. The three women sat motionless, listening to the rain, waiting for someone to begin.

"Why don't you tell us what you're feeling?" Elizabeth finally asked, gently.

When Maggie did speak, Elizabeth was struck by how very young she was. Her voice quivered. She was a little girl crouching in the dark, confused and terrified.

"He said it could happen to me. He said it would for sure if I told."

"Who's he?" asked Peg.

"Uncle Edgar."

Peg shifted uncomfortably in her seat. It was as if they all knew what was coming next, as if they had known from the minute they had entered the trailer.

Maggie told them about her uncle's threats, his taunts, his unrelenting demands.

Princess Doe, he claimed, had been no runaway, no accident. She was a girl who had gone bad, had done what Maggie had done and had been punished for it.

Elizabeth rubbed her hands against each other for warmth. Suddenly she felt the chill. She was only seconds away from knowing.

Maggie's words echoed against the thin walls of the trailer; they swept through the air, moving in ever-widening circles until there was nothing else but the child and the truth she was about to reveal.

Peg set her mouth in a hard line, freezing her features until her face became a mask upon which nothing showed.

Edgar Rice had been having sexual relations with his niece for almost a year.

It had all begun innocently: a fatherly embrace, a kiss that lingered on the lips, touching that became increasingly insistent. Maggie knew it was wrong, but Edgar had told her it was all right. He had given her presents, showered her with favors and attention.

Then the body of a young girl had been found. This triggered Maggie's guilt. Princess Doe became a symbol of her evil, her badness. She no longer wanted to meet with her uncle in the small office behind the used-car lot.

When he forced her, bruising her with his fists, she threatened to reveal their relationship. But Edgar guessed Maggie's fears; he helped shape her most terrible fantasies. He told her he knew who had killed the girl, who had crushed her skull and dumped her beside the riverbank. It would be easy, he said, to arrange for Maggie to suffer the same way.

Then he had described the torture, detailed the ways in which Princess Doe had been raped, sodomized, beaten, and humiliated.

When she could no longer tell the difference between her uncle's fantasies and her own, Maggie had run away. But she was afraid Edgar might find her. She sought refuge in Lucian's trailer. She had known him since she was a little girl and trusted him, but still she had revealed nothing about what had happened.

Maggie's voice became stronger as she spoke. Her fantasies were a child's collection of dark, omnipotent demons, her reality an ordeal of abuse and exploitation. It would take a long time before she could begin to separate one from the other.

The small room in which the three women sat became a world apart from all others. The rain clouds that had gathered outside the window, blotting out the light, no longer mattered. The only darkness that mattered now was the horror that had crept into Maggie's life.

Elizabeth had seen this horror before; she had heard the confessions, had witnessed the denials of fathers, uncles, brothers, cousins. Not for a second did she doubt that Maggie had spoken the truth. Her descriptions of Edgar, cajoling, insistent, and threatening, were part of a predictable pattern of abuse. But Elizabeth also knew something else. She knew Edgar had been lying about the murdered girl.

As Maggie spoke, Elizabeth's memories of the cross and the clothing triggered her recollections of what George had told her about the case. She knew Princess Doe had not been raped. She had not been sodomized. There had been no torture, only a series of fierce and merciless blows to the head. Elizabeth wasn't sure if telling Maggie this now would make any difference. The girl was obviously tormented, not only by her uncle's threats but by the unspeakable acts he had forced her to perform in the office where he conducted his everyday business.

An eerie silence moved into the room until Elizabeth felt she could no longer breathe. And that's when the words came, words intended to ease the pain, wash away the guilt.

Peg was talking too. She covered Maggie's hand with her own and assured her she had done nothing wrong. No one could hurt her. Her uncle Edgar would never touch her again.

Relieved of her burden, Maggie slumped against Peg's shoulder. There were no more tears to shed.

"Is there a phone here?" Peg asked. Maggie shook her head. "I can't go home. Not yet."

"Let me at least tell your mother we've found you and that you're okay."

A heat rose in Maggie's face, a terror so real, both Peg and Elizabeth could feel it.

"What about Uncle Edgar? What will he do when he finds out I've told you?"

That's when Peg and Elizabeth realized that Maggie had no idea her uncle was missing. Perhaps he was out searching for his niece, or perhaps his disappearance was merely a coincidence.

"He'll do nothing," Peg said. There was a meanness in her face Elizabeth had never seen before. A hatred that made her whole body rigid. "Don't ever think about him again—"

Elizabeth interrupted, sensing that Peg was treading a thin line between helping Maggie and expressing her own rage.

"We've got to tell someone that you're here and you're okay. Who would you like me to contact?"

Maggie stared down at the floor. "Do I have to go back now? Everybody will know."

"No one will have to know except me and Peg, your mother, and," she hesitated, "the authorities. You see, what your uncle made you do, what he did to you, was not only cruel, it was a crime."

Maggie nodded. She knew all this, but the words weren't penetrating. It was clear the girl needed some time. Elizabeth was aware of the questions George would have to ask, detailed questions that would bring back every moment, every excruciating time Maggie had been molested by her uncle.

"Where's Luke?" Peg asked, acknowledging that Maggie could not stay in the trailer by herself.

"He's out back in the woodshed. He said he would wait."

In an instant, Peg was out the door. When she returned, Lucian Milk was by her side. He was tall and lanky, blue-eyed, and pleasant-looking. He brought with him the smell of wet leaves and warm summer air. But he was swallowed up by the world inside the trailer. Maggie's nightmare was there. An untouchable, sacred thing, it filled the empty spaces, pushing against the walls, the furniture, and the four people who stood close to one another.

Elizabeth felt Peg's hand on her arm. She looked directly at Maggie as she spoke. "I'm going to leave you here with Luke for a while, if that's all right with Miss Kern." Peg looked at Elizabeth for approval.

Elizabeth assumed Peg would want to speak with her in private before they contacted Mrs. Rice and the police department. But when the two women were finally alone in the car, speeding down the dirt road, Peg was silent. Elizabeth was careful. She still couldn't be sure just how close Peg really was to Maggie, or to Edgar. She decided not to discuss what Maggie had told them. Instead, she found herself talking just to ease her own discomfort.

"I'd sure like to find Edgar Rice," she said, noticing how the trailer had completely disappeared in the distance.

"Find him," Peg said, jamming her foot against the accelerator. "I'd like to kill him."

36

AFTER SHE DROPPED ELIZABETH OFF, Peg drove past the used-car lot. The cars were lined up neatly in long rows; numbers and dollar signs were painted on the windshields. She stared at the office where it had all happened. Through the small window she could see Bill Stosh sorting papers at a desk in the corner.

Then she drove past Edgar's house. She tried to picture his wife inside, dusting the furniture or putting a chicken in the oven.

Peg couldn't get the images out of her head. Edgar Rice, his big swollen hands, his fat, soft belly, his penis, long and pale. And she had let him make love to her, willingly. She tried not to picture those same hands on Maggie's body. She tried not to think about how he had violated a child.

She was burning now, a rage that made her speed past every place Edgar might be. She looked for his blue Pontiac, the one that smelled of cigar smoke and cheap perfume.

And then she thought of driving out to the Pines Motel. She hadn't been there since that time she had let him touch her, let him move his fat belly over her body, let him grunt and thrust until he'd relieved himself inside her.

It didn't matter that the police had been looking for him or that she had no idea what she could do once she found him. She just drove, propelled by the notion that somehow he was waiting for her and that finding him might make a difference.

It took just under twenty minutes for her to reach the place. Nothing had changed. The marquee still had a lighted sign that said, "Vacancy." There was a space where the letter *P* was missing from the word *Pines.*

The Pines Motel consisted of twenty-eight rooms, fourteen on either side of a long, rectangular building. Each room had its own entrance and parking space. She saw his car in front of Room 27.

Without thinking, she parked beside it. The backseat was littered with newspapers and coffee-stained Styrofoam drinking cups. She stood staring inside the car until the burning subsided. Then she calmly approached the door. It was locked. She remembered the thick metal bolt he had slipped shut, grinning at her before he began taking off his clothes. If it was locked from the inside, there was no way she could get in. Maybe this time he had been careless.

Peg walked into the small glassed-in office marked "Manager." The young boy behind the counter was watching a game show on a portable television. Contestants jumped up and down, ringing buzzers and shouting answers. When she asked for the key to Room 27, saying she was expected, the boy didn't even look at her. He pushed the key across the counter as if this was something he did every day.

She followed the narrow pebble path that led to the room. There was no way she could know, no way she could remember if this was the same room he had taken her to. It didn't matter anyway. It didn't even matter if he was inside with someone. Nothing could stop her. There was a pounding in her head, a pain that ran down through her belly. It was as if Maggie were her own daughter. Right now, there was no difference in her mind. Edgar had killed something in Maggie, something that could never be repaired. It was the same as if he had bludgeoned her and left her for dead.

The door yielded easily when she turned the key. It was not bolted on the inside.

The lamp on the chipped night table was on. The bed was still made. There was no noise. Not a sound. Wallpaper bulged and curled along a loose seam. Perhaps he had gone out; perhaps he had never really checked in at all. But she had seen the car. She was sure it was his.

Then she saw the red. It ran in a small stream from the bathroom onto the worn beige carpet. She followed it until her shoes were on the tile floor. When she looked down, she was standing in it. It was on the walls. And it was splattered in crazy patterns between the sink and the tub. Beneath the shower curtain there was a large, wet puddle. She reached down and tasted the red with her fingers. She accidentally wiped her hands on her blouse, staining it with color.

She didn't have to look, but she wanted to. Pushing the shower curtain aside, she saw him. She stared, unblinking, until she was sure he couldn't move.

He had drowned in the red.

Huge, self-inflicted gashes ran from his elbows to his wrists. The red liquid she could still taste on her lips filled the bathtub, overflowed onto the floor and out the door.

Peg was standing in Edgar Rice's blood.

She watched herself draw the curtain closed, watched as she walked over to the telephone and requested an outside line. The voice she heard ask for Lieutenant Murphy was her own. And her hands were steady as she placed the receiver back on the hook.

It might be a few minutes until the lieutenant could call her back, he was in a meeting. Was it an emergency? The woman on the other end asked.

Peg glanced at the bathroom. There was no need to rush. She gave her name and the location of the motel.

"I'll wait for him here," she said.

Suddenly, she felt tired, as if she had finally put down something heavy she had been carrying for a long, long time.

Peg stretched out on the bed. No one was going anywhere.

Edgar was dead.

He had killed himself before she had a chance to do it for him.

37

THE ROOM WAS FILLED with cigarette smoke. Chief Norris leaned forward, trying to get as close to Elizabeth as possible. He had the rugged, swollen features of a man who drank too much. George was tipped back in his chair, his feet propped up on the desk. The two men had been listening to Elizabeth's account of Maggie's confession for the last forty-five minutes.

"She did say he had roughed her up," Norris said, lighting another cigarette.

"But only one time, and only because she had threatened to cut him off or tell someone—or both."

Norris shot George a look. "What the hell else do we need? The guy was molesting a teenage girl and he displayed a pattern of violence. He told the kid he knew about the murder. Shit, he's practically handed us a confession."

George was going to fight Norris on this. Elizabeth could see it in the set of his jaw, the way he stared up at the ceiling, trying to collect his thoughts.

"Pushing Maggie around a little as a result of a sexual encounter is a far cry from outright, violent murder. And, remember, the girl we found hadn't been assaulted sexually. All the things he told Maggie were made up specifically to frighten her. Edgar no more knew about Princess Doe than any of us knew about what had been going on between him and his niece."

"Yeah," Norris answered, ready to challenge George until he backed down, "then why the hell did Rice skip town? My guess is he knew the kid would lead us to him, implicate him in the murder."

"Come on, it's completely obvious that Rice cut out because he suspected Maggie had run away and was ready to reveal their relationship."

"And do you think that would bother a guy like Rice?"

"Child abuse is a crime. And not only that. Edgar's connected around here, a member of the Rotary. A revelation like this would ruin him."

Norris was skeptical. "Every time I've ever busted one of those bastards, they deny it. Act real high and mighty, claim the girl was asking for it. Sometimes they convince themselves that what they've done is within their rights as a father or an uncle. And plenty of people believe them. No, I just can't see Edgar being afraid of a teenage girl's confession."

"In my opinion," George said, "he wasn't only afraid, he was terrified. If this information ever became public, Edgar Rice would die of shame."

"He was doing this in broad daylight, for Christ's sake, and in his own goddamn office. Now, tell me Bill Stosh and some of Rices' woodchuck buddies didn't suspect anything. Shit, they probably had front-row seats!"

Elizabeth listened quietly as the two men fought it out. It didn't take much to figure out what was going on. Norris wanted the murder case closed—forgotten. Although he wasn't the ideal suspect, Edgar Rice was good enough. But she agreed with George. The evidence just wasn't there. Rice's main interest in Maggie had been sexual. If he had been involved in the murder, they would need more hard facts. The stories Edgar had told Maggie about the torture of Princess Doe were completely false. Clearly, he just wanted to frighten the girl, prevent her from exposing him.

"I've told you everything I know," Elizabeth said. "For what it's worth, I agree with George. I think Edgar wanted to terrify Maggie, and I think he succeeded. Maybe he just went too far and that's when she couldn't take it anymore. It's going to take a long time until that girl can understand she wasn't guilty of anything, and that Princess Doe has nothing to do with her. In her mind, the unidentified victim was murdered for what *she* had done. It sounds crazy, I know, but that's what we call 'magical thinking.' Old Edgar knew just how to key into that."

George lit another cigarette. He was grateful. She could see it on his face. Right now, Elizabeth was his only ally. He wasn't fighting Norris just to make points; he really cared about this case. She had to respect that. She just wasn't sure where respect ended and love began.

When the phone rang, all three of them were relieved. It was as if the deadlock between George and Chief Norris had been temporarily broken.

George wrote something down on a piece of paper as he cradled the receiver against his shoulder.

"Strange," he said as he hung up. Then, looking at Elizabeth, he asked, "Where do you think Peg went after she dropped you off at the diner?"

"I don't know. Home I guess."

"Guess again. She just called from a place called the Pines Motel. Wants me to come out there right away. Says she'll wait."

Elizabeth was uneasy. The idea of Peg waiting for George in a roadside motel disturbed her. She assumed it was official business, but still . . .

"How did she seem when she left you?"

"Pretty calm, I thought. I'm guessing that she's close to Maggie Rice. Most people would be enraged, but Peg was cool. She barely showed any emotion."

"Did she say anything, anything that might indicate what she was up to?"

Elizabeth thought for a moment. "Sure, she said something, but it wasn't anything I would take seriously."

"Just for laughs, tell me."

She sensed George was impatient, worried about the call.

"She said she wanted to kill Edgar."

Chief Norris stood up. "I'm sending Hurley and Greene out there with you."

"Listen," George said, almost pleading, "give me a little time with her first. Peg and I go back a long way. She'll talk to me."

Norris seemed weary. He suspected he had been losing against George all along. This was just one more concession.

"Okay. I'll give you a half hour head start. Hurley and Greene will be right behind you. Nothing heroic. Understand?"

Elizabeth was confused. She followed George out into the hallway. As she bent close to whisper in his ear, she felt a sudden urge to put her arms around him.

"What are you so worried about?" she asked.

George restrained himself from embracing her. He had felt her slipping away from him since that afternoon in New Jersey. But there just wasn't time to talk about that now.

"It's not an uncommon reaction. Peg is confused. She feels guilty, angry. She might do something to hurt herself or someone else."

"What has she got to feel guilty about?"

George knew what he was telling Elizabeth was confidential information, but she was already involved. In a way she was as much a part of this as any of them. She had a right to know.

"Peg had a brief affair with Edgar."

Now Elizabeth understood. Peg's stony silence, her rage, the way she froze when Maggie had told her.

"Let me come with you," Elizabeth said. George was sure that this time that was a bad idea. Peg was ashamed about what she had done. Elizabeth's presence would only intensify that shame.

"I don't think so. You just heard Norris. He's on my ass as it is. And, besides, I think it would be easier for her to talk to me. I already know."

Elizabeth didn't argue. She knew George was right. As he walked away, she wanted to run after him, just to touch him one more time. Instead she shouted "good luck." He waved as he hurried toward his patrol car.

He started to remember things as he drove past Bakersville on his way to the motel. Two other women had mentioned having sex with Rice at the Pines. Why hadn't he thought of it? Again, George got the uneasy feeling that he had been missing something. He tried to figure it out. Why had she gone there? To relive what had happened between herself and Edgar? No, he thought, that was unlikely. She must have gone there to find him. And she had phoned the police station. That could only mean one thing.

Edgar Rice had been in the Pines Motel all along.

George stepped on the accelerator. There was no need to turn on his siren. The roads were empty. A summer afternoon in the country. The only traffic he was likely to encounter was a farmer hauling feed or manure.

* * *

He had never actually been inside the motel, but he had passed it several times. It was the type of place you see along roadsides everywhere, the type of place that looked like a thousand others. Completely forgettable, it was perfect for Edgar's sordid little encounters.

He saw Peg's car parked beside Edgar's blue Pontiac in front of Room 27. George paused for a split second before knocking on the door. He knew if anything had happened, if Peg had done something violent, it would be on his head. He should have checked this place out himself.

When no one answered, George turned the knob. The door swung open.

Peg was sitting cross-legged on the bed. The room was small and shabby. There was an odor, something familiar, something he had smelled before. Then he noticed the bloodstains on Peg's blouse.

"He's in there," she said, pointing to the bathroom.

A trail of blood led from the sink to the tub. Two straight-edge razors rested on the floor. Instantly, George knew what had happened. When he pulled the shower curtain aside, he was not surprised to see the body.

George reached down and felt for a pulse. The gashes along Edgar's arms were deep and furious. He had attacked himself like a wild animal. His bloody fingerprints dotted the white tiles around the tub. George could almost picture him—bleeding, scrambling wildly to escape, slipping on his own blood—dying, while he grasped violently at the slick tiles.

There was no pulse. Edgar Rice had been dead for hours.

*   *   *

Peg was still sitting calmly in the shadow cast by the small lamp beside the bed. George touched her gently as he reached over and called for an ambulance. There was nothing left for him to do.

Hurley and Greene would arrive shortly. He wanted to get Peg as far away from the Pines Motel as he could.

"Are you all right?" he asked.

Peg turned to him, her face perfectly composed, her breathing steady.

"I'm fine," she answered.

George knew she still wasn't feeling it. The scene she had just discovered would haunt her for years. At least, he thought, he could help her make it through the night.

When the ambulance bearing Edgar Rice's body had left, he gave Hurley and Greene a brief report, and they checked the room for evidence. Then George turned to Peg.

"Can I take you somewhere?"

She was still so stony, so eerily silent. George didn't want her to be alone when it hit her.

"Where is there to go?" she asked, looking at him blankly.

"How about a cup of coffee? I bet it's been hours since you've had anything to eat."

Peg sat beside him in the patrol car. George couldn't be sure if she could hear him, but he kept on talking. Anything was better than the silence; anything was better than wondering what Peg was thinking.

They drove past acres and acres of farm country. It had stopped raining, and a cool breeze blew through the open window. They were nowhere—on a partially paved road between Crescent Springs and Bakersville—when Peg motioned for him to stop. She opened the door. Tipping crazily from side to side, she ran toward a cluster of apple trees. He watched as she moved deeper into the grove. George knew it was coming. She gripped a tree trunk for support. He looked away as she vomited.

The horror had broken through.

She was sobbing when he finally approached her. A dusty light spread across the damp ground. Everything smelled clean again. He put his jacket over her shoulders. She shivered in the heat.

"Come back to my place," he said. "It's going to be a rough night."

It didn't take Peg long. George was surprised. After a couple of whiskeys, a cigarette, and a good cry, she was able to talk about it.

"I was crazy going there," she admitted. "I really didn't know what I'd do. I just had to see him. I felt like I could kill him with my bare hands. And then to find him like that. The blood. I've never seen a dead man before. I mean, outside of a funeral."

George nodded. It was a grisly scene. He had seen worse, but that didn't make it any less hard to take.

They sat in George's kitchen, drinking whiskey and listening to the sound of each other's voice. He was tired, but he knew she needed to talk it out.

He poured himself another drink.

"You don't think he had anything to do with that girl who was murdered?" Peg couldn't bring herself to say Edgar's name.

"Can't see it," George answered, hoping to get off the entire subject. Peg had had enough nightmares for one day.

He stood up and looked out the window. Sometime between the moment he had found her in the motel and now, daylight had disappeared. The moon was a small, fading circle anchored in an unmoving sea. George thought about Elizabeth. He hoped Hurley had called her as he had asked him to.

"I think I can sleep now," Peg said. She was standing behind him. He could feel her whiskey-scented breath along the back of his neck. When he turned, they were only inches apart. She swayed toward him, and his first impulse was to reach out for her. But he stepped back, creating a distance that said more than anything he could explain verbally.

"You're in love with her, aren't you?" Peg asked.

He knew she was speaking of Elizabeth. "I'm not sure. It's just not that simple."

Peg smiled. The corners of her mouth turned up, and for an instant he was sorry he had reacted as he had.

"Nothing's simple, or easy. Especially love."

George nodded. "I've got to work on this one. Not like with my wife. I let her go too easily. Know what I mean?"

"It's probably hard on her too. You being involved in all this. It has to get in the way."

"Maybe," George said. "But I get this feeling it's something more. I just don't know what."

"Someone else?" Peg asked.

Never once had he considered that possibility.

"No, I don't think so." He shook his head.

"Whatever it is, she's probably feeling pretty bad too. I don't know much about her, but there's one thing you can be sure of. Women love harder than men, and hurt longer too."

Then they had one last drink together. There was nothing more to say. They sat in the dreamy stillness listening to the trees rustle in the breeze as darkness covered the landscape.

Although he offered to, Peg insisted on being the one to sleep on the couch. "After all the whiskey I just drank," she said, "I could probably sleep on a bed of nails and not feel a thing."

George agreed, even though he knew better.

38

HE STOOD OUTSIDE in the cool night air and he listened. The men in the tavern were talking about the missing girl. There was no need for Gary to go inside. The voices filtered into the darkness. Everything was clear as a bell. Another girl had disappeared from Bakersville.

He revved the Harley. A narrow band of moonlight spread across the handlebars. He wasn't sure what he should do next. No one knew anything about the girl. Her name was unimportant. Gary didn't care about that. But he did care that she was gone.

He sped into the evening. There was a phone booth just down the road in a small convenience store. He could call Elizabeth from there.

The anger made him take chances, wild, reckless chances. He cut off a gang of teenagers in a sports car. Taking a curve too sharply, he hit gravel and nearly tipped into a ditch.

Damn it, Gary thought, they have to find that kid.

He couldn't stand the idea of anyone touching his photographs.

*   *   *

Elizabeth couldn't get the images out of her mind. Hurley had called her and told her what had happened in the motel. God. Why did Peg have to be the one to find him? She tried to picture the scene: Edgar with his arms, slashed and bloody, slumped in the bathtub of a cheap motel.

George had been right. He did die of shame.

She wanted to call Celia. There was so much to understand: Maggie's confession, Edgar, Peg, her own changing feelings about George. Elizabeth stared at the telephone. Celia was always so sensible, so rooted. What would she think about all this? So many nightmares tangled up in one another. Would they ever be able to sort it out?

When the phone rang, she was sure it was Celia. ESP. Close friends were like that.

She didn't recognize his voice.

"It's me, Gary," he said. There were background noises: cars, voices, a door slamming.

"Where are you?" she asked.

"I'm in a phone booth not far away. I need to talk to you."

She wanted to talk to him too. Gary was the only one who wasn't part of the nightmare. Except for Celia, he was the only outsider she could turn to. All he knew about the murder was what he had read and the little she had told him. Maybe, if he made love to her, she could stop thinking, even for a little while.

* * *

The gentle purr of the engine broke through the silence; a slice of moonlight lit his way. He appeared suddenly. The black Harley floated on the first dark tide of night. She walked out to meet him, and, for a moment, Elizabeth believed he was coming to save her.

She breathed him in before she said his name, before she touched him.

"I heard about the missing girl. I got here as soon as I could."

She didn't want to talk about Maggie Rice. Not now. There was so much else to say. He put his arm around her shoulders as they walked into her house.

"The girl's been found. She ran away."

Gary seemed to relax. She was surprised he had even been interested.

"Where was she?"

"In a trailer, with a friend. Let's just say she had problems."

"What kind of problems?"

Elizabeth felt uncomfortable. What she knew about Maggie Rice was confidential. She didn't want to think about her professional responsibility now, but she sensed Gary was only asking out of curiosity. She gave him the barest details.

"Family stuff. Kids run away all the time. This just happened at a moment that made it look a lot worse than it really was."

Gary nodded.

Elizabeth poured herself a glass of wine. Taking the bottle from her hands, he glanced at the label. "I'll have a glass myself."

"I thought you don't drink."

"Tonight's an exception," he said.

When they had finished nearly the whole bottle, Elizabeth told him about the seeing.

"Ever since you explained it to me, everywhere I turn there's something I hadn't noticed before. Even in my own office. I must have spent forty minutes watching the light creep across a stack of folders on my desk. And it changed, rippled, moved. And then today I had the oddest experience."

Gary watched her closely. She was beginning to understand now. Soon he could tell her everything. He felt himself tip and sway. Not yet. Not quite yet.

"I was in a trailer. The place where the girl had run away to. It was so bare, so empty. I remembered what you said about rooms keeping secrets, bearing the imprints of their owners, but that's where the seeing failed me. It was just a plain bed, a chest of drawers, a coatrack."

"Did you look everywhere?" Gary asked.

"Well, I just sort of glanced inside. I mean the owner wasn't far away, and there were people in the next room. It was a tiny place. I couldn't look under the bed, if that's what you mean."

"That's not what I mean." His green eyes were shining now. His face seemed almost flushed. "Remember what I told you about a photographer being like a thief? The room yields its secrets only when you're alone. When you can explore. The images must be stolen."

Maybe it was the wine, but Elizabeth didn't understand. Images weren't real. How could something that was not real be stolen?

Gary moved closer. He placed his hand on hers. The darkness had a different dimension now. It was as if the space between them had expanded, making room for something urgent, a secret that pushed against them, wanting to reveal itself.

Streams of reddish light fell across his face. She watched as the words formed on his lips.

"I stole something from you and I left something of myself."

Elizabeth was silent. He wasn't talking about sex or love. Somehow she knew that.

"I came here, when your house was empty. I took pictures in my head. We knew each other before we ever touched."

It was as if she had stopped breathing. She couldn't be sure exactly what he was saying, yet she knew what he meant. It frightened her that she could no longer tell the difference between madness and art. Was there a difference?

Fighting against the wine and the slow, dizzy feeling it gave her, she gripped the table.

"You mean you were here? In my house, without me? When? How?"

"Before you knew me. I slipped the lock. It was easy. Everything here excited me. Couldn't you tell? Couldn't you sense it?"

She wanted to deny it, to say that he had gone too far, trespassed, and that his behavior was unacceptable, intrusive. But it was true, she *had* sensed it. She remembered the uneasy feelings she had attributed to fear, to her involvement in the murder. His presence had been that strong. It had broken through what was visible. It had remained long after he had departed.

"I was always going to tell you," he said. "But you can see now why I had to wait. There's something between us. Something different."

She was no longer sure what was real. The room seemed to be floating, spinning. He had shown her things she had never seen, and now he had told her something impossible and she believed him.

She was aware that they had just crossed an invisible line. She had no idea where it would lead them.

When he reached out for her, she did not resist. She let him unbutton her blouse, unzip her jeans. She let him carry her naked into the bedroom.

He was different this time. Grasping both her hands in one of his, he held her arms above her head. His beard was coarse, his teeth nipped at her flesh. Unable to move, she became his prisoner. His fingers were rough, insistent. Her nipples ached. There were scratches along the inside of her thighs. She squirmed, but he held her down. He bruised her lips with his kisses. She was wet. The violence excited her. He rubbed his penis, swollen and erect, against her breasts. He didn't wait like the other times. He knew she was ready. When he entered her, he let go of her hands. She dug her nails into his back, his buttocks, leaving marks on his perfect skin. He moaned as he thrust deep, pulling her up to him. But the rhythm was his. The hunger, the need, all his.

He said her name as he came. She held on to him, dreading the moment when he would pull away and they would be separate again.

And then she slept. The wine, the sex, the images of her day, Gary's confession pulled her into a deep and continuous blackness. His body, warm and moist, lay beside her. But now she was alone, entering a place where there was no light, no shadow— only truth.

*　　*　　*

She was underwater, someplace dark and cold where the orchids grew. They were transparent. White and purple, they strained upward. Sheets of ice shifted along the freezing surface.

She swam toward the night-blooming flowers, searching for roots to free so the petals might reach the sun. But the roots were long and fiercely anchored. She pulled at the blackened stems. They partially gave way, revealing their source. Faces. Buried faces. Mouths filled with indigo soil, eyes glasslike and blind. She dug frantically with her fingers. There were thousands of them: lips twisted in agony, heads bludgeoned and crawling with yellow maggots.

She saw the ice reforming on the surface. Seamless and solid, it would soon close her in with the flowers that grew beneath.

Elizabeth swam frantically. When she broke through the ice, the dream ended. She was soaking wet. Her perspiration had left long streaming stains on the sheets.

He was still sleeping beside her. She slipped into a cotton nightgown and a blue terry cloth robe she had thrown on a chair beside the bed. The keys to his motorcycle lay in a jumble on her dresser. She slipped them into her pocket.

She laced up a pair of sneakers she had left beside the door of her house.

Then she walked into the night.

Her fingers trembled as she unlocked the first luggage box. She had a right. He had explored *her* secrets. There were still images left to steal.

She ran her hands along the black portfolio, the one with the photographs of fields and flowers. There were cameras, film containers, lenses, and something hard and cold. She reached deeper, outlining the object with her fingertips. She didn't need to see it. Gary carried a gun. But then that did not surprise her. Handguns and rifles were common in rural areas. She pressed her hand against the ridges of the barrel, tracing it in the darkness. It was a .38.

A smoky mist settled around her ankles as she opened the second luggage box. It did not yield easily. Elizabeth moved the key gently, until the lock reluctantly gave way.

There were several loose photographs printed on flat paper. Holding them up to the moonlight, Elizabeth saw black and white images of empty rooms, neatly made beds. There was a shot of the outside of the New Chicago Lunch, looking strangely ominous in the shifting shadows of late afternoon. Then there was a photograph she had seen before. A skirt and a sweater, a glint of gold shining through a cascade of dried leaves. There was no figure, only the clothes.

The chill crawled from her neck to her spine. She had touched those clothes, had held that shining thing in her hand.

Elizabeth knew this was not a dream. Her dream was over. But now, time and space, day and night seemed suspended. She couldn't stop herself. She reached further into the luggage box.

She was holding the jeans in her hand. Then there was a blouse, underpants, and a cotton bra. Everything was covered with dried blood. The blood had formed a thick brown scab, covering the cloth until the colors were hardly visible beneath. Her fingers scraped frantically against the bottom of the box. There was something more. Thin rectangular objects that she seemed unable to grasp. Finally, she pulled them out.

Postcards.

Elizabeth moved into a luminous curve of light. There was only the moon to read by.

The postcards were cheap color shots of western scenes. She turned them over, expecting to see blank spaces. But the spaces were filled. Black letters crawled across the white surfaces. It was hard to focus now. The photographs and the blood-stained clothes were lying at her feet. The messages were almost all the same, predictable, ordinary. One even said, "Wish you were here."

A cricket stirred in a nearby bush. She could feel the ice breaking. She was falling deeper into the cold. When she saw the signature—identical on all the postcards—she knew there was no escape. This was a nightmare, and it was real.

The postcards were all signed, "Love Ya, Jamie."

39

SHE ONLY KNEW SHE was driving. She had no idea when, or how, she had begun. Her car moved automatically over familiar roads. Everything she had found was resting on the seat beside her. It was as if they were alive: the photographs, the clothes, the postcards. She was taking them somewhere, rescuing them.

Elizabeth knew these were the clothes the dead girl had worn. The skirt and sweater, the gold cross in the photograph belonged to Princess Doe. And then there were the postcards. It all fit together somehow, but her mind couldn't work.

She was running for her life.

She could still see the pictures. The ones he had put there, and the ones she now saw for the first time. They were shrinking, growing, swimming in dark pools of light. Images from her dream mingled with reality: the orchids that lived on rotting flesh, decay, death, the bloodstained clothes, the postcards written in the childish scrawl of a young girl on vacation. She wanted to pull over, to run into the woods until the trees swallowed her, until the fading night became day and she could understand. But Elizabeth knew there wasn't time. Her breasts ached from his touch, her thighs tingled. Part of him was still warm and alive inside her.

He was back there in her house. Sleeping in her bed. Perhaps he already knew that she had discovered his secret.

Elizabeth began to drive crazily, swaying from side to side, speeding up, slowing down. The perimeters were no longer clear. She couldn't be sure where the road was straight and where it curved, where the pavement ended and the drainage ditches began. She forgot to shift gears and the car made a loud grinding sound.

There was a telephone in an all-night grocery about two miles down the road. Her mind clicked into action. There was probably some loose change in the glove compartment. But who would she call? It was very late—around 3:00 A.M. She was alone, fleeing from a nightmare that pursued her, a waking dream that refused to end.

Had he meant to kill her too?

*　　*　　*

The man behind the counter of the grocery looked startled when she entered. The lights were too bright. Everything smelled of potato chips and popcorn. She blinked her eyes. She realized she was wearing a nightgown and bathrobe. She wished she could go back to her childhood bed, back where she could hear her brother breathing in the next room, and be comforted by her mother's voice.

She dialed Celia's number. "This is a collect call for anyone from Elizabeth," she told the operator.

Be home, she prayed.

Celia picked up on the first ring. She accepted Elizabeth's call.

The words didn't make sense, but she said them anyway.

"I found everything," she said, gasping for air. "Clothes covered with blood. Photographs of the skirt and sweater Princess Doe was found in. And he had postcards already written and signed."

Celia was calm. She asked for more details, but Elizabeth couldn't hear her. Something was rushing in her ears. She shouted over the noise.

"And there was a gun."

"I want you to listen to me," Celia was saying. Elizabeth strained to hear. If only the sounds would stop.

"I want you to get out of there right now and drive to George's house. Can you do that?"

She thought of the winding roads, the way her hands trembled on the steering wheel.

"I think so," she said. The rushing sounds were louder now, almost deafening. Celia's voice sounded very far away.

"You must not go back to your house. Promise me, Elizabeth. Promise me you'll drive to George as soon as you hang up this phone."

She was a little girl again. It was easy to promise her mother anything, easy to be good and follow all the rules.

"I promise," she said.

When she walked past the man behind the counter, she wondered if he noticed how small she had become—and how terrified.

*　　*　　*

George got up to use the bathroom. He saw that the couch was empty. Peg had left him a note, but he was too tired, too hung over to read it. He swallowed four aspirins and tried not to look at his reflection in the mirror.

When he saw her, he thought she was part of his dream. Dressed in a nightgown and bathrobe, she shivered in the darkness. She was shouting and gesturing in the air. He rubbed his eyes. No, this was really happening. Elizabeth was here, on his doorstep. She dropped some things at his feet. He took her hand and brought her inside. She pulled away, fighting him.

"No," she said. She was screaming now. The hysterical screams of someone out of control. Without thinking, he slapped her face. She stood motionless, stunned. Her cheek bore the imprint of his hand.

"I know everything," she said. Then she began talking about orchids and darkness and things that grew underground.

He went to get a drink of water. When he returned, she ran out to where she had dropped the bundle she had been carrying. She handed him jeans and underwear, a photograph, and a pile of postcards.

He thought she was mad until he saw the dried blood. She was silent as he stared at the picture of the paisley skirt and the brown sweater. He could see the gold chain beneath the leaves.

"What is all this? Where did you get it?"

"The postcards," Elizabeth said. Her eyes were wild with fear.

They were all addressed to Peg Moore, and they were signed by her daughter.

He tried to get her to take a drink—water, coffee, whiskey, anything. She was no good to him like this. Her lips were blue with cold. He drew her to him, hoping he could soothe her long enough to begin to understand. He stroked her hair. She buried her face in his chest. After a few minutes she spoke. She was forcing the words, but at last they began to have an order, a meaning.

"I found these things," she said, "in the luggage boxes of a motorcycle. Those clothes belong to Princess Doe. He killed her."

"Who's he?"

"A man," she said. "A man I know."

"Where is this man?"

"He was in my house. I'm not sure he's still there."

Please don't ask anything else, she prayed. Please don't ask me what he was doing there with me, in my bed.

George got up. "Stay right here." His voice was firm. She was afraid to breathe.

When he came out of the bedroom he was wearing jeans and a tee shirt. He carried his jacket and his gun.

"Maybe you had better wait here."

She began shaking uncontrollably. "Please," she said. "He'll find me. He's taken pictures. He sees everything."

George couldn't be sure. She might have gone off the deep end, or she might be telling the truth. One thing was clear. Somehow, Elizabeth had stumbled onto something—something important.

He threw a blanket over her shoulders. The air was an odd, amber color. The sun would be rising soon. The sky looked as though it was streaked with blood.

As they drove toward her house, he tried to ask her more questions, but she stared straight ahead as if he weren't there. He decided not to probe. He would have his answers soon enough.

They pulled up in front of her house.

"He's gone," she said.

"How can you tell?"

"The motorcycle. It was parked right there."

"What kind of a motorcycle?"

"A big one. Black. A Harley-Davidson."

Then George began to remember. He had seen that bike. It had been following him the day of the autopsy. The rider had been cocky. And then the day of Kiley's funeral he was sure he had spotted it again.

The suspicions that he had been missing something were no longer vague. The motorcycle rider had appeared shortly after he had discovered the body. But what was Elizabeth's connection? Why was she here now, shivering beside him.

"I'm going inside. Stay here."

"He might be hiding. He'll do anything." She was terrified.

George loaded his service revolver.

She tried to stop him, but he pushed her away.

George walked around the house first. There were no lights, no signs of movement. He drew his gun as he stood to one side of the door. Reaching out with his foot, he kicked it open. It was unlocked.

"Police officer!" he shouted.

But he knew the house was empty. In the dim light he could see the fresh tracks the Harley had made in the shale. He went inside.

He had been here so many times before, but it seemed different now. He glanced into the kitchen.

Her clothes were lying in a heap beside the table. Things were fitting together. Things that had seemed muddled before.

He stood in the doorway of her bedroom. The sheets were twisted, the blanket fell to one side. The bed smelled of sweat and sex. He closed his eyes. The pain was sharp and sure, his worst nightmare coming true. Of course. It had been happening all along. Only a blind man could have missed it.

"Thank God," she said as he opened the car door. "You were right. He's gone."

Elizabeth nodded her head.

"Hand me those postcards."

She reached over and gave them to him. He was careful to look away. He couldn't let her see what he was feeling.

"Where are we going?" she asked as he turned the key in the ignition.

"To the diner."

*   *   *

It was like one of his photographs. Black and white. Ugly shadows moved across the walls. Peg's Diner was empty except for Bernie who pushed a soiled rag along the countertop.

Elizabeth followed George inside, clutching the blanket like a child.

Bernie nodded as if he had been expecting them. He was only half-awake and moved slowly as George reached up and took some of the postcards down from the mirror over the cash register.

He spread them out in the yellow light. Elizabeth looked over his shoulder.

"These are all from Jamie. Just like the ones you found. The handwriting is the same."

Elizabeth stared at the curling letters. They both realized it instantly.

The last three postcards bore photographs of northern California. They were postmarked "Crescent Springs, New York."

Bernie was staring quizzically at them. "Got any hot coffee?" George asked. Wordlessly, Bernie passed them two steaming mugs.

The warmth sizzled against Elizabeth's lips. She blinked, hoping she could transform the diner into a place she knew, hoping she could escape Gary's images.

"Can you talk now?" George asked.

The colors were coming back. The coffee warmed her from inside.

"Tell me his name."

"Gary Rolf."

"Where does he live?"

"He travels. He takes pictures."

"Do you know where we can find him now?"

Elizabeth shook her head.

George ran his fingers through his hair. He looked at her for the first time since he had seen the bedroom. He wondered how long this had been going on and how deeply she was involved.

"Wait," she said, glancing around the diner, "there is a place he might be."

George stood up. She leaned against him for support. He slipped his arm around her shoulders. He didn't care what she had done, or with whom. He loved her, and he couldn't let her go.

"I can't explain it," she whispered, "but I can show you the way."

40

THE SPEEDOMETER SAID 95 MPH. He gave it gas and kicked the bike up another gear. Without his helmet, the wind stung his face, biting into his flesh.

When he awoke, alone in her bed, he knew instantly what she had done—what he had always suspected she might do. It had been a risk. But it had been worth taking.

Gary felt the exhilaration of the moment. He was escaping. She was in pursuit. He closed his eyes. One, two, three, he counted. He loved the danger of it—the frantic pace. He could see clearly now. Trees glistened in the dawn. The sun was a purple bruise creeping slowly upward into a pink sky. He was alive. He could feel everything. The blackness was behind him.

And that was what it had been all about.

He was one with the road. It passed beneath his wheels and vibrated through his body. It had been just like this with the girl. He saw her face now in the wildly shifting patterns of light. The way she looked at him, the way she sat staring blankly.

He had picked her up just north of Rochester. He was heading south. So was she. She was on her way to the bus station. Still tan from her vacation in California, she looked older than her age. She told him how her father had paid for her ticket home. When she changed planes in Chicago, she cashed in the ticket and decided to travel on her own. She took buses and hitched a few rides. She had been careful, she told him, and now she was almost home and there was money to spare.

She looked as though she'd fit into the clothes.

He bought her coffee, and she never stopped talking. Her voice was high-pitched, with a grating quality he found annoying. She told him how she had written out dozens of postcards in advance. That way her mom wouldn't worry. When she decided to leave two weeks early, she had conned her dad into mailing them from California. She wanted to surprise her mother, she told him.

*After that he didn't pay much attention
to what she said.*

*There were more postcards,
all written out, in her purse.*

He closed his eyes again. The wind stung his cheeks. One, two, three, four, five. He was getting better and better. It was another way to prove he was still invisible.

* * *

Just before he had met her, he had lost his invisibility. Lost it completely. It was the closest to dying he had ever come.

He had been in a house in Buffalo, a tiny, ugly, brown house. He was looking at beds. He was trying to capture the forbidden. There had been a sound. Footsteps. Voices. A hand on his throat. He could still smell the putrid stink of scotch and sweat. Someone had come home early. They hadn't understood what he was stealing. They thought he wanted their television, their toaster, the twenty dollars they had hidden in a jar on top of the refrigerator.

When the cop had seen the cameras and the photographs, he had let him go. He had called him a crackpot. But it didn't matter, because by then the blackness had moved in. There was no more seeing. Nothing at all. He had felt this before, on and off, but never as strong as this time.

He was completely blind.

After that, he had been sucked back into the ordinary. He took assignments. He created technically perfect photographs of things he couldn't see. He thought he'd never emerge from the darkness.

Then he met her.

She had said "wow!" when she saw the motorcycle. She had begged him for a ride. Her name was Jamie. He remembered that because it was a name that sounded like her. Jamie. It reminded him of ice cream cones and merry-go-rounds.

She never stopped talking, even when he was speeding into the wind. She would lean over and shout into his ear. Of course he didn't listen. And he was still blind, so he barely noticed the way she straddled her long legs around the bike, or how gracefully her hands locked into one another.

He didn't see all of that until much later.

He had found the clothing in a rummage sale. It was an idea he had been playing with before the blackness. Rooms without people. Beds without dreamers. Why not clothing without bodies? He had filled a cardboard carton with the stuff: discarded garments, woolen caps, toreador pants, soiled nightgowns, faded madras trousers, earrings, necklaces. He toyed with the props, arranging them, imagining them in different combinations. The brown pullover and the paisley skirt reminded him of the sixties, of girls with long brown hair and tanned lithe legs. He spread the clothes beneath the dried leaves, recreating his memories. The chain with the cross was a last-minute touch. It glistened in his lens. He had taken other shots as well, but this was the only one he had saved. It haunted him. And although he was blind, he carried the photograph and the clothes with him, hoping that when he regained his sight he might use them somehow.

*She was the one
who suggested they stop for a rest.*

He was tired too. The coffee shop was attached to a motel. He hardly noticed, but she must have.

She told him she was a virgin.

He knew what she wanted, but he was not interested. He explained that he was impotent. She asked what that meant. He told her it meant his penis couldn't get hard. He couldn't fuck her. She stared down at her food, embarrassed she had ever said anything.

He felt good saying the word. He was blind, but he couldn't explain that to her. Impotent would do. It was probably the truth anyway.

She asked him to take her picture. He clicked at her with a camera. There was no film inside. She smiled and posed.

It was hideous and he hated her.

There were two beds in the room. Singles. He stretched out on one, throwing his boots to the floor.

He watched as she polished her fingernails. One, two, three, four, five. He closed his eyes. She was still talking. She told him she lived in Bakersville. They were almost there. He hated her voice. He wanted her to shut up.

It got worse.

He could see inside himself. It was as if he had become one of those plastic models with transparent skin. Beneath the plastic there was a machine: a heart, lungs, a brain. But he was outside looking in. Completely disconnected.

It was totally black. He had to get back inside himself—out of the darkness.

He picked up the tripod that rested on the floor next to the bed. The steel felt heavy in his hands. But when he touched it, the first finger of light tingled behind his eyelids.

She must have thought he was going to kiss her. She turned her face up at him. Her smile was a grimace.

He heard the sounds
as he crushed her skull.

Then they were in the silence together. The light was searing. White. The blackness burned away in an instant. He was alive again. Inhabiting his own body.

He dressed Jamie in the clothes he still carried with him. Her blood thickened on his fingers as he closed the clasp on the chain he hung around her neck. He stood back, staring at what he had done. He saw then that her hands were beautiful, that her legs were long and girlish.

He made a circle
with his thumb and forefinger.
Click.

When he placed her body along the riverbank, the landscape was his only witness. But he already knew the trees would say nothing. They remained tall and straight, protecting him from view.

Once again he was invisible.

Over and over, several times a day, he made the circle with his fingers, and he was able to relive the moment.

He heard the sounds as he crushed her skull.

Then the photograph he stored in his head began to vibrate with its own energy. There were people, a town. He had created all of them from a single vision. And then he entered that vision, became part of a living composition.

Never before had he been so alive. Never before had he seen so much.

The afternoon he discovered the diner and saw the postcards, he knew he had a way to make it last.

There were more postcards, all written out.
And he had saved them.

Gary wanted it to go on forever. When he encountered Jamie Moore, when he brought the steel down on her skull, he had freed himself. He knew he no longer needed to journey halfway around the world to snap images of the orchid.

He had broken through to a new kind of seeing.

He had experienced the ecstasy—
the beauty—of the forbidden.

He couldn't stop now.

41

Had he meant to kill her, too?

The question wouldn't go away. Elizabeth stared at George as he drove out of Bakersville. His jaw was set. His face was a mask. How much did he know?

She could feel Gary's presence. It had broken through before and she felt it now, coming closer. He had had so many opportunities. All those times: in the field, in her bed. No one would have known. No one had ever seen them together.

Had he planned it that way all along?

The morning approached slowly. Elizabeth was impatient. The night seemed endless. But her dreams had rescued her. It had begun when she saw herself in the dead girl's clothing. And then tonight when she was swimming beneath the ice and discovered the orchid. It was beyond reason, she knew that now. In her dreams nothing was reasonable, there were no rules. And that had saved her.

Elizabeth realized the dead girl had been beside her all along. She had been there that first night when Gary offered her a ride in the moonlight. She had been there with them in the field. Every time he made love to her, Princess Doe had been the unseen presence. This had been his deadly secret. The stolen images, the exquisite flower that lived in blackness. Had he been warning her all along—or had it been an invitation?

Was it the same invitation he had offered Jamie Moore before he bludgeoned her to death?

Elizabeth couldn't be sure of anything. She did know that Gary had offered her a fantasy. Like a runaway girl, she had been enticed, seduced. What would have happened if her dreams had not intervened?

Where would he have taken her if she had accepted his offer?

* * *

George didn't dare move his eyes from the road. If he did, he would have to look at her, and he couldn't do that now.

He could still smell the sweat and the sex.

Another man had never occurred to him. And that man had been a killer. George wondered now how he could have intuited so much—the connection between Maggie Rice and Princess Doe, his conviction that Edgar was uninvolved in the murder— while missing everything that mattered.

Elizabeth had been sleeping with the man he had been searching for, the man who had killed the girl.

George knew now that Jamie Moore, Peg's daughter, was that girl. How could she have remained unidentified? He had asked Peg about the clothes, the cross, that very first day.

Nothing made sense. He had his gun and his shield, but that wasn't enough. It hadn't been enough for Princess Doe, and it hadn't protected Elizabeth. But she was here. Somehow, she had escaped and now she was trusting him with her life. He knew that meant something.

"Turn left," she said. There were no road signs, and she was amazed that she remembered the way. But now she was remembering everything. He had always just appeared, as if he could sense when she needed him.

Had he been stalking her?

But he had been so gentle, so loving.

Except for that last time.

She moved her hand over her breasts. They still ached. Yes, he could be brutal. He had that power. She should have guessed it when he told her the seeing could be dangerous. But she thought he had been speaking only of art, of light and shadows. There was a danger. There were lines to cross. And Gary had felt it, experienced it. When he killed Jamie, battering her with wild, ferocious energy, he had entered a place from which there was no return.

She remembered now how he had told her that the camera made him numb, replaced his eyes. He needed to feel danger, fear, excitement. Those were his own words. He had told her that the only real photographs were the ones in his head.

Murdering Jamie had restored his vision.

How long would that vision last and what might he do if it began to fade again?

Elizabeth realized just how close she had come.

*　　*　　*

It looked like a painting. The red neon sign, the orange sunrise—his motorcycle, a solid black rectangle outlined against a liquid sky.

"That's it," she said. "He's in there."

"What is this place?" George asked. It was called the New Chicago Lunch. He had never seen it before.

"It's an all-night cafeteria."

She had been here. With him. "What does he look like?"

"He's tall, over six feet. Green eyes, black hair. He usually wears jeans and one of those leather motor-cycle jackets."

"Will I recognize him?"

"Immediately," she said.

George took a deep breath.

"You can't go in there alone. Can't you call someone?"

She listened as he spoke into the radio. He was notifying headquarters of his location. He was calling for a backup. She thought they would wait together.

Then she felt him. She gripped George's arm.

"He's coming," she whispered.

He turned and looked at her for the first time. But her eyes were closed.

A figure, blue beneath the glowing neon, walked slowly across the parking lot.

George opened the car door. He drew his gun.

There was no sound in his picture, so he didn't hear a thing when the man with the noose shouted,

"Halt! Police!" He didn't hear it when the other one screamed, "He's got a gun."

This was a very old picture—his first. He had been a boy then, and he had watched silently, invisibly, as they murdered a dog.

*   *   *

He knew why they were here. They wanted to get him inside the cage. They wanted to kill him. They came closer than they should have. They cornered him like the dog, but he stood his ground. He refused to dodge or run.

He saw the revolver.

It was just like that first time, and he knew what was coming.

This was a very old picture, and he had not forgotten.

He moved the gun out from beneath his jacket. He saw it gleam in the orange light.
The sound of the shot lingered in the air. There were a thousand images. Everything was painted red. He made a circle with his thumb and forefinger. It was odd how he was falling into his shadow.

Click.

George's aim had been perfect. His hand was steady. One shot had been all he needed.

The man lay facedown on the pavement.

George knew he was dead. He turned him over.

The shot had been clean. The bullet had pierced his heart.

The man was exactly as Elizabeth had described him. He had died with his fingers frozen in a circle around his eye.

*　　*　　*

There were flashing lights and sirens. Elizabeth stood beneath the neon sign and waited. She watched as George talked to Hurley and Greene. They nodded as they wrote on their pads.

She watched them put his body on a stretcher and place it in the van. Like a dead animal, she thought.

*　　*　　*

Morning had come. The sun was a flat yellow circle radiating through cubes of blue. She realized that night would return, but never would it seem so dark again.

Elizabeth looked at George's tired face. She touched his hand as he turned the ignition and started the car. This was real. She was alive. She faced him and saw the questions that had not been asked.

They were going home. There would be plenty of time for answers.